Suitable

for

HANGING

Selected Stories

MARGARET MARON

Suitable for

Selected Stories

MARGARET MARON

Crippen & Landru Publishers
Norfolk, Virginia
2004

Cover painting by Carol Heyer

Cover design by Deborah Miller

Crippen & Landru logo by Eric D. Greene

ISBN: 1-932009-10-8
Printed in the United States of America
Crippen & Landru, Publishers
P. O. Box 9315
Norfolk, VA 23505-9315

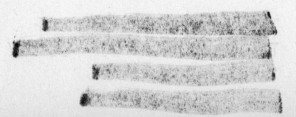

For
Carlette and David Moser,
Celeste and Johnny Blankenship,
and
Scott and Beth Honeycutt,
who are as varied as these stories yet bound with love.

Contents

Introduction

In putting together this second collection and thinking of how these stories originated, I am reminded of my young granddaughter's crafts box: a big tub filled with scraps of colorful felt shapes, glow-in-the-dark stars, googlie eyes, shiny paper, buttons, feathers, tubes of glitter, a rainbow of markers and crayons. She reaches into the box, pulls out the bit she wants, trims away the excess with her blunt-tipped scissors, secures it in place with a generous blob of glue, then fills in around the edges with color and glitter.

My head is stuffed with similar odds and ends: a snippet from the morning paper, a certain slant of light, a smug smile on a stranger's lips, oddball factoids. Example: the other morning, my husband was reading a letter from a friend, who wrote that "I'd rather kill myself on a double black diamond than die safe in bed."

"What's a double black diamond?" my husband wondered aloud.

"An extremely dangerous ski trail," I replied.

He looked at me as if I'd glibly rattled off an alchemist's formula for turning lead into gold. Neither he nor I nor anyone belonging to us has ever been on skis.

"How the hell do you know that?"

I haven't a clue. But if I ever need to kill off a skier in one of my stories, that little bit of esoteric knowledge may be just what I need.

My granddaughter doesn't always know what she's going to make and more often than not, the execution doesn't come close to her conception; but when she's finished, she's created a picture suitable for hanging on the door of any refrigerator.

Me, too. (I hope!)

Margaret Maron
Johnston County, NC
Summer 2003

The Early Retirement of Mario Colletti

I have always worried about men and women who face old age without a pension or enough savings … (And I am saddened to realize anew how much personal freedom we've lost vis a vis air travel since wrote this story thirty years ago.)

At precisely 11:38 A.M., Central Standard Time, Mario Coletti nosed his rented red Mustang into the heavy traffic of State Street and headed for O'Hare International Airport, right on schedule. On the white leather seat beside him lay a battered pigskin briefcase neatly packed with large bills—the Syndicate's monthly juicy slice of all the dirty pies which bubbled and seethed in Chicago's underworld.

As he drove, weaving in and out, expertly gearing his pace to the lights, Coletti occasionally checked the rearview mirror. Not that a tail would have bothered him at this point, but he liked to know when the cards were stacked. So far, he had followed procedure down to the tiniest detail. He was Coletti, 'the Collector', making the usual monthly pick-up—as he had two days before in Atlanta, as he was scheduled to do tomorrow in Detroit.

Tall, slump-shouldered and almost completely bald at fifty, you could look at Coletti and see the usual overweight businessman, well on his way to his second million and third coronary. His neck strained within a too-tight collar and his shirt gaped open between the buttons where his stomach bulged against and spilled over his belt.

You might dismiss him as a soft harmless man until you noticed his eyes, cold and flint gray behind steel-rimmed glasses.

Then you would remember, if you ran in the right circles, that he had earned the name 'Collector' long before the upper echelons of the Syndicate had assigned him this present position.

In those earlier, bloodier days before the country had been carved up into so many corporate duchies and settled into its present, almost workaday routine, Mario Coletti had collected other than money for the organization.

Obedience, for instance, and men's lives when they rebelled against the new order. And he still kept his hand in, as the occasional need arose.

At 12:25, still on schedule, he handed over the keys to the Mustang at the rental agency's desk in the busy terminal, then hurried over to a local airlines counter where he bought a one-way ticket to Detroit and confirmed that the next flight left at 12:45.

At 12:40, he surrendered his ticket at the gate and was checked off the list. It was encouraging to note that the flight was going to be crowded. Later, it would be difficult to prove he hadn't been aboard. Just before boarding the plane, he snapped his fingers as if suddenly remembering something important.

"Be right back," he muttered as he pushed back through the gate.

This was his first deviation from schedule.

His experienced gray eyes canvassed the crowded terminal and still no one seemed interested in his actions.

Confidently, he crossed to the Pan Am counter and asked for a ticket to New York. As the clerk turned to check his listings, a hand fell on Coletti's shoulder.

"Thought you were going to Detroit, Collector."

He hesitated only a split second before turning to stare coldly at Lexy Larsen, one of the lesser figures who'd been present at the 'business meeting' on State Street.

"Following me, Lexy?" he asked, his voice dangerously pleasant.

"Naw!" the little man denied hastily. "Kelso's old lady's coming in from L.A. and he told me to meet her. I just got a little curious when I saw you standing here."

Coletti appeared to unbend a bit. "I checked in with home base just now and they told me to get back today. Something's come up."

At that moment, the clerk returned. "One ticket to New York, sir."

"New York?" exclaimed Larsen. "They moved home base lately?"

"Not New York," Coletti snapped to the clerk. "Newark. *Newark!*" He emphasized his Jersey accent so that the two names sounded almost identical.

"Excuse me, sir," said the nettled clerk and flounced away to get a ticket for Newark.

"Happens to me all the time," Coletti complained to Larsen; but whether or not the little man was convinced he couldn't tell for the loudspeaker announced the arrival of TWA's flight from Los Angeles and Larsen had to hustle.

"The old lady's eighty-six," he explained, "and she's liable to get on another plane if somebody don't grab her."

Coletti accepted the ticket to Newark with bad grace and cursed the day that Kelso's loony old mother'd been born. Still, he reflected, Larsen might not mention the incident to anyone immediately and by then it would be too late for the Syndicate to stop him.

Of course it meant that his false trail to Detroit had been laid down for no use, but he'd never expected it to divert them for long. And maybe a ticket for Newark would be more puzzling than one for New York. No, he'd go ahead with his plans and quickly, before Larsen passed back through the terminal.

He paused in front of a bank of lockers, withdrew the gray suitcase he had stashed there that morning upon his arrival in Chicago and carried it with him to the men's room. Inside one of the cramped cubicles, he methodically stripped off his tight gray plaid suit and folded up the constricting shirt.

Nine months ago, he had suffered a mild heart attack and his doctor had sternly ordered him to lose weight or else. That was when he'd suddenly conceived what had to be a foolproof plan.

Paola was always telling him that he looked fatter than he was because his clothes were too tight; so when the layers of fat began to peel off, he had haunted the secondhand clothing stores, duplicating his clothes, keeping them always two sizes smaller than his body actually was. Paola had not noticed the change; perhaps she had grown as bored with their relationship as he had.

Too, he had emphasized the slump of his shoulders of late and carefully cultivated the impression of a bulging belly. Now, encased in a new well fitting brown suit and standing with his shoulders thrown back, he already looked like a different person. Not enough to pass even a cursory inspection, but getting there.

He reached into the suitcase again and unwrapped an expensive wig of thick brown human hair with medium length sideburns. Last, Coletti discarded the steel-rimmed glasses and substituted tiny contact lenses. Their green tint softened his eyes and effectively masked the flinty color.

Carefully, he re-packed the gray suitcase, hollowing out a nest for the briefcase and his wallet with all its identifying cards, and locked it. As a final touch, he sheathed the suitcase in a zippered protective case of brown plastic.

As he left the cubicle, he checked his appearance in the bank of mirrors over the wash basins. Perfect. He resisted the impulse to touch his hairpiece. He must be careful not to pick up any such betraying mannerisms.

Feeling as if the moment of truth had arrived, Coletti took a deep breath and pushed open the door. He walked out into the main hall, a tall, square-shouldered man who looked quietly prosperous and no older than forty-five. At that point he would have welcomed Larsen's presence just as a test.

He was one among many at TWA's counter, where he bought a one-way ticket to New York; and once aloft, Coletti began to relax, to allow a bright flame of triumph to blaze inside him.

Few executives ever retired from the Syndicate. He was not misled by the corporate air of legitimacy which surrounded organized crime these days. True, the old violence was mostly a thing of the past and things were generally run on a business like basis: the hours were good, the rewards substantial the higher one rose and a bright young man could advance rapidly.

But as for pension plans, forget it. Especially for someone as near the top as he was, who knew where so many of the bodies were buried, who indeed had buried more than a few of those bodies himself.

No, the Colettis of the Syndicate don't exactly go around inquiring about retirement benefits.

All this he had accepted years before, as one can when one is young and invincible, when death is only a vague eventuality and old age something that happens to other people who somehow aren't very smart anyway.

But when the years slipped away as irrevocably as his hair, Coletti had to face the unpleasant fact that strong, courageous, intelligent or not, old age came to everyone, even to him.

The question was, what to do about it? Would he be a Gimpy Saluciano, eking out a welfare existence as shop steward of a minor Jersey union? Or like Joe Colombo, who'd had a heart attack while making a hit in upstate New York?

Certainly he didn't intend *not* to have an old age; he wouldn't repeat Carlo Murphy's mistake. Carlo'd complained once too often about his arthritis, about his fallen arches, about being too old to keep making certain rounds; and he'd wound up 'slipping' in front of a bus.

Remembering Carlo's startled yelp, the way he'd flung his arms up to shield himself from the huge green and white bus made Coletti sigh; and the stewardess, an alert child, bent over him solicitously and asked if she could bring him a pillow. He opted for scotch and soda instead.

As he sipped his drink and enjoyed the startling contrast of hard blue skies and intensely white clouds outside the vacuum sealed windows, Coletti recalled how inevitably the choices had narrowed to this solution.

He wasn't the first to attempt it. Several had the nerve and wit and opportunity to try to get out with a bundle, to run so far and so fast as to almost make it. *Almost* because the Syndicate couldn't afford too many successes without the organization's falling apart. Those who tried had to be made an example of, and Coletti became something of an expert in tracking them down.

Like a scholar working on a Ph.D. thesis, he researched their methods—how they fled, what sort of hole they were likely to bolt for, and most importantly, what had given them away.

He came to know that if a man on the run openly bought a plane ticket for Canada, it was three to one he'd gone to Mexico. Likewise, if he'd sung the praises of New York just before fleeing, he would be run to earth in San Francisco or L.A. Although once, Coletti almost overlooked the poor sap who bought a bus ticket for his home town and actually went there.

Lifetime habits are not easily shaken off either. If a man's been spending every Saturday of the past twenty years at a racetrack, he may have the will power to lay off for a few months till the heat cools down, but eventually he'll convince himself that an occasional day at the track won't hurt. Who'll notice him among all those thousands? But word drifts around and whammo!—there's another stiff who couldn't beat the Syndicate.

Or the fugitive would be naive enough to take along his latest flame; and if there were such a thing as a glamorous woman willing to disguise her beauty and go permanently into dull hiding, Coletti had yet to meet her. That was why he had never considered asking Paola to come with him, had never let her suspect he was getting ready to run.

Paola. Tall, leggy and beautiful, with Coletti's favorite color combination: hair of midnight darkness and clear blue eyes. As far as Coletti was concerned, he would trade all the lovely blondes and red-heads in the world for one well-built brunette with blue eyes. It had been a wrench when he'd first faced the fact that Paola would be one of the things he'd have to leave behind, for he'd still loved her when his planning began and blue-eyed brunettes are not easy to find.

But he had to look at the record. To his personal knowledge, only two men had beat the Syndicate. Two men, out of all who'd tried, who had successfully vanished without even a rumor threading back that they'd been found and knocked off. Five years ago, one had abandoned a charming wife and two adoring children; two years later, the other left a very bewildered and heartbroken blonde who cried on Coletti's shoulder and swore that the man had loved her completely.

However, as the months of planning took tangible form, Coletti could look at Paola dispassionately, realize how incredibly shallow she was, see her avarice when the jewels and clothes he gave her weren't lavish enough, her petulance when he was too tired to take her dancing.

"First you look like an old man, now you start acting like one," she jeered from her vantage point of youth, totally ignoring his heart condition.

Well, Paola was as he'd known her to be when he'd picked her out of a two-bit show over a year ago—young, inane, greedy for life's goodies. He didn't blame her; he *was* getting older and it was that knowledge which had put him and a bag full of the Syndicate's money on this plane today.

Overhead, the warning light blinked its command to fasten seatbelts and from a concealed speaker, the pilot informed them of their approach to Kennedy Airport.

He strode through the terminal with his stomach sucked in and his shoulders back, without bothering to check the place for stray members of the Syndicate. Who would connect a tall, well proportioned brown haired man of forty-five with a stoop-shouldered, fat, bespectacled baldy of fifty? They wouldn't even know he was missing until tomorrow when he didn't show up in Detroit.

At the taxi stand, he took the first cab in line and gave the address of an apartment house on the West Side. He was Anthony Lazzo now, with a wallet full of cards to prove it—credit cards, driver's license, Social Security card, bank statement; all issued within the past eight months.

Therein lay the success of his plan. Too many of the others had failed simply because they had prepared no place to run to and had stuck out in their new locations like Eskimos in a nudist colony.

Seven months ago, wearing his present disguise, he had rented a furnished apartment in his new name; and to account for his long absences, he had told the superintendent that he was an insurance salesman from Chicago, newly assigned to the eastern territory. It was accepted without question.

At least once a week after that, he would spend a night at his new apartment establishing his identity. He bought cold cuts at the corner delicatessen, had a drink in the bar across the street, took his new suits to the local cleaners down the block, picked up his mail, and exchanged pleasantries with the other tenants on his floor.

Old Mrs. Fairchild across the hall thought it was disgraceful that he had to do so much traveling and mothered him with homemade cookies whenever he was there; the Smiths in the front apartment greeted him cheerfully in the elevator now; and even Kathleen in the rear apartment had begun to smile at him tentatively.

Kathleen—Mrs. Morgan to him—was a wild, unlooked for blessing, a gift from the gods, a shining omen of his success. A childless widow of about thirty-seven, with a great high-breasted figure and shoulder length black hair, there was a humorous light in her eyes which bespoke intelligence.

Of course it was her eyes which held him, eyes the color of a still sea under a deep clear sky, a hint of green overlaid with melting blue. From the moment Mrs. Fairchild introduced them in the elevator with a "Have you met our new neighbor?", Coletti ceased to regret pretty, empty-headed Paola.

After her eyes, the thing he most noticed as the elevator ascended too quickly was her clean spicy smell. Whereas Mrs. Fairchild baked twice a month, Kathleen Morgan seemed to bake twice a week; and Coletti longed for an invitation to try her spaghetti sauce. Often, as he carried up his cold cuts, the insistent aroma of garlic, olive oil and well-browned tomato paste would be hanging in the hall, enticing him.

But after six months of commonplaces as they met in the hall, elevator or lobby, no such invitation had been forthcoming; and she turned aside his gentle compliments and half-voiced suggestions of a closer friendship with a pleasant smile which promised nothing. Kathleen Morgan was no doll to be picked up at his leisure.

He liked her all the more for her ladylike reserve, however. A woman worth having should value herself. She hadn't actively discouraged him and if he went slowly …

There was time. Surely fifty was not too old an age to marry?

Dreaming of his new life, the Syndicate behind him, and Kathleen filling the stretches of his golden years, they had driven through the Brooklyn Battery Tunnel and up the West Side Drive without his noticing.

"This the place, bud?" the cabbie asked as he double-parked in front of Coletti's new home.

It was 5:28 P.M. Eastern Standard Time.

Hefting the suitcase which contained his pension, Coletti got out, paid the driver and hurried up to the apartment building. So intent was he on getting upstairs—maybe he could knock on her door and ask to borrow a cup of sugar?—that he almost collided with her as she too reached for the door of the building.

"Why Mr. Lazzo! What a surprise to see you now!" she exclaimed as he apologized and picked up her packages.

"I mean," she stammered, blushing deeply, "you usually get back to town later in the week, don't you?"

Elation blossomed inside Coletti as he realized that she at least cared enough to note his going and coming and it emboldened him.

"Today is special," he said as he ushered her into the elevator and pressed the button for their floor.

"Oh?" Her lips curved in a smile of interest.

"Yep. I retired today. Decided I'd had enough traveling to last me a lifetime."

"But you're so young," she began and then blushed again.

That second blush destroyed his diffidence.

"Look," he said as the elevator reached their floor, "I don't want you to think I'm fresh, but today *is* special for me and I don't have a soul to help me celebrate. Won't you come in and have just one drink with me to inaugurate my new life of leisure?"

"I'm sorry, but …" Then she lifted her blue eyes to him and smiled. "Right, Mr. Lazzo. Give me ten minutes to put away my packages and freshen up and then I'll join you for that drink."

Excited by this second success of the day, Coletti entered his apartment and stuck the suitcase in his bedroom before going into the kitchen to check on his supply of ice cubes. As he filled an extra tray, he noticed the small bottle of pills on the sink ledge, another careful piece of his forethought.

Upon taking the apartment, he'd placed himself under the care of a doctor whose office was on the ground floor of the apartment building next door. And that reminded him: from an inner breast pocket, he removed a duplicate vial of heart medicine. Its typed label carried the last remaining evidence in his identity as Mario Coletti. Carefully, he emptied the pills into the bottle on the sink, soaked off the tiny label and rinsed it down the drain.

Now let them find him!

The doorbell rang as he carried a large tray with glasses, ice and whiskey into the living room, and he opened the door eagerly. She had taken the time to brush her dark hair and change into a simple cotton dress which matched her eyes and had large patch pocket embroidered with green leaves of the full skirt.

Now that she was here, she seemed shy and tense; so Coletti bustled about the room, mixing drinks and keeping up a steady flow of conversation to put her at ease.

"I'm sorry I can't offer you anything but scotch or bourbon, Mrs. Morgan; now that I'm going to be here I'll have to lay in more of a variety."

"Bourbon is fine," she smiled. "And if we're going to be seeing more of you, you needn't stay so formal. My name is Kathleen."

"And I'm Tony." He bowed ceremoniously and they shook-hands with mock seriousness, their laughter blending easily.

He handed her a tall glass and hoisted his own.

"To a new life!" he said and added boldly, "For both of us."

"For both of us," she echoed and lifted the glass to her lips. Suddenly her hand jerked and some of the liquid splashed onto her dress. "How clumsy of me!"

"Wait," Coletti said, "I'll get a cloth." He set his glass down on the coffee table and hurried into the kitchen.

"You must think me very awkward,' Kathleen said as he gave her the cloth. "Perhaps I'd better go now."

"Please don't," he begged. "I could never think of you as anything but graceful. You couldn't look clumsy if you tried."

She smiled at him gratefully and learned back in her chair while he retrieved his drink and sat down on the couch. If only he could draw her out, get her talking, perhaps she might stay for a second or even a third drink, at which time it would seem natural to ask her out to dinner.

"Tell me about yourself," he said. "What were you like as a child? I'll bet you were a tomboy."

"The world's most incorrigible," she laughed and launched into a long anecdote concerning an amusing childhood escapade she and her two older brothers had been involved in.

Coletti sipped his drink and only half listened as he watched the interplay of her lips and eyes. This was the first opportunity he had had to study her expressive face and his eyes devoured her, memorizing every detail. She was a bit older than he'd thought at first, probably early forties instead of late thirties. Not that he minded. Paola had cured him of young party types; Kathleen's maturity only made her more desirable.

Suddenly he realized that she had asked him a question. "Sorry," he mumbled. "What did you say?" Strange how thick his tongue felt after only one drink.

"I asked if you felt all right," she said anxiously. "You look so odd all at once."

"I-I don't know." He tried to stand and realized that his whole body was growing numb. The glass tumbled from his hand onto the floor.

"Heart condition," he gasped. "Get Dr. Stein next door."

"No, Collector," she said quietly and reality crashed in on Coletti like a three-pound blackjack.

"But you! A woman?" he managed to get out.

She shrugged. All traces of shy hesitancy had disappeared. "You might say the Syndicate is an Equal Opportunities Employer now; no sex differentiation. Last year someone on top wondered if your zest for running down traitors was really in the interest of the organization or in the nature of practical research.

"It wasn't hard to make friends with Paola. Was her never-ending chatter one of the reasons you deserted? Of course she didn't know what she was saying, but she babbled about your being away overnight occasionally when I knew you weren't scheduled for a pick-up. It wasn't enough to take to the bosses. You could have had another woman, but still it made me wonder."

"How?" he choked.

"How did I find out for sure? I'd like to say it was clever deduction on my part, but actually it was just old-fashioned bad luck for you. I was waiting for a friend one evening in the bus terminal when I saw you come in and case the place. That made me curious. Then when you took a suitcase out of one of the lockers and went into the men's room, I was even more curious. I ignored the arrival of my friend's bus and waited for almost two hours but I never saw you come out.

"So I started doing a little research myself. Naturally you never considered a woman tail, you only scrutinized men. Then too, I'm a blonde and you don't notice blondes, do you? Just brunettes with blue eyes. Anyhow I followed you as far as the bus terminal twice before I tumbled to your disguise. It really is excellent."

Coletti managed to acknowledge the compliment with a wry jerky nod as the paralysis enfolded him.

Helplessly he watched her pull a pair of thin white gloves from her pocket and put them on. As she polished the arms of the chair in which she sat, he realized that it was the only thing she had touched in the room besides her glass. That object she now picked up along with his own and carried them into the kitchen, where he heard her wash them and put hers back in the cabinet.

She returned with his glass, mixed half a drink and pressed his unresisting fingers around it, then set it on the coffee table.

Moving quickly now, she searched him for the key and disappeared into the bedroom, emerging with the suitcase.

"Back in a minute," she whispered and he caught the spicy scent of her perfume as she passed by on her way to the front door and her apartment.

A minute! How many did he have left? His eyes focused on the clock across the room. 6:15. Taking into account the hour's difference in time zones, his retirement had lasted exactly four hours. It didn't console him to remember that that was four hours longer than Carlo Murphy'd had.

Kathleen returned without the suitcase and looked around the room, examining the scene she was setting.

At last she let her eyes rest on him and for a moment, he knew she felt regret.

"Won't get away," he gasped with painful effort.

"Ah, but I will," she said conversationally. "I was told the drug stimulates a coronary and is practically undetectable unless specifically tested for. In a few minutes I shall call your Dr. Stein and explain how I discovered you in the throes of an attack. He'll arrive too late, of course. I doubt if he'll think twice about issuing a death certificate.

"Tomorrow I'll tell everyone that I'm so upset at having discovered you that I have to get away for awhile. Then I'll take two suitcases and go."

"No use," Coletti said, speaking his last words and she understood his meaning as he had understood hers. Well, he'd never doubted her intelligence and perversely he almost hoped that she would make it now that he couldn't.

"You may be right," she said, "but I'm forty-nine and I have to try."

Mike Shayne Mystery Magazine, December 1970

Devil's Island

This story was a bit of an intellectual exercise to see if I could write one in less than five hundred words. (It's actually less than three hundred.)

Only ze most vile, ze most dangerous are sent here," said the captain in his thick colonial patois. "Criminals more low zan ze lowest. Beasts. Men in name only. No decency, no—how do you say?—humanity. How will one such a one as you exist where only madmen survive? You will go mad yourself."

The prisoner shrugged and looked down at his hands, uncallused nobleman's hands. "I used to enjoy woodworking as a child. Perhaps I'll take it up again." He tossed off the last of his wine, then leaned across the table to clasp the strong hand of the man who had become his friend during this long voyage to the most brutal penal colony in the empire. "Don't worry, Captain. I'll survive. The Emperor credits me with a traitorous ability to lead, to rally men to a cause. If he's right, I can help these wretched remnants of mankind—for they *will* be men, no matter how sunken in bestiality."

Before the captain could reply, a junior officer entered and saluted. "The patrol craft approaches, sir."

The captain stood heavily. "I must return to ze bridge."

He wanted to offer the prisoner words of optimism, but when he looked at the finely bred boyish figure dressed in the absurd uniform of the colony—white robe, blue cloak, rough leather sandals—all optimism died.

There was a jarring metallic clangor as the airlock of the patrol ship matched that of the starcruiser. The exchange was effected, then the patrol ship fell away, descending to the penal colony. In less than an hour, the captain received official notification:

Prisoner released in that sector known to inmates as Judea.

And all the way back to the civilized planets of the Empire, the captain wondered what form the prisoner's madness would ultimately take.

To Hide a Tree

The civil rights and anti-war protest demonstrations of the early 1970's sparked the idea for this story.

The temperature hit 82 degrees that day—unseasonably warm for early April; but, as had become more usual all over the country these past few years, spring's first warmth brought out more marchers and demonstrators than daffodils, even in small cities like this one. Here and now, soft vernal air was split by the shrieks of fire engines, ambulances and patrol cars.

It was almost 7:30, well dark, and only a few cars scurried through the streets. Most of the city's inhabitants were complying with the mayor's request for a self-imposed curfew; and on South Winston Street, the fire which raged through an abandoned tenement had been brought under control. There was nothing to do now but watch it burn and hope that no one else felt like exterminating rats with flames.

Three blocks south, an even grimmer situation unfolded as the driver of a late-model Chevy slammed on his brakes, causing the beat-up Volkswagen behind to crash into him. The accident itself wasn't serious; and the VW's owner, Ken Sperry, was more angry than hurt when he jumped out of his car to tongue-lash the idiot in the Chevrolet. His anger died, however, when he saw the man's white face, heard him yell in a ragged voice, "My wife! Somebody's shot my wife! Get down! There's a sniper up there somewhere!"

Ducking down by the closed door, Sperry glanced inside the car and saw a woman, her body held erect by the safety harness while her head slumped forward.

Her husband clutched Sperry's arm as he strained to listen for another shot from the vacant windows of a condemned tenement opposite them. Only sirens in the near distance could be heard. An elderly couple in a sedan pulled up and the man joined them, quickly comprehending what had happened.

"Stay here," Sperry told them. "There should be a cop up at that fire."

Ordinarily, there would have been several at such a major conflagration, but these were not ordinary times, and the city's police force was spread thinly that night. In the confusion of hoses, falling sparks and sullen onlookers, Sperry finally spotted a young, inexperienced patrolman, told his story, and waited while he radioed for help.

A small crowd had gathered around the Chevy, but they fell back obediently as the young policeman took out his notebook and began jotting down preliminary facts. Through the windshield, the dead woman's eyes glistened dully. Street lights made her skin a greenish white and her lipstick appeared a lurid purple. Dark hair helped hide the darker hole in the right side of her head.

"She wouldn't listen," Philip Watson kept repeating. "She wouldn't *listen*. To die for a lousy bridge game!" Just under six feet, Watson was a thin man in his late forties. He wore lightweight gray slacks and his sport shirt was drenched with perspiration and clung to his body, revealing a slight bulge at his waist. Except for that sign of middle age, Watson carried himself with military precision; but the control implied by his posture was betrayed by the way he repeated, "If only she'd listened to me!"

At last another patrol car appeared and experienced officers took over. They moved back the curiosity-seekers, began a cautious search of the vacant building from which the shot must have come, and sifted the crowd for witnesses. No one seemed to have heard the fatal shot. The block was one of many which had suffered by the exodus of business from city to suburb, and consisted of small warehouses, boarded-up shops and run-down tenements. Except for an elderly deaf widow, everyone seemed to have been up at the fire. Sperry had been closest, of course, but because of the fire engines he had not heard the shot.

Silently, Watson watched police procedure unroll, blinking as the flashgun of a police photographer illuminated the car's interior. He saw ballistics experts work out the angle of trajectory from the shattered car window; he watched the medical examiner touch his wife's still-warm body, then saw it lifted into a police ambulance. He heard the young patrolman report that they had flushed no one in the deserted building.

Finally, as a city tow truck pulled Watson's car away, Lt. Albindi came over to him and said with gruff consideration, "We'd like you and the other main witnesses to come down to headquarters with us for complete statements." Albindi carried his jacket over one arm and his shirt was damp with sweat, for the evening was still quite balmy.

He had collected Sperry, whose VW was now out of commission, and given an escort to the elderly couple, a Mr. and Mrs. Grayley. As they walked toward a waiting squad car, Watson asked, "This isn't going to be on a newscast, is it? My daughter—she's just fifteen—she's spending the night with a friend. I'd hate to have her learn about her mother like that."

"I don't think so," Albindi said. "With so much happening, I doubt they've picked this up yet. What a night!" He pitied Watson, one of many who would suffer tonight.

"Mildred never listened," Watson said, as they drove downtown. "She always had to have her way. I told her it wasn't safe to go out tonight, but it was our regular bridge night at her sister's and nothing was going to stand in the way of it. And I don't even like bridge. Or her sister," he added glumly. "If just this once she'd listened to me, she'd still be alive. All this rioting and demonstrating, and my daughter saying we have to understand! She gets that at school, but what can I do? I can't afford private schools on my salary."

Watson lapsed into a bitter silence, and suddenly Albindi pitied him less.

Headquarters was an organized maelstrom. Phones rang constantly and tired officers, working sixteen-hour stretches as the overload of emergency calls poured in, strode through the halls. Albindi found a deserted office and motioned the Grayleys in first. Their statement was not very informative and Sperry's offered little more. "I was thinking about the riot," he said, "and deciding that I'd better turn off at the next block to get around the fire. Sure, my windows were down—it's like June outside—but I didn't hear the shot. First thing I knew, Watson slammed on his brakes and I piled into him."

Watson had his emotions under tight control and answered Albindi's questions almost coldly. Reading between the lines, Albindi got the impression that Watson's marriage had been a failure. Only when he spoke of his daughter did his tone thaw. Despite the riot, Mrs. Watson had insisted on keeping their weekly bridge date. Her sister and brother-in-law lived on the southwest side of town; the Watsons lived on the northeast. To get there, they had to drive through the fringes of the riot area.

They'd left home around seven, as usual. "She said it would be safe, that we weren't going through the worst part. We weren't involved—you know how it is, you think these things won't affect you." Watson seemed to watch his words. Perhaps he had sensed the subtle change of attitude his outburst in the squad car had produced in Albindi.

"One minute Mildred was talking about the riot and the next minute I heard the window shatter and she was dead. Gone—just like that!" He shook his head as if to deny the suddenness of death. "Do you think you'll find the killer?"

Albindi leaned back in his chair wearily. "I just don't know, Mr. Watson. You see, most people are killed by someone who knew the victim well and wanted him dead for a reason—love, hate, jealousy, greed, fear, you name it. Nine out of ten killings are simple. We ask around the victim's neighborhood, talk to his family or friends, and usually come up with the murderer right away.

"But when it's impersonal—some crackpot shooting at random …" Albindi threw up his hands. "If we don't catch him immediately, on the scene, where do we start in a city this large? We'll go over that tenement again with a microscope tomorrow. Maybe we'll be lucky. But don't worry, sir, we won't write off your wife's death without trying."

Watson nodded and stood up. At the door, he paused and asked, "What about my car? When can I pick it up?" He seemed almost apologetic. "I use it to commute, you know."

"We'll let you know as soon as we've finished going over it. I'll try to expedite it for you."

Albindi sat looking at the closed door for a long moment after Watson had gone. To his credit, Watson hadn't pretended a grief he didn't feel; but could the man really continue to use the car in which his wife had been killed? Flexing tired shoulder muscles, Albindi swiveled in his chair and began typing reports.

Although it was his Saturday off, Albindi came in at noon the next day, determined to whittle down his stack of paper work. Last night's violence had petered out with a drop in temperature, but he had gotten far behind.

"Need a good secretary?" gibed his partner, Jake Whittaker, riffling through Albindi's backlog.

"Your figure's lousy, but you're hired," Albindi said as he scanned the top sheet. "Hmmm. Ballistics report on last night's sniper: M-1 rifle; elevation, twenty feet; distance about fifty."

"Yeah, I saw that. A Mrs. Watson killed, right? Her husband called just now and asked if we'd released the car yet."

"I forgot. I told him I'd get the lab to hurry it up. Did we get a report on that tenement where the shot was fired from? Oh yes, here it is." He read aloud, skimming the pages: "*Building condemned. Used as a flophouse by area bums. Oh, great! Windows from which shot could have been fired all broken. No positive evidence. Multiple latents on all surfaces.*" He groaned. "Want to bet they don't all belong to winos who saw and heard nothing because they were all passed out in gutters on the other side of town?"

"No takers," Jake said.

The phone rang and Albindi answered. The conversation was short and he turned to Whittaker as he hung up. "Watson again. He forgot to ask when we would release his wife's body; and, by the way, could I tell him how much longer we'll be keeping his car?"

He leaned back in his chair. "Tell me, Jake, what do you think of a man who's more interested in his car than his wife's body?"

"That it's too early in the year to go fishing," Whittaker warned. "So he's not all cut up by her death. We see a lot of men like that. What's it prove? Or did you see something last night that doesn't show up in the reports?" he asked shrewdly.

"I don't know. Guess I'm just tired and a little discouraged to think our city's going the way of Chicago, Detroit and L.A. Sure, we have our share of racial unrest, of kids marching against the war; and someone set fire to some empty buildings, *and* there was some minor looting on Dexter Avenue last night. But we haven't had a lot of violence in these demonstrations and we sure as hell never had a sniper before. I just don't like to think our little city's getting to be a jungle."

"And Watson rubs you wrong?"

"That, too," Albindi admitted. "Plus the fact that more women are murdered by their husbands than by snipers."

"Well, not in this case. Not unless Watson's a magician," Whittaker said as he shuffled through the reports. "The woman was shot from a distance, by a rifle, *while* her husband was driving. No one can be two places at one time, Al."

"I know, I know. But he could have set her up for it. He said they drove the same route every week at the same time."

"You've been watching too much television. This isn't New York or the wild West. Where does a man like Watson hire a killer?"

"You're right," Albindi said. "I guess I'm reaching." He rolled another set of report forms into his typewriter and began pecking at the keys with two fingers.

Whittaker started to do the same, then paused. "You know, Al," he said slowly, "I don't see Watson hiring a pro, but what if someone else had it in for her? That regular drive *would* put her in rifle range every Friday night. It's worth a look."

April had become skittish; temperatures plunged and topcoats were a necessity again as Albindi and Whittaker dug into Mildred Watson's background.

They began by driving out to the Watson home Saturday afternoon through a bone-chilling spring rain. The house was located in an older section of town where property had held its value. The '30's construction had mellowed well and mature trees and shrubbery muffled all but the loudest traffic noises from the nearby freeway.

Set on a half-acre lot, the Watson home was typical of the neighborhood. It was a comfortable, two-story brick surrounded by tall, full-branched maples and screened from its neighbors by dense plantings of evergreens and over-grown privet. A blacktop drive along one edge of the yard led to a small garage in the back and flared into a circular turn-around there.

After leaving Whittaker a few doors down to interview the neighbors, Albindi parked in the Watson driveway. The garage was too small for a modern car and, judging from the clutter of cartons and tools inside, Watson probably used it as a storage shed and kept his car parked in the turnaround.

The rain had slacked off to a misty drizzle and Philip Watson looked like an ordinary do-it-your-selfer on his day off as he rounded the corner of the house with an extension ladder of lightweight aluminum on his shoulder. He broke step momentarily at the sight of Albindi, who called, "Need a hand with that?"

"Thanks," Watson replied, "but it's not heavy, just cumbersome." He slid it into the garage, closed the doors and turned to Albindi. "Yesterday was so warm, I thought I'd do a little yard work. Clean out the gutters, lop off a few dead limbs. Now, though …"

They looked across the deep yard to the back where a tall thick hedge of forsythia sported an occasional bright yellow blossom. "Mildred said they meant that spring was really here, but I guess it'll be another couple of weeks yet." He shivered slightly as he led the way out of the chill into a warm, neat kitchen.

The young girl who stood with her back against the refrigerator held herself as erect as Watson and had his slim frame. Her light-brown hair was as long as any teen-ager's; but her clothes were an abnormally dark-hued assortment, as if her pathetic attempt to show mourning had been frustrated by the gaudy wardrobe of youth. A navy bodystocking clashed with her purple and black jumper, but she crossed the room with dignity when her father introduced Albindi, and offered her thin hand firmly.

"Have you found out who did it yet, Lieutenant?"

Briefly, Albindi explained the lack of clues offered by the tenement. "I was hoping you or your father would know if your mother had any enemies who knew about that standing bridge date."

Ellen Watson looked blank, but her father stiffened. "Are you suggesting that anyone we know could do a thing like that? You think we socialize with arsonists, rioters, snipers? You know where to look for that element, Lieutenant, and it's not among our friends!"

"Daddy, please!" the girl cried.

He glared at her. "It's your own mother they've killed! Are you going to preach to me now about understanding murder?"

She flinched, but stood her ground. "Rage and frustration aren't limited to any one class, Daddy. You don't know why Mother was killed and you shouldn't judge until you do."

Watson's anger changed to bafflement as he looked at her. "Okay, Ellie, that's enough. Why don't you finish getting ready? Nora said she'd be here soon."

To Albindi, he said, "Ellen's going to stay with my wife's sister till after the funeral." He sighed when the door had closed behind her. "I just don't know any longer. You have kids, Lieutenant? Do they listen when you try to tell them how things really are?"

Albindi shook his head. "I try to let them find out for themselves. Besides, my truths may not be theirs."

"You sound like Mildred. Truth is truth, isn't it? And everyone knows—"

"If you don't mind, sir, I'd rather discuss your wife's enemies."

There were none, Watson repeated. People might have gotten a little angry at some of Mildred's radical ideas, but nobody took her seriously and he'd put his foot down on her joining any of those "commie" groups or taking part in any demonstrations.

"Except that it was getting harder to keep her under control," Whittaker said when they met and compared notes afterwards. "The neighborhood consensus is that they were on the verge of divorce."

"Over politics?" Albindi asked dubiously.

"Well, except for that bridge date with her sister, they pretty much went their separate ways. Watson moves in rather conservative circles and she was becoming an embarrassment. For instance, at a company party last month, she started sounding off about tax deductions to businesses and how they were nothing more than welfare for the rich. Watson's boss was livid. Mrs. Watson thought it was funny, but Watson told someone it cost him a promotion."

"So what was holding up the divorce?"

"The kid," said Whittaker. "They both wanted her and she's old enough now to choose which parent she'd live with. Friends say the daughter was always a daddy's girl and Mrs. Watson wouldn't take the chance; but recently they've heard the girl call him a narrow-minded bigot, so Mrs. Watson was putting on pressure."

"Even so …" Albindi mused.

"Right," Whittaker agreed. "We still come back to the fact that he was driving while she was shot. Did you tell him about the rifle? I wondered what he'd say."

"Yeah. He didn't turn a hair. Just said he used an M-1 in Korea twenty years ago and was surprised any were still around."

"He didn't happen to bring one home as a souvenir, did he?"

"He says not. I talked to Mrs. Watson's sister alone when she came to pick up Ellen and she doesn't seem to be a member of Watson's fan club. I asked if she'd ever heard of his having a rifle and you could see the wheels turning in her head. I got the feeling she'd have loved to say yes."

"But?"

"But nothing. She and her sister were very close. Restricting firearms was another of Mrs. Watson's hobbyhorses and she's sure she'd have heard about it if Watson had a rifle in the house."

"So there we are," Whittaker said. "Might as well face it, Al, our little city's in step with the bigger ones. Riots and now snipers. Unless you can nail Watson carrying an M-1 and put him in two places at the same time, it can't be a private kill. Nobody else seems to have been that bugged by Mrs. Watson. They just put her down as a misguided nut, and sympathized with Watson for having to live with her."

"I guess you're right," Albindi said regretfully, shaking his head.

They spent the next morning in the unheated tenement on South Winston, hoping for a clue to their anonymous sniper which the lab crew might have overlooked. As they worked, they were joined by one of the building's squatters, a seedy old man with rheumy eyes, shaky fingers and an obvious hangover.

"Ain't you guys ever gonna finish with your scraping and measuring?" he complained. "Yesterday and again today—this is the second Sunday in a row you guys been stomping around up here with your tapes and things. A person's got a right to sleep, ain't he? Ain't I got a right to sleep Sunday mornings?"

Whittaker, who was examining the baseboard under the broken windows, ignored the wino, but Albindi asked, "The *second* Sunday? We weren't here last Sunday."

"Same difference," the little man said belligerently. "You're all on the city payroll, ain't you? Fat lot any of you care about a person's rights. Where's a person gonna find another flop this good? You think the city cares?"

"What's the city got to do with it?" asked Whittaker.

"Nothing!" the bum cried triumphantly, and sat down on the floor beside Whittaker. "That's exactly what I told him. I said, 'What right's the city got wrecking a person's life?' "

It took them twenty patient minutes to get a coherent picture. The aggrieved bum ("Call me Charlie"), had been awakened early last Sunday by someone kicking debris around in the room overhead. Worse, whoever it was hadn't closed the door properly and it banged every time the wind gusted. As the condemned building's steadiest tenant, Charlie had staggered upstairs to lay down some house rules and found a building inspector taking notes on the condition of the place. He'd told Charlie that the whole block was to be torn down as part of the city's urban renewal program.

Before Charlie could start grumbling about his rights again, they asked him how he knew the man was a building inspector.

" 'Cause he said so. And he was measuring things and writing 'em down like all you guys do."

Whittaker lifted his eyebrows, Albindi nodded, and they invited Charlie to headquarters. His objections dwindled abruptly when they hinted that the city often rewarded helpful citizens.

Downtown, Whittaker settled Charlie in front of a selection of mug shots while Albindi went off to make a few phone calls. When he returned, his face wore a look of satisfaction. "Good news, Charlie! That firetrap of yours won't be bulldozed any time soon." To Whittaker, he added, "No building inspector's been in the place since it was condemned three years ago. It has to be our sniper getting the layout. Any luck with those pictures?"

"Just what you'd expect," Whittaker said sourly. "He narrowed the first fifty I showed him down to twenty-five. No two alike."

"What about this one, Charlie?" Albindi asked, shoving a newspaper photograph under the old man's rheumy eyes.

"That's him! That's the guy!" Charlie exclaimed, using both shaky hands to hold the picture steady. "Those others sorta mixed me up, but this is him, I promise you!"

Abruptly, Whittaker stood up, fished a bill from his wallet and hustled Charlie from the room with the city's thanks for his commendable citizenship.

"Forget it," Whittaker said when Albindi started to protest. "So he just identified Watson as his phony inspector. Terrific! You weren't here when he was almost as positive about two dozen others. Can't you just see our Charlie on a witness stand? A first-year law student could laugh him out of court.

"Granted, he might be cleaned up and dried out and made into a half-credible witness, but so what? Even if the jury believed him, what difference would it make, since Mrs. Watson wasn't killed last Sunday? In case you've forgotten, Al, she was shot *Friday* night while riding with her husband, and three much more reliable witnesses than Charlie will swear to it. You're acting like a green rookie who can't see the woods for the trees."

"But what if Charlie's right and Watson was up there last Sunday?" Albindi argued. "Somebody was. Charlie's not bright enough to make up a story like that for no reason. That means the murder was planned in advance, and who's the only one in sight with a motive?"

"Mr. Watson," Whittaker said patiently. "But you're the one who said politics made a poor reason for divorce. What makes it a better reason for murder?"

"Losing his daughter," Albindi said, remembering the way Watson had looked at her.

"Yeah, well ..." said Whittaker, who had no children, as he picked up his overcoat. "You've still got to show me how he managed it without leaving any evidence behind. Me, I'm going to spend the rest of *my* day off at home."

Albindi reached for his own overcoat and left with Whittaker.

Although he tried to put the case out of his thoughts and spent the rest of the day acting like a husband and father, his mind kept toying with the problem, and he went to sleep that night with fantastic diagrams of electrically-detonated, self-destructing rifles running through his head.

It was still cold and rainy the next day. There were going to be a hell of a lot of May flowers if it didn't let up soon, Albindi reflected, as he stopped in at the police lab.

Jarrell, the technician on duty, hooted when Albindi asked if Watson could possibly have shot his wife while driving. "See the way the window's smashed from the outside in?" he asked, leading Albindi out to the Watson car. "Everything lines up with the angle at which the bullet entered her head: twenty feet up, fifty feet away. Sorry, Al, there's no way he could have done it."

Discouraged, Albindi took the elevator and entered their office behind Whittaker. His resolve to forget about the Watson case until after he'd caught up on some of his other work was canceled by a knock on their open door. They looked up to see the familiar face of Gerald Hartford, claims investigator for a large insurance company.

"Heard you two had the Watson case," Hartford said, "and I just wanted to check it out with you—make sure everything's kosher."

"Any reason why it shouldn't be?"

"Not really," Hartford said cheerfully. "Just that we never lost a policy-holder to a sniper before and, of course, double indemnity does bring it up to a nice round figure."

"How round?" Albindi asked softly, while his partner groaned.

"Sixty thousand," Hartford said, quirking a brow at Whittaker.

"Ignore him," Albindi said. "He refuses to believe in the impossible. I know inflation's hit everything, but isn't thirty thousand a lot to carry on a housewife?"

"Not really. Not when you consider that there's a minor child, and what a housekeeper costs these days."

"But the girl's fifteen. She wouldn't need a nursemaid now."

"Make him happy," Whittaker said. "Tell him Watson took out the insurance policy last week."

"No," Hartford said slowly. "The original policy was issued twelve years ago as part of a family-coverage plan, but for the more usual five thousand. Last month, Watson reviewed his policies and upped them all: an extra five thousand on the daughter, fifteen on himself—"

"And twenty-five on his wife!" Albindi interrupted happily. "The other two were camouflage."

"It has to be," he repeated to Whittaker when Hartford had left. "I bet if we check, we'll find that Watson decided to 'review his policies' the day after that party when she insulted his boss and lost him a promotion."

"Coincidence," Whittaker said, but without conviction. "Besides, why would he need extra money? We've turned up no signs of heavy debts or expensive tastes."

"Everyone needs money, Jake. What if he were counting on that promotion to put Ellen into a private school away from public school contamination? Sixty thousand pays a lot of tuition."

"Okay, I'll grant you motive; I'll admit he's familiar with an M-1; hell, I'll even believe Charlie saw him in the building last Sunday. But you still have to—"

"Show you how he did it," Albindi finished. "You're starting to sound like a stuck needle. It's probably too late, but I'm going to get a search warrant and have a look for that rifle."

Right away, Albindi ran into a stone wall. Captain Fulner was sympathetic but said, "Unless you give me at least a theory as to how he could have done it, a search warrant's out, Al. People are touchy about their rights these days and I'm not going to have this department open to charges of high-handedness without good cause.

"I'm glad spring decided to hold off a while longer," he said, softening his denial. "Crazy weather, but at least no one marches on city hall in the sleet yet."

Albindi glanced at the window where freezing rain had begun to coat the panes with a thin film of ice. "Well, we knew it was just a matter of time. Everyone's been saying this was the year our city would feel the effect of protest movements." A germ of an idea wiggled in his brain. "That's it!" he said and hurried out.

"Don't you see?" Albindi asked, back in his office with Whittaker. "Everyone *expected* riots here this year. Remember that old riddle, where do you hide a tree? In a forest, of course. And where do you hide a private murder? In a night of impending public violence!

"Except for that standing bridge game at her sister's, the Watsons had quit going out together, right? So why did he make that exception if it weren't to have an excuse to drive through an area everyone knew was ripe for an explosion?"

"Why?" he repeated an hour later, facing Watson in his own livingroom. Albindi had driven through icy streets to watch Watson's reaction to that question. "Neighborhood gossip had you two in a divorce court. You say you hate bridge and can't stand your in-laws. So why, Mr. Watson?"

More than ever, Albindi was aware of the man's rigid control as Watson eyed him steadily. "I could tell you we kept up appearances for my daughter's sake, but you probably wouldn't believe me." He shrugged.

"We have a witness who saw you in that tenement last Sunday figuring out the angle of fire."

"A reliable witness?" Watson asked coolly. "I thought that place was a flophouse for drunks and hopheads."

"But you did hate her, didn't you?" Albindi needled. "She knocked you out of a promotion and she was taking your daughter away from you. Well, *wasn't* she?"

Watson ignored the bait. "Isn't this where you're supposed to inform me of my rights, Lieutenant? Or do you reserve your kid-glove treatment for the kind of scum who killed my wife?"

His voice became icy as his anger deepened. "Listen, cop, and listen carefully: arrest me or get out! We may have been planning a divorce, but Mildred was still my wife when she died. I want her body released for a decent burial and I want my car, and if I don't get them you're going to see what kind of a stink law-abiding citizens can raise. We're still a majority in this city!"

Stymied, Albindi retreated to headquarters where he spent the rest of the afternoon filling out reports.

Whittaker had gone to recheck the three witnesses and returned just before five, gloomily predicting that he'd probably caught pneumonia in the process. "And unless everyone's lying his head off, there's no collusion. None of those three ever met Watson before. He was definitely in the car when Sperry rammed into him and the Grayleys were right by his side till we came, so he couldn't have disposed of any trick weapon."

To make matters worse, Captain Fulner was less than pleased when Albindi and Whittaker gave their progress report Tuesday morning. He began with a brief physics lecture ("Nobody may occupy two separate places at the same time, dammit!"), elaborated the more basic points of crime detection, reviewed proper procedures for questioning decent citizens and concluded by phoning Watson to announce the release of Mrs. Watson's body. "And your car will be returned this afternoon," he promised.

"It *is* in good enough condition for you to drive it over, isn't it, Lieutenant?" Fulner asked pointedly.

"He'll cool off," Whittaker consoled as they took the elevator down to the garage in the basement.

"I guess," Albindi agreed glumly, "but why does Watson feel so *right* to me? I've been less certain on far more evidence than this before. And now I've got to take his car back and all but apologize for suspecting him."

They picked up the keys to Watson's car, signed the necessary forms and Albindi slid behind the wheel. Whittaker was to follow in a squad car. Except for a small stain on the upholstery, the spider-webbed window and a crumpled rear bumper, there was nothing to show that a woman had died in this car four days ago. The Chevy cranked easily and cornered smoothly as Albindi drove it through the city streets. It was a comfortable car, one of the higher-priced models; and he could almost sympathize with Watson's desire to get it back.

The April rain had finally stopped and the sun was out, but the mercury remained low. The heater felt good as it warmed the chilly interior, and Albindi could feel it draining away some of his tension. He had just taken one hand off the steering wheel to loosen the buttons of his topcoat when it hit him.

Abruptly, he pulled the Chevy into a bus stop beside a telephone booth, waved a dime at Whittaker, who'd eased in behind him, and called Jarrell at the lab. He asked one question, received a negative reply and shouted to Whittaker, "Back to headquarters. Jarrell just told me how Watson could be in two places at one time!"

In their office, while Whittaker began laying out all the pictures the photographers had taken the night of the murder, Albindi tracked down Dr. Caird, chief medical examiner, by phone. There was a lengthy silence on the other end of the line when Albindi had outlined his theory, then Dr. Caird said cautiously, "I'll have to recheck all my figures, but technically, there's no reason to disagree. Damn it! I must be getting old not to have noticed it myself."

As Albindi hung up, Whittaker laid a photograph in front of him and tapped the significant feature with his finger. "There it is!" Together, they tackled Captain Fulner, and this time there was no hesitation in the issuance of a search warrant.

If Watson were surprised to see them when they arrived with a search party, he was too disciplined to let them see it. He accepted the warrant and opened the door for them as coolly as if it were a social occasion. "May I ask what you expect to find?"

"The warrant states what we're looking for, Mr. Watson."

He read the paper he held. "An M-1 rifle? So you've decided I was in the building shooting my wife at the same time I was driving with her in the car?"

"Not at the same time and not from that building," Albindi said. "I rather think it was a half hour earlier and out in your back yard. What reason did you give her for keeping her waiting in the car while you climbed one of those big maples on your extension ladder? Did you tell her you'd left your pruning shears up there and it looked like rain?"

"Am I under arrest?" Watson asked, turning the warrant in his hand.

"Not yet," Whittaker answered as they listened to the sounds of the searchers moving through the house.

"We know you were in that tenement last Sunday studying the angles so you could duplicate them here," Albindi said. "We have a witness."

"A decrepit old drunk! Three people saw me in the car when Mildred was killed."

"A clever bit of misdirection, but no one heard a shot."

"The fire engines—" Watson began, but Albindi interrupted.

"Not good enough. We could buy it except for one small point: it was a warm evening. Your shirt was still wet with sweat when I first saw you, but it didn't register because mine was damp, too. On the other hand, I wasn't riding around that night with both windows closed *and a heater going full blast*. You were, Watson. You thought of everything—even to closing the car door when Sperry rammed you and you jumped out to begin your act—but you forgot to turn off the heater. By the time you remembered, it was too late. You couldn't open the door and turn it off with Sperry and the Grayleys there. I noticed how powerful it was when I started to return your car today. The only thing is, I hadn't turned it on."

"One of your people could have done it."

"Sorry," Albindi said. "The witnesses all confirm that the windows were up, and photographs taken that night before your wife's body was moved show the heater on its highest setting. The medical examiner says it would be enough to push the time of death back at least a half hour, maybe more."

The search party came downstairs. "No luck, Lieutenant," one of them said.

"There's a garage out back. Lots of boxes and cartons, so take your time."

Albindi and Whittaker trailed along as Watson walked slowly through the house to halt at the back kitchen windows. Crisp sunlight filtered through lightly-leaved trees outside and was mirrored in the line of forsythia across the back where, despite the last few days of cold weather, more yellow buds had opened. The room was silent, then Watson pulled a letter from his pocket and crumpled it.

"It came today," he said, tossing it into a wastebasket. "A letter from Creighton Prep saying they had a vacancy for Ellen." He had heard the running footsteps across the yard outside.

A young detective stuck his head in the door. "We found it, Lieutenant! Up on one of the back rafters."

Albindi turned to Watson. "Mr. Watson, I'm arresting you for the murder of your wife. You have the right to remain silent—"

Watson held up his hand to stop him and, for the first time, Albindi saw his shoulders slump.

"All these past months, my daughter—Ellen—she's been so quick to understand and make excuses for every no-good, lazy malcontent in the country." He looked at them despairingly. "I wonder if she'll understand all this—or me?"

Albindi couldn't answer.

Croquet Summer

Technically, this is not a crime story, although there is a small domestic mystery—not whodunnit, but whydunnit? Readers familiar with my Deborah Knott books may see an echo of my continuing fascination with family dynamics.

Your turn to set up the course," says Barry, balancing dinner plates and vegetable bowls precariously along his left arm. "Dad and I'll clear away."

Liz Miller would just as soon stack the dishwasher herself, but her son has become very ritualistic these past few weeks. It seems important to him that they meticulously rotate their turns to lay out the croquet course and, since this is his last summer before he goes away to college, Liz doesn't argue. She's a bit apprehensive about the coming changes herself, but knows Barry will have to discover on his own that ritual and routine do not hold his world together. In the meantime, she trundles the wheeled croquet stand outside and pounds the starting post into the ground beside the patio.

Barry has kept the grass cut all summer without their nagging, but an English enthusiast of the game would still be appalled by their scruffy yard. Tufts of crabgrass, patches of clover, and a network of mole runs defeat any pretensions to billiard table smoothness. Nor does the layout of their wickets follow any official standard. Barry likes a long game and always puts the starting post on the other side of the drive with the turning post up against the back hedges; Sam likes to stick the hoops immediately beside or behind a tree; and, although her course is often shortest, Liz is not above putting some of her wickets on a tricky downslope.

The Millers are not terribly athletic, but their play is fiercely competitive and the tree-shaded yard around their old farmhouse bears the scars of past battles. Through the years they have played badminton, horse shoes and lawn darts; these days, it's croquet. Last summer they didn't play much of anything because Barry worked at the nearest fast burger place twelve miles away and spent most of his money and all his free time with Callie Ann Edgecroft.

This summer he's driving a tractor for a farmer at the end of their rural dirt road and saving everything for college. He goes to his room early most nights to sort through the eighteen-year accumulation on his shelves and in his closet. Sometimes Liz thinks he's trying to fit his whole life into that metal trunk he's taking to a college dorm.

Callie Ann married someone else just before graduation in June. It still shocks Liz. Even though several of her own classmates were wed before they finished high school and even though eighteen is considered adult, no way will she concede that today's high school graduates are mature enough to make their own way in the world. Barry still has to be reminded to take back library books, to put gas in the car, to remove his guitar from the middle of the living room floor.

All the same, time does have a way of creeping up on you, thinks Liz as she pushes a wire wicket into a bald patch of ground. Barry and his friends used to shoot baskets from this very spot in their pickup games. Sometime in his sophomore year, though, his basketball developed a slow leak and no one cared enough to buy a new one when it finally died. The post that held the backboard and hoop is long gone, but grass hasn't completely covered that hard packed dirt yet.

Sam and Barry come out to take a few practice shots while she positions the last two wickets. The sun has sunk behind the pink crepe myrtle trees, but it's still hot and muggy.

In the flower border, the pink and yellow four-o'clocks are starting to open; and as Liz walks across the shaded part of the yard, the grass feels cool to her bare feet. All three of them are in shorts, but Barry and Sam have on shoes because part of their game is sending someone halfway around the house in vicious croquet drives. The last time Liz tried it, she smashed her foot so hard that she limped for three days; now she confines herself to subtle position shots.

It's Sam's turn to go first this evening. He clears the first two wickets in one shot and makes it through the third before sending his ball wide of the middle wicket. Liz goes next. She also clears the starting wickets, but gets hung up in front of the third. Barry is able to use her ball to get through the third and hits it again coming out. When his turn finally ends, his ball is squarely in front of the turning wickets.

The three of them were fairly evenly matched at the beginning of summer.

Liz plays with conservative skill; Sam alternates between brilliance and incredible lapses. There are times when he can hit one of their balls from thirty feet away, times when he misses at three. Barry is the most consistent. He can't duplicate his father's long shots, but he strokes firmly and confidently with muscles strengthened by the summer's manual labor, and his game has steadily improved until he wins more often than both his parents together.

"I don't know why I bother to play anymore," Sam grumbles. Sales are way off this summer and, as personnel manager, he's the one who has to call employees in, who has to keep explaining that pink slips are just a matter of economics and nothing personal.

He tells Liz and Barry that hiring is a lot more fun than firing and there are new lines in his face. He will be forty-nine in September.

"Forty-nine!" Barry looks at Liz, knowing she's only five years younger. Forty-four. They see the startled awareness in his eyes. "Hey," he says, "I don't want you guys to get old."

"Who's old?" Liz smiles.

"Got a better alternative?" asks Sam.

Even though Liz and Sam gang up on him near the end, Barry wins the first game easily. Liz wins the second through a combination of good shots on her part and poor judgment on Barry's when he decides to shoot for the end wickets instead of sending her ball down the drive. Sam slips in second that time, but he's still grumbling about missed shots as they begin their third round.

By now, the sun is a fat orange blob settling into the horizon and the four-o'clocks are fully open, a mass of deep pink and brilliant yellow, buzzing with hummingbird moths and sleepy bumblebees.

Barry's having trouble with his approach shots and Sam calls encouragement to him through the lengthening shadows. These last few minutes between daylight and dusk are Liz's favorite time of day and she remembers other summer evenings when Barry wasn't much bigger than the baseball bat he swung with so much determination. "That's the way!" Sam would call as he lobbed in easy pitches. And Liz, squatting behind Barry with a catcher's mitt, would say, "You almost got your bat on it that time, honey. Keep swinging level."

Liz glances over to where their pitcher's mound once lay, but Little League days are so long past that it's only a slight hump now, covered by thick grass. It's the same with the depression under the old tire swing still hanging from the limb of the pecan tree. There was a time when the ground beneath was scuffed so bare that she never expected to see grass there again. She gives herself a mental shake, knowing these bittersweet memories are only because Barry will be leaving for college in five short days; and, since she's not paying strict attention to Sam's twenty-foot putt toward the next wicket, she catches a small movement of Barry's foot from the corner of her eye and is profoundly shocked.

Cheating?

They all like to win, yes, but Liz has thought their games were mostly for the fun of playing together. She is shaken to think they've made Barry so competitive that he would nudge his ball into a better position when no one's looking.

Sam gets the wicket. "Great shot, Dad!" calls Barry and his voice sounds normal and happy. Liz decides she must have been seeing things.

Cocky now, Sam tries a nearly impossible drive around a dwarf apple tree and his ball slams into the trunk so hard that four apples tumble to the ground.

The three of them burst into laughter and Liz takes her turn. From this closer stand, she can see that the angle is a little too great for Barry to get his ball through the hoop in one stroke. Sure enough, he misses and she is able to go ahead of him her next turn.

Sam has emerged from the turning wickets and is heading down the backstretch unperturbed by their gibes and insults.

"We gotta get him, Mom," says Barry and aims for her ball. For once he makes the long shot and, with the two extra strokes, hits Sam's ball, where his skill runs out. In trying to send Sam's ball off-course, Barry's mallet lands awkwardly and he winds up leaving his own ball so close to Sam's that he's actually helped his father instead of hindering.

"Here's how it's done," laughs Sam and croquets Barry's ball neatly back to Liz, which enables her to get through the turning wickets, too.

She's still uneasy though and lingers at that end to watch Barry make his way through the double wickets to the turning post and back out again. His approach to the next hoop is at an acute, but not impossible, angle. Sam is back through the middle wicket and nicely positioned for the last side hoop. Liz strokes through smoothly and looks back at her son.

His ball has definitely moved.

There is now no way Barry can get through that wicket in one shot and he's griping loudly about sticky wickets in a phony English accent while, from two hoops ahead, Sam gives amused advice about keeping his head down and following through.

Liz holds up her end of the chatter and laughter, but her peripheral vision gets a good workout and she reevaluates Barry's "poor judgment" that let her win the last game. Sam has never been devious himself, so he doesn't suspect a thing. Anyhow, Barry's very subtle about it. He mixes good shots with bad and when he goes ahead of Sam on one turn, he slips back the next so that the game ends in a glorious, down-to-the-wire finish. Sam is exultant in victory, the most relaxed he's been in days.

"The old man's still got it!" he chortles and Barry snorts in mock derision, vowing vengeance tomorrow night.

The moonflowers trellised beside the patio have uncurled into wide white circles eight inches across. Sam and Barry rack the balls and mallets as Liz moves across the grass gathering up wire wickets. Through the twilight she listens to the bantering give-and-take of those two male voices and something twists inside as she allows herself to realize how very much they're going to miss Barry next week.

At least she doesn't have to worry anymore about whether he's mature enough to handle things. Somehow that makes letting go a little easier.

"... That Married Dear Old Dad"

It's been said that every man marries his mother. This story is where that particular train of thought ended up.

I didn't know old-fashioned girls like Jessica still existed," Florence Weston had said when her only son abruptly eloped seven months ago and cheated her out of the fun of a big splashy wedding.

Of course, it's the bride's mother who always gets to run things, she reminded herself. The groom's mother has to stand where she's told, tell the bride's mother how lovely everything is, and buy a beige dress. Mrs. Weston hated what beige did to her skin, so maybe an elopement was just as well. Besides, if James had been made to wait through engagement party, showers, teas, tuxedo fittings and all the other formalities connected with a big wedding to a *good* girl—

No mother wants to think that her only child is that strongly influenced by his ... um, libido; but when she considered that string of really unsuitable young ladies—*Ladies*? Strumpets, more like it—that James seemed to attract—well! Foregoing "O Promise Me" and being escorted down the aisle (in a beige dress, don't forget!) seemed a small price to pay if James's hastiness brought her dear little Jessica as a daughter-in-law.

James had inherited the family real estate firm when he was only twenty, and surely it showed an underlying strength of character that he *did* work as hard as he played? Nevertheless, when he first started talking about settling down and taking his rightful place in the community, Mrs. Weston had been afraid he meant to try and housebreak that flashy (trashy) Sherri Conrad; so afraid, in fact, that she'd insisted upon attending one of Miss Conrad's performances.

And performance was certainly the right term for what she did with that cordless microphone right there in the Holiday Inn's cocktail lounge. Mrs.

Weston conceded a certain earthy charm to her smoky voice, but those vulgar lyrics! Mrs. Weston might be a lady, yet she was shrewd enough to see that the golden spotlight lent the young woman pseudo-sophistication and glamour; and judging by what the creature was willing to do in public, James probably wasn't strong enough to resist what she was no doubt willing to do in private.

Like father like son, Mrs. Weston worried. (A good man, but too prone to the weaknesses of the flesh. Had he controlled his appetites, he might have avoided that acute ptomaine—or was it botulism one got from indulging in oysters out of season?)

She invited the young woman to Sunday morning brunch; and, just as she'd expected, bright morning sunlight was less kind than subdued spotlights. The singer's makeup looked tawdry, her nail polish garish, and she could certainly stand to scrub her neck and elbows.

Mrs. Weston liked to think it was that brunch that opened James's eyes to Miss Conrad's unsuitability. In truth, Miss Conrad turned out to be as indiscreet as a Harvey Wallbanger.

She'd been booked to sing for a week at the Blue Star Lounge down in Wilmington, and when James went down to surprise her, he caught her in bed with the Blue Star Lounge's piano player. He'd stormed off to a party at someone's beach house, found Jessica in the kitchen slicing brown bread, and, entranced by her quiet wholesome beauty, swept her off to the nearest preacher.

With his pick of the town's houses, he had installed her in a Victorian cottage that suited her old-fashioned charm.

A perfect daughter-in-law, thought Mrs. Weston, watching Jessica knead bread dough in her sunny kitchen. No need for *her* to shrink from sunlight. Everything about the child radiated well-scrubbed cleanliness. "I do hope James appreciates you."

"He does," Jessica smiled. "You know he does. But he's so worried about the business. Even with the lowered interest rates, if this recession keeps up … I really ought to look for work myself."

"Surely not now?" said Mrs. Weston and was absolutely delighted to see her suspicions confirmed by Jessica's rosy blush. Impulsively, she jumped up and hugged the girl. "My dear! I'm so pleased. Have you told him yet?"

"No, not while he's under so much pressure." She blushed again. "Besides, it's been such a lovely secret. I'm glad you've guessed though. With my own mother dead …"

Teary-eyed, they hugged again.

"I always envied my friends who had daughters," Mrs. Weston said shakily. "And now I finally have a daughter of my very own."

Contentment wreathed the kitchen as Jessica returned to her kneading. She broke off a lump of dough and shaped it into a miniature ring.

"What's that for?" asked Mrs. Weston.

"Dessert. James is crazy about sweet rolls with my special honey-nut topping."

"You spoil him," Mrs. Weston beamed.

But that's what a wife should do, thought Jessica as she tidied the kitchen after Mother Weston left. Marriage was a partnership, wasn't it? If the husband wanted to spoil the wife by going out to earn their living singlehandedly, then why shouldn't the wife spoil him back with a perfectly ordered house and delicious little treats?

Dreamily, she pictured James's reaction to her news. He claimed not to want children, but she knew exactly what he'd say. He'd be tender again, solicitous, anxious for her well-being. She would smile indulgently, assure him she felt fine, that the doctor had said ...

Jessica stopped daydreaming and considered doctors. Perhaps an up-to-date obstetrician?

No.

Old Dr. Mills was a GP who'd been the Weston physician for almost forty years, and Jessica believed in family traditions. He'd brought James into the world and he could certainly deliver James's son, too. Besides, Dr. Mills was such a sweetie and so considerate of her fears; had even scolded James for taking too many barbiturates when the real estate business worsened.

"Less alcohol and more exercise!" he'd ordered.

She should probably start exercising, too. That afternoon, she wrote a note to her sister about the baby. The post office was twelve long blocks away, but the walk would be good for her.

"For both of us," she emended happily as she rummaged through James's desk in the den for a stamp.

Outdoors, it was a glorious spring day. She walked briskly past yellow forsythias and purple hyacinths, past drifts of daffodils and flowering dogwoods, thinking positive and beautiful thoughts. Inside that secret recess of the mind never touched by intellect, Jessica superstitiously believed one could prenatally mark one's baby for good or ill; so she dwelt on butterflies and blossoming crabapples and blue skies overhead.

At eight-thirty, when James let himself in through the garage door, the house was redolent of freshly baked rolls and a perfect *coq au vin*. Because he often had to show houses at odd hours, Jessica never knew when he'd get home, so she'd learned to cook things that were all the better for being reheated.

She threw aside her apron and rushed to kiss him. James gave her a squeeze, sniffed the air and asked, "When's dinner?"

"You have time for one gin and tonic," she said, handing him a tall chilled glass with a slice of lime perched on the rim just as he liked it.

But by the time she brought in their plates to the candlelit dining table, he was gulping down the last of a second drink; and while they ate, Jessica noticed puffy bags under his eyes. "You're working too hard," she said. "You look tired."

He gave another of those impatient sighs. "Would you stop being the perfect attentive wife for just once? Quit babying me, okay?"

"Maybe I'm getting into practice," she said demurely.

"In practice for what? Oh, my God!"

Jessica saw his dismay, and tears flooded her eyes.

James laid aside his fork and patted her hand. "Look, I'm sorry, Jess, but dammit! I thought we agreed. I mean, with business so rotten—don't cry. It complicates the hell out of things, but I'll manage. Somehow."

"You mean *we'll* manage, right, darling?" she asked, trying to smile through her tears.

"Yeah, yeah, sure." He patted her hand again. "Got any more of this chicken stew left?"

He mixed himself another drink as she refilled his plate and then put dessert in the oven.

It took twenty minutes for the yeasty confection to bake, for the viscous mixture of honey, walnuts and spices to seep down the edges and permeate sweetly through the soft crust.

James greedily eyed the second portion. "Aren't you having any?"

"I have to watch my diet now," she said. For the first time she really looked at his faint double chin, saw how self-indulgent his mouth looked as he chewed.

James was sipping his fourth drink as she cleared away the dishes, which was probably why his mind seemed to wander from his favorite program. Much earlier than usual, he rose, yawned, and said, "I've got a couple coming to see that house over in Dobbs after they get off from work, so I'll probably be late again tomorrow night. Guess I'd better turn in early."

"Me, too," said Jessica.

She was in bed before him and had almost drifted off to sleep when she heard James fumbling with the sleeping pills in the bathroom. Another, she thought dreamily and wondered if that many would seem credible? Still, Dr. Mills *had* warned him how easy it was to overdose while drinking.

In memory, she read again the letter she'd found in James's desk and which now lay strewn like confetti along her walk to the mailbox:

> *James luv—*
>   The earrings are gorgeous!!!! Of course, I'll forgive you for thinking a two-bit piano player could ever—but I won't talk about him if you won't talk about that man-stealer who tricked you into marriage just so she can stiff you with a big divorce settlement. Surprise! I'll be singing at the Dobbs Tavern all this week and I'm just dying to have my sweet baby show me some more houses. I won't wear *anything* but my new gold earrings!!!!
> *Love and kisses forever,*
> *Sherri*

James stumbled clumsily into bed and turned out the light as Jessica reviewed her neat kitchen. She'd thoroughly scrubbed all the dinner dishes, especially the dessert pan. Not that anyone would even think of checking. Not after Dr. Mills confirmed how freely James mixed barbiturates and alcohol. There'd be no more suspicions about James's accidental death than when James's father had died.

Of ptomaine, was it?

("And a good thing, too, if you ask me," Mrs. Weston's sister had confided shortly after she and James were married. "Florence would have just *died* if she'd known that he and Mable Byrd's oversexed teenage daughter bzz-bzz-bzz.")

An absurd speculation leaped to mind, but she dismissed it firmly, closed her eyes again, and, as James slept himself to death beside her, Jessica folded her hands protectively over her still-flat stomach and began to think beautiful, positive thoughts.

Craquelure

To celebrate the 50th Birthday of the North Carolina Museum of Art, I was asked to select a picture from the museum's collection and "write a response." Some authors wrote poems, some described a picture factually, some (like me) wrote stories. I chose a 14th Century painting, Madonna and Child *by Segna di Bonaventura.*

This story should come with a warning sign since it is a fictionalized version of how I got inside the head of a character in one of my Sigrid Harald books. If you haven't yet read Fugitive Colors, *you might want to skip this story for now.*

Beautiful, isn't it?"

Startled, she looks around and sees a guard, a pleasant, smiling, gray-haired man, slightly smaller than his dark gray uniform.

She smiles back politely. "Yes, it is."

"You really like these pictures, huh? I saw you here yesterday, didn't I? And maybe last week, too?"

"Yes."

Heretofore she's been unbothered in this quiet room of the museum. Italian primitives don't seem to be high on the pop charts of most visitors.

"You taking an art course?" the guard persists. "Maybe writing a term paper?"

She glances down at her note pad. A reasonable guess. The pages are covered with scribbled notes and crossed-out possibilities.

"Not exactly."

"Reason I ask, not a lot of people stop for a second look unless it's for a course or something."

That figures, she thinks. Despite the brilliant colors and all the gold, everything in this small gallery has an austere religious cast. This might be the Bible Belt, but the Bible of authority is the King James Version, the imageless Bible of Calvin and Wesley, not the illuminated gospels of medieval Catholicism.

"Actually," she says, "I'm researching a book. Is there someone here who could talk to me about a picture?"

"That Madonna?"

"Yes."

Once the Renaissance hit its stride, Mary would soften into a real mother with rosy cheeks and rich blue robes and she would gaze fondly at a chubby pink infant straight out of a Gerber baby food ad. In the early 1300s though, Mary was an unsmiling, abstract idealization and in this case, the baby that balances stiffly on her boneless hands has the solemn brow of a miniature adult.

She decides abruptly that she has wasted enough time wandering through the museum's collection of religious art. This picture will fit the needs of her current book as well as anything else. The period is off-beat enough to interest the character who is slowly taking shape in her mind and surely one primitive Madonna is much like another.

Isn't it?

"You might could ask somebody at the front desk," says the guard.

"Oh, I'm so sorry," says the receptionist. "Our curator of painting will be in Italy all summer, but maybe one of our interns could help you."

The receptionist summons a young man who appears knowledgeable about the period.

"Researching a novel you said?" he asks when they are standing in front of the picture she's settled on.

"Yes. A mystery novel. I need a picture that someone would kill for and I thought a Madonna might make an ironic contrast to the modern art setting I'll be using. This one looks interesting, but I need more information so I can sound as if I know what I'm writing about."

"Well," he says dubiously, "it's certainly a fine example of the period. Are you going to have it stolen from us?"

"No, no. I'll fictionalize a legitimate sounding provenance. Maybe change a few details. After six hundred years, you can't prove that this artist didn't paint one more picture, can you?"

"Probably not," he says. "Especially since uniqueness wasn't a great virtue back then and artists rarely signed their work."

The young man is steeped in knowledge recently acquired in pursuit of a Ph.D. and he is happily voluble about the techniques the artist must have used. He explains how the wooden panel was prepared to receive paint, why the gold leaf around the Madonna's head was applied over a base coat of red, why the flesh tones are now the greenish gray of *terre vert* instead of a rosy pink, and he discusses the problems of restoration and maintenance. He even explains some of the symbolism inherent in the picture. "Her face, her head, her halo—those three concentric circles echo the Trinity, and the red swaddling clothes foretell the crucifixion."

He is patient and he answers her questions without patronizing, but she goes away vaguely dissatisfied, feeling as if she's just been released from an Art 101 lecture.

She borrows library books about fourteenth-century Italian art. Several are literate and lively, and all are full of technical terms and aesthetic speculations that bring her no closer to the nameless *something* that she senses she is lacking.

She returns the books and spends the rest of the summer writing, hoping that the killer's passion for the picture will become clearer as his personality emerges.

She decides to make him an international art dealer. European.

French?

Too bloodless.

Italian then?

Yes. Mature and cultured and a lover of beautiful things. A citizen of the world who moves easily between his gallery in Milan and a smaller, satellite gallery in New York. A decent, well-respected man who makes a comfortable living dealing in 20th Century European art; a warm man, well loved by his friends; a man she herself would enjoy knowing.

"Why would someone like you kill for a Sienese Madonna?" she asks him.

He gazes back at her with intelligent brown eyes and does not answer.

Summer passes, autumn arrives, and she continues to doubt the validity of the motivation she has, by default, given to her character. She goes back to the museum and stands again in front of the picture and is pleased to realize how much she has learned since she first chose it.

Thanks to that young intern and the books she has read, she now has more knowledge—more vocabulary, anyhow—with which to assess the picture. She knows this is the central third of a wooden triptych, she knows that *craquelure* is the technical term for the fine red lines of the *bole* ground that show through the cracked gold leaf around the Virgin, and she can see clearly how the proportions of the figures have been altered to fit the religious requirements of the age. "Hieratic medieval theology wrapped up in a single painting," she can tell herself glibly.

But she's no closer to the essence. Something is still missing and she wonders if she's too far removed in time and temperament. Perhaps she should choose a more accessible work? One of the French Impressionists or maybe an American realist like Copely or Eakins?

And yet—

"You ever talk to the curator about that picture?" asks the guard, who has approached unnoticed.

"No."

"I hear he's back from Italy now."

She takes a second look at the man and is dismayed by the changes three short months have made.

He's shrunk even more inside his uniform and his skin is now almost as gray as the Madonna's.

"Fugitive colors," she thinks and doesn't realize she has spoken out loud until he nods.

"Yeah, that's what he called it," he says. "I asked him once how come so many of the faces have that ashy green skin and that's what he said. I forget exactly how it worked-something about how the artists used white for light and put in the shadows with green and then painted over both of them with some pink to make it look like real skin? But the pinks, they didn't hold up good—fugitive colors, that's what he said."

He gazes at the picture with proprietary pride.

"You like it, don't you?" she asks, surprised. (And is immediately ashamed of the snobbery implicit in her surprise.)

"Yeah," he says simply. "The real colors may be gone, but you can still imagine how she looked when she was first painted—all pink and red and gold. That's twenty-four-carat gold, you know, and it must've really shined when it was new. And I like it that she's serious. See the way her fingers curl around that little foot, all sweet and tender? She *knows* she's the Mother of God."

His gaunt face echoes the same certainty.

"Sometimes, when nobody's in here, I think about what it must've been like back then, back when it was new and had all its parts. It used to have two little side panels, you know? See where they hinged? They folded down over this one and when it was shut, it must have looked like a plain wood box. I think about a gloomy little stone chapel where the good priest comes to say mass. He stands the closed box up there on the altar, then he lights the candles and opens it up and the Queen of Heaven glows like the golden promise of salvation in a world all dark with sin and disease and—"

His bony fingers sketch the glory of his imagination and she wonders if he knows he is dying.

He sees her staring at him and breaks off. "Sorry. I guess I shouldn't be bothering you and you trying to look at the pictures."

She assures him that he isn't bothering her and to encourage him, she says, "It's too bad that the gold leaf has cracked so badly."

"Oh, I don't mind that. It's like one of those pictures you see in medical books, isn't it? Where they show somebody without his skin and you can see like a net of healthy red blood vessels?"

He gazes intently at the delicate red lines that spiderweb the gold.

"Blood of Christ," he whispers, almost as if he's forgotten she's there. "Blood of life."

Yes, she thinks. He knows.

And suddenly her elusive character stirs within her. For the first time, she who has no faith can feel the depth of his.

And the core of his despair.

"Now you know, too," he tells her.

The Store of Joys, 1997

Lost and Found

This was another exercise in the short form, occasioned by reading one news-paper article too many about poor-but-honest people who find large amounts of money and virtuously turn it in.

Mike Ozment stood outside the Ripton police station, turning in his hands an envelope that held enough money to last a drifter like him for six months.

After a spring on the road, he was ready to light for the summer months and build up his grubstake again.

Ripton seemed as good a place as any for that. Large enough to support a minor league team yet small enough to retain the illusion that everyone knew everyone else, the little city's main flaw was a suspicion of drifters, and after two weeks, Mike had found no steady work. He'd been a medic in Vietnam, and having come through that alive and unmaimed, he found his wants modest enough. All he asked of Ripton was a clean bed, decent food and an honest job.

That's why he hesitated in front of the police station and asked himself why he didn't just go back to his boardinghouse with the envelope. Why not spend the summer lounging in Ripton, take in *all* the ball games and forget the prom-ises he'd made to himself about not lowering his standards? The temptation was strong, but Mike faced it down and walked into the station. He laid the envelope before the desk sergeant on duty, a woman not quite 40 and sturdily attractive in her dark blue uniform.

"What's this?" she asked.

"I found it lying near the corner of Elm and Martin about twenty minutes ago."

The sergeant looked inside, and her eyes widened. "Did you count it?"

Mike nodded. "Three thousand dollars."

Sergeant Mary Stith dumped it out and made her own count. The money was divided into three packets of twenties, each held by a blue rubber band. There was also a silver religious medal tied to a red plaid ribbon. Nothing else. No writing on the shabby envelope and no identification inside.

The sergeant stuffed everything back inside and reached for a form. "This much money, someone's sure to report it, but I'll give you a receipt. Maybe there'll be a reward. Name and address?"

"Well," said Mike, "that might be a problem. I've got a room over on Pierce, but if I don't land a job by Saturday, I have to get out."

"Broke?" asked the sergeant.

" 'Fraid so."

Mary Stith took a second look at Mike's faded jeans, worn shoes and neat salt-and-pepper hair. "Broke, no job, yet you hand in three thou without a second thought?"

"Oh, I had a second thought or three." Mike grinned. It was a friendly, open grin, and the sergeant found herself smiling back.

A reporter from the Ripton *News* wandered over. "What's up, sarge?"

In minutes, he had the whole story despite Mike's modesty. Yeah, he was an unemployed ex-medic down to his last 10 bucks, but he wanted no halos hung on him. "Whoever lost that money might be in worse trouble—old, maybe, or sick. At least I'm strong and healthy."

Next morning, Mike's picture appeared in the *News* with the caption " 'Honesty still the best policy,' says jobless vet," and a local TV station featured him on the evening news.

If the attention was more than Mike had expected, he had to admit one side benefit: Smiling into the camera, he confided that his landlady had said he could stay till he found a job. The next day, job offers poured in, including one from Ripton's mayor. The mayor's father had suffered a stroke in April but was now recovered enough to manage in his own home if a suitable companion could be found. An ex-medic would be perfect, especially one so honest. Mike's only duty would be to tend his patient, a feisty old gentleman who loved baseball even more than Mike did.

With the doctor's consent, Mike soon had Mr. Larkin and his new wheelchair back in his box at the ballpark.

At one of the night games, Mike spotted a familiar face in the crowd a few rows back, Sergeant Mary Stith's.

"Do you come to all the games?" he asked when they met at the concession stand during the seventh-inning stretch a few nights later.

She gave him a friendly smile. "My husband got me hooked on baseball. He used to love it."

"Used to?" asked Mike, thinking how nice she looked in sneakers and jeans.

He liked the way her dark hair was feathered with wisps of gray and the way her eyes crinkled when she smiled.

She shrugged. "Still does, I guess. We were divorced four years ago."

"I'm sorry," said Mike.

"No need to be. A man and woman probably need more than a common love of baseball to keep a marriage going."

"How do you feel about fishing?" he asked. Mr. Larkin had told him about a secret stretch of the river and offered Mike the use of his fishing rods. "I'm off tomorrow."

Mary looked at him a long, considering moment, and then her eyes crinkled again. "You bring the bait, and I'll bring lunch."

Mr. Larkin's secret fishing hole didn't yield any fish worth keeping, but Mary's cold chicken sandwiches were delicious, and afterward, they lay on the grass under a shady oak and talked until sundown. Mike couldn't remember a time since Vietnam that he'd felt so deeply contented. "I guess you thought I was crazy at the time," he said, "but look what turning in that money got me: a place to live, a perfect job and now you." He looked at her shyly. "I'm not the only one feeling this, am I?"

Her blue eyes met his. "For how long, though, Mike? Another month? Two months? You're a drifter. I don't want to be anybody's summer fling."

"Maybe Ripton's where I finally set anchor."

"Let's not push it, Mike. Let's just see what happens." She began to repack her picnic hamper. "In any event, Ripton may not be a total waste. With a little luck, you might even get the money."

"No one's claimed it yet?"

"Oh, there've been lots of claims. We had people coming out of the woodwork, but none of them got the details right. You and I and Daws are the only ones who know about the blue rubber bands and that religious medal."

"Daws?"

"Jim Daws, our property clerk."

"Oh, yeah." Mike vaguely recalled a pudgy, young man in a blue uniform. He helped her fold up the blanket as the sun set over the river. "You'll still let me know if anyone does show up for it?"

"Sure," said Mary Stith and gave him a teasing look. "If you're still here."

Summer dwindled into autumn, and afternoons at the ball park gave way to televised football in Mr. Larkin's cozy den. At the old gentleman's invitation, Mary Stith occasionally joined them. In other years, Mike would have been two states away by Thanksgiving, but this year, the siren call of the road had faded to a faint whisper. Christmas found his stocking stuffed with bonuses from Mr. Larkin's grateful children, but shortly after New Year's Day, Mary telephoned. "I'm sorry, Mike. Somebody claimed the money today."

"*What?*"

As soon as he could, Mike appeared at the police station, and Mary showed him the receipt the claimant had signed that morning. "He's a salesman. Said he lost the money here last June."

"If you lost three thousand dollars," said Mike, "would you wait six months to come looking for it?"

Mary shrugged. "All I know is that he identified it down to the plaid ribbon on that religious medal."

"Did he now? The only ones who knew that detail were you and me and your property clerk."

"And the owner." Mary stared at him coldly across her desk. "Say what you mean, Mike. You think I'm so anxious to keep you in Ripton that I'd help someone claim the money?"

"Not you, my love, but what about Daws?" He saw a slight frown in her eyes. "Ever had shortages? Any prisoners ever claim they'd had more money than his receipts later showed?"

"Mike, give it up," she said, unwilling to let him know he'd struck a nerve.

"I want to see your boss."

She started to refuse, then saw the *News* reporter ambling toward them and quickly ushered Mike into the chief's office.

Only minutes later, Daws was summoned. The property clerk kept his gaze steady as Chief Waite repeated Mike's assertion that Daws had told a friend how to claim the money, but his voice squeaked when he asked Mike. "What makes you so sure that guy was lying?"

Chief Waite handed Daws an envelope that had been sealed with tape until a few minutes earlier. Across the tape was a date and the words, "Please hold till asked for."

"This was mailed to me in June," said the chief. "Three days before Ozment 'found' the money. Let me read you the letter."

Dear Chief Waite,
     If I don't find work soon, I will put my emergency fund ($3,000)

in a manila envelope and pretend to find it. Maybe that will attract enough notice to help me get a decent job for the summer. So you'll know the money's mine, it'll be in three packs of twenties held with blue rubber bands. There'll also be a red plaid ribbon tied to a medal of St. Christopher, patron saint of travelers and drifters like me.

Michael Ozment.

"Now then, Daws," Chief Waite concluded, "would you tell us who really has Mr. Ozment's money?"

Woman's World Magazine, February 1988

Shaggy Dog

According to Merriam-Webster, a shaggy dog story is "a long drawn-out story concerning an inconsequential happening ... whose humor lies in the pointlessness or irrelevance of the punch line."

What you have to understand is just how much Arthur MacHenry and Gillian Greber loved Emily, okay?

And each other, too, of course.

Arthur is the successful, hard-driving owner of an earth-moving company and I suppose you could say that Gillian is his trophy wife. She is certainly twenty years younger, five shades blonder, and three sizes slimmer than his first wife, who let her hair go gray and started wearing slacks with elasticized waistbands about the time Arthur and Gillian met.

This is not to say that Gillian's a trinket to be dangled from any man's key ring. She's an equally hard-driving stockbroker who ruthlessly fought off several other fast-trackers for the MacHenry account when it was up for grabs, and she didn't permit herself to fall into Arthur's bed until she'd upped the return on his investments by several percentage points, okay?

Arthur was as much her trophy as she was his—trim, distinguished, and as utterly besotted with her as she with him—a marriage made in heaven and blessed by Wall Street.

But not by children.

On this point, they were both clear: no kids. She claimed to have been born without a mommy gene and of his three grown children, one was into drugs, one was into a survivalist cult somewhere in Montana, and the third was convinced that her corporeal body was actually in an alien spacecraft on its way to Alpha Centauri and that what was still walking around on Earth was a telepathic projection.

As for his desire to take another swing at fatherhood, "Three strikes, I'm out," said Arthur.

The first few years of marriage were blissfully carefree. Their lifestyle was modestly lavish—a large Victorian jewel inside the beltway in the older part of town where hundred-year-old oaks arch above the streets, a weekly cleaning service, a yardman, catered meals that tasted almost homemade. She kept her name and job, his company won a major contract to clear and grade the land for a hundred-acre retirement village, and their combined personal portfolios topped the goal she'd set for them a whole year earlier than she'd planned. They scheduled quality time for each other in their calendars: they travelled when both could get away, Mexico or the Virgin Islands in the winter, wilderness adventures in the summer; they subscribed to the symphony; they attended the Episcopal church every Sunday morning and even based their tithes on actual income.

Until Emily showed up on their doorstep one day, they felt no lack in their lives. Once she was there though, hoo-*boy*!

Overnight, those two objective, articulate, career-oriented adults morphed into baby-talking, overindulgent Mega-Mommy and Doting Daddy.

And for what?

Emily?

Even for a dog, she was a dog.

Beyond ugly.

Picture a thirty-pound cross between a spitz and a spaniel, with an uneven black and tan and yellow coat that's been groomed with hedge trimmers. Picture hind legs slightly longer than the front so that she always looks ready to pounce. Picture the raggedy ears of a spaniel, the mouth of a Doberman, the nose of a poodle.

"Ah, but wook at dose big bwown eyes. Her's a shweetie, yes, her is," Gillian coos, cupping the dog's homely face in her slender hand and kissing its poodle nose.

"Her's Daddy's clever widdle Emily," Arthur beams as the dog obligingly fetches, shakes hands or offers to share a squeaky rubber duck.

Clearly Emily is intelligent. I mean she *did* pick Gillian and Arthur's doorstep, didn't she? And she did know how to ingratiate herself instantly, didn't she?

Gillian and Arthur were smitten from the first, but being the decent, high-principled people they were, they tried not to become too attached too quickly. Such a loveable dog as this, they agreed, must have owners who would be griefstricken to lose her. She wore no collar, so they notified the local animal shelter, put an ad in the Lost and Found column, and read every homemade

LOST DOG sign they passed. They themselves posted a few FOUND signs at strategic crossings.

Nothing.

While they waited, Arthur bought a handsome red leather collar and leash so that they could safely walk her around the neighborhood and ask if anyone recognized her.

Still nothing.

Cautiously, Gillian bought a wicker basket with a goosedown cushion.

"Emily has to sleep somewhere."

"Emily?"

"She was always my favorite poet," Gillian said shyly.

That afternoon, Arthur visited the mall near his office and came home with a pair of beautifully engineered stainless steel food and water bowls and a leatherbound copy of Emily Dickinson's poetry.

"Something for both my girls," he said.

Both smothered him with kisses.

There was an upscale pet boutique near Gillian's office and when an early frost was predicted the following week, she bought an expensive plaid coat and hat for Emily.

"The clerk said it was the MacHenry tartan," she told Arthur.

By Thanksgiving, it was as if they'd had Emily from puppyhood.

Gillian had never been particularly craftsy, but for Christmas, she knitted matching scarves for Arthur and Emily.

Not a week passed that one of them didn't bring Emily something special: buffalo hide chew bones, a raincoat, neckerchiefs, doggy shampoo, Velcro-tabbed boots to protect her paws from ice and salt, and dozens of toys.

Yellow rubber ducks were her favorite. She would toss them in the air, catch them in her Doberman teeth and clamp down so quickly that the ducks seemed to give a surprised quack. Occasionally, a startled Gillian or Arthur would step on one of the squeaky things by mistake and Emily gave such a wolfish grin when they jumped that all three enjoyed the joke.

Unfortunately, those sharp teeth meant a short lifespan for the ducks. As soon as the toy had too many tooth holes, Arthur would replace it so that Emily wouldn't choke on pieces of yellow rubber. The pet boutique began giving them discounts on ducks by the dozen.

In the year that followed, Emily's morning and evening walks introduced the MacHenrys to a different side of their neighborhood. There were the pleasures of being outside in all weather, of greeting the morning when it was dewy and fresh, of peeping through cozy lighted windows on frosty winter evenings or greeting the humans attached to Spike and Goldie, a grumpy English bulldog and a sweet-tempered golden retriever.

(Spike's "daddy" invited Arthur to join his club. Goldie's elderly "mommy" turned out to hold the purse strings of a large cosmetic company that Gillian's company had been wooing. When Gillian walked in with the account, she was promoted to full partner.)

That summer, they took Emily hiking with them in the high Sierras. For walking sticks, they ordered a hand-carved alpenstock for Arthur and a sturdy little shepherd's crook for Gillian. From the same chichi outdoors catalog, they ordered a special salve to keep Emily's pads from cracking on the trail, a collapsible/inflatable water bowl and packets of freeze-dried sirloin.

The trip almost ended in disaster though. On the second day out, Gillian glanced back to speak to Arthur and her foot came down on a twig.

Except that the twig writhed beneath her foot.

She looked down and froze as a young timber rattler gathered itself to coil for a strike.

Emily gave one sharp bark, then moved so rapidly that she was a blur of yellow, black and tan. They could only watch in amazement as she slung the snake into the air as if it were a rubber duck, caught it by the tail and then slung it again so hard that it cracked like a whip and fell lifeless to the cliff below, broken and bloody.

"My God!" said Arthur. "Are you all right, sweetheart?"

"She saved my life," said Gillian, throwing her arms around Emily. "Oh you wonderful, brave baby!"

Since this trip had been planned before they found Emily, the MacHenrys were now firmly convinced that Fate had sent her to them as a guardian angel.

It was a lovely idyllic vacation after that and when the MacHenrys returned refreshed to town, they continued to carry their walking sticks on Emily's daily outings.

Living in one of the oldest, most historical sections of the city meant living not too far from some of the oldest, less desirable sections; and Goldie's owner had been mugged while they were away. She wasn't hurt, merely shaken up a bit, but it was enough to make everyone uneasy. A stout walking stick seemed a sensible precaution.

"Not that anyone would bother me with Emily," Gillian assured Arthur.

Golden retrievers were not much protection, Arthur agreed, and Goldie had lost most of her teeth anyhow; but Emily was young and assertive and her Doberman teeth were a formidable deterrent.

"Look at how she handled that rattler," they told each other. (The length and girth of the rattlesnake had increased with each telling of the story.)

So when Gillian went out that wet autumn night to walk Emily, she was not at first concerned with the man who stopped and stared at them from across the street as they passed beneath a corner light even though the man's tight jeans and flashy jacket immediately signalled that he was not of this neighborhood.

Nor was she overly apprehensive when he turned and began walking along in the same direction as they, still staring.

When he crossed the street to intercept however, she shortened Emily's leash and tightened her grip on her sturdy shepherd's crook.

"Warty?" he said tentatively when he was only a few feet away.

"I beg your pardon?" said Gillian.

"I'll be damned," said the man. "It *is* Warty!"

He patted his thigh, inviting Emily to jump up on him. "Where you been, girl?"

Emily declined to jump, but neither did she growl as she normally would when Gillian drew back from strangers.

"That's my dog," said the man.

"*Your* dog?"

"Yeah. I lost her about a year ago. Right after we moved here." He gestured toward the east, where the large, carefully restored, turn-of-the-century homes gave way to a blue-collar neighborhood of bungalows and tract houses. "I figured Warty tried to get back to the guy up in Pennsylvania that gave her to me, but he said she never turned up. And here she is."

All the while he was talking, Gillian could feel him sizing her up, from her Italian boots to her English slicker.

"Can you prove this is the same dog?" she asked coldly.

The man snorted. "You kidding? You think there's another dog in the world like her, uglier than a warthog? It's Warty, all right. I'll show you. C'mon, Warty, shake hands."

Emily hesitated and then, with something very like a human sigh, she put out her paw.

Gillian felt her heart begin to break. Clearly the man spoke the truth, but just as clearly she knew she could not bear to give Emily up.

"Please," she said. "My husband and I—Could we buy her?"

"Gee, I don't know, lady." Again, that appraising stare.

"Oh, please. Any price. She's like a child to us and if you didn't have her long to begin with—"

"Five grand," the man said flatly.

"Five thousand dollars?" Gillian was taken aback. "But she's not purebred."

He gave an sardonic sneer. "She's one of a kind, lady, and that's the going rate. You give me five thou, I give you a bill of sale."

It was extortion pure and simple and they both knew it, but then Gillian looked down at Emily, who was looking up at her with such beseeching, humiliated eyes.

"Very well," said Gillian. "If you want to come now, we'll—"

"No checks," the man said sharply. "Cash."

"Then it will have to be tomorrow," Gillian said, just as sharply. "We certainly don't keep that much on hand."

A light mist began to fall as they exchanged names and addresses. He was Mike Phipps and Gillian saw that he lived about six blocks to the east of them.

"My husband and I will be home after six tomorrow," she told him and started to move away, but he grabbed Emily's leash.

"We'll see you at six-thirty then," he said and, despite her protests and pleas, he hauled Emily away with him.

Emily tried to resist, but Phipps gave the leash a vicious jerk and the dog reluctantly heeled.

The mist had turned to rain by the time Gillian returned home, but her tears were falling faster. Arthur lowered his newspaper as she came into the den, took one look at her distrait face, and hurried to her.

"Sweetheart, what's wrong? And where's Emily?" Images of wet pavement, bad brakes, and a small shaggy heap of fur lying limply in the gutter flashed through his mind. "She—she isn't hurt, is she?"

"No, she's fine, but oh, Arthur!"

Between her sobs, she told him all that had happened and Arthur was indignant and outraged at the man's effrontery, "But if she *is* his dog—?"

Gillian nodded. "She knew him when he spoke to her."

"Then we shall just have to pay him. Cheer up, sweetheart. It's only money, and if it brings her back to us—"

"But he was so awful. You can't know. Poor Emily. No wonder she ran away from him."

Arthur went to the bank next day and that evening, they both came home early. It had been an unhappy twenty-four hours, but soon it would be behind them.

The doorbell rang promptly at six-thirty. Mike Phipps was on time, but he came alone.

"Where's Emily?" Gillian asked anxiously as Arthur ushered him into the den.

Phipps just stood in the doorway. His hands were thrust into his jacket pockets, but his greedy eyes touched every lovely object in the room with a pawnbroker's cold assessment.

"Well, it's a funny thing. I got her home and it's like I forgot how much a dog can add to a man's life, you know?"

Bewildered, Gillian could only stare, but construction work had kept Arthur at street level. "How much?" he asked.

Phipps grinned appreciatively. "I like a man that can cut straight through the crap. Ten thousand dollars."

Arthur laid a stack of bills on the polished oak table. "There's the five thousand you and my wife agreed on last night. Either take it and bring the dog back or get out because we won't pay a penny more."

"Oh, I think you will. Look at your wife, man."

Gillian was white-faced, but her sense of right and wrong was just as strong as Arthur's and her chin came up bravely. "We will not be blackmailed, Mr. Phipps. You have our phone number. When you are ready to stand by the bargain we made, call us."

Yet thinking of poor Emily alone with this awful man who would probably chain her up outside with nothing but scraps to eat, Gillian gathered up some of the dog's possessions—her wicker basket with the goosedown cushion, a bag of her special food and some of her favorite toys.

Phipps took them with a sardonic sneer. "You don't fool me, lady. You're bluffing, the two of you. You said Warty's like your child? So just think of it as her adoption fee."

"Warty?" asked Arthur when Phipps was gone.

Tears spilled down Gillian's lovely cheeks and she shook her head. It was bad enough that she had to know why Emily's owner had given her that ugly name; she could at least spare Arthur that indignity.

Next evening, there was a message from Phipps on their answering machine when they got home. It was not a message they wanted to hear. The man sounded drunk.

"Somebody here's missing her mom and pop. Say hey to 'em, Warty. Speak ... come on, dammit, speak!"

There was the sound of something falling, a muffled curse and then Emily gave a sharp yelp of pain.

"Hear what she's saying? You don't come up with her adoption fees, I might decide to donate her to science. Knew a guy once that washed out of vet school when he operated on a dog and the dog died."

"Sweetheart, please," Arthur said, trying to loosen her hand from his.

Gillian looked down and saw that she'd squeezed his hand so tightly that her nails had left little red half-moons on his palm.

Both of them had read of the experiments done on dogs and cats over the years in the name of science and cosmetics and that Phipps could even consider it—!

"He's just trying to scare us," she said, with a shaky little laugh.

"Of course, he is," Arthur agreed briskly. "Pathetic really, trying to make us think he'd pass up our offer and just give her away."

"We were merely firm with him yesterday, weren't we?" she asked, needing reassurance. "He wouldn't feel that we tried to emasculate him, would he?"

"So that he'd give up five thousand on principle? Believe me, love—when it comes to money, men like Phipps have no principles."

He said it with more conviction than he felt.

"Be brave, sweetheart. We cannot give in to extortion. He'll come around. You'll see."

But Phipps's message left them with little small talk and after dinner, Arthur murmured something about contracts that needed his attention in his office.

"Maybe I'll take a walk," said Gillian. "Unwind."

"Shall I come with you?"

She shook her head. "I think I need to be alone."

He nodded so understandingly that she felt like a complete fraud when she stepped out into the autumn night.

A low pressure system had hung over the city all week, bringing intermittent showers that left the sidewalks adrift in fallen leaves. She had picked up her shepherd's crook by habit and was glad for its support when her feet nearly slipped out from under her on the wet leaves.

The damp night air was chilly and as she reached into her slicker pocket for gloves, her hand brushed the thick envelope that she'd hidden there. If she went through with this, it would be the first time she'd ever gone behind Arthur's back and the thought of deceiving him pained her intensely.

But what if Arthur's wrong, she thought. What if this Phipps creature *did* mean to carry out his threat? Could she stand idly by and sacrifice Emily for their own principles?

It was a simple plan. She would go to Phipps and throw herself on his mercy. "Arthur will never pay you another penny," she would tell him. Then she would give him the five thousand in cash which she'd drawn out of her personal account this afternoon and beg him to tell Arthur that he had decided to accept their original offer after all.

Phipps would get his ten thousand, Arthur would retain his principles and Emily would come safely home.

A simple plan and yet she couldn't bring herself to do it. Indeed, she spent the first twenty minutes walking in the opposite direction from Phipps' house. Eventually, though, her feet turned eastward and less than an hour after she'd left the house, she found herself staring into the front window of a small bungalow.

The curtain hadn't been drawn, but there was no light in the front room, merely a dim glow from somewhere beyond.

She went up onto the dark porch and pushed the bell button, but it appeared to be broken, so she knocked with more confidence than she actually felt.

Immediately, she saw Emily race into the room. As soon as the dog caught sight of Gillian, she seemed to go mad with joy, leaping up at the window, thrusting her little poodle nose through the mail slot, giving soft little yelps until Gillian slipped her gloved fingers under the brass flap.

But where was Phipps?

Gillian rapped again. With all the noise Emily was making, surely he must hear her?

Emily was whining now, begging Gillian to dissolve the barrier between them.

Helplessly, Gillian touched the old-fashioned latch and, to her surprise, the door swung open. Emily was all over her in an instant, jumping, racing in circles, tugging at her gloves.

"I know, lovey, I know," she whispered, calming the dog. "It won't be long, I promise."

A cold draft swirled through the room and suddenly, as if she'd forgotten an earlier appointment, Emily trotted across the dark room and out into a narrow hall. After a moment of hesitation, Gillian followed, still clutching her shepherd's crook.

The light of the all-white bathroom dazzled her eyes at first. Emily was dancing in excitement again and Gillian was dumbfounded by the man who crouched in front of the old-fashioned white porcelain sink. She gasped and he pulled himself erect with the aid of his sturdy Alpenstock.

"*Arthur?*"

Then her eyes adjusted to the bright lights and she saw that the dark object on the white tiled floor beyond him was not a scrunched up rug but the sprawled figure of Mike Phipps.

He lay face down in a puddle of blood.

Head wound, she thought automatically and looked at Arthur's stick.

"Is he—?"

"Yes."

"Oh, Arthur," she moaned.

"It's all right," he said decisively. "No one will think twice about it. They'll think he fell and cracked his skull on the sink or tub. An accident, pure and simple. My car's out back. I'll get Emily's basket, you find her leash and toys."

Quickly, efficiently, they cleared the house of all traces of Emily, then slipped the latch on both the front and back doors and got in the car unnoticed by any of the neighbors.

Emily sat between them, blissfully happy even though her humans were silent on the circuitous drive home.

Gillian knew she should be shocked and appalled by what Arthur had done, but instead she felt an almost atavistic glow of pride. He was Man, she was Woman and he had protected the clan of his cave with a primal club.

"Phipps was an evil man," Arthur said at last and reached past Emily to squeeze her hand.

"The world is better off without him," Gillian said, hoping that the squeeze she gave him in return would make it clear that she would never reproach him for this night.

He stopped on a deserted back road where there was a steep drop into a wooded ravine and reached into the back seat. A moment later, she heard the sharp crack of breaking wood, then the clatter of something hitting the rocks below.

But what—?

When Arthur got back into the car, she was touched to realize he was not quite as calm and efficient as he appeared. Somehow he had confused her shepherd's crook with his alpenstock. No matter, she told herself. She would take off early tomorrow evening, chop it into kindling with their camping hatchet and have a cozy fire warming their cave by the time Arthur came home.

Sex had always been good for them, but that night it was sensational.

Afterwards, when they had let Emily back into their bedroom and all three were lying cozily in bed, Arthur said, "You didn't leave fingerprints anywhere, did you, sweetheart?"

"I had on gloves the whole time," she reminded him. "What about you?"

"I didn't touch anything except the doorknob and Phipps's neck to see if he was still alive." He pulled her closer with a satisfied sigh. "So we're safe then. Nobody will ever connect your crook to—"

She pulled upright. "My *crook?* But it was *your* alpenstock!"

"You mean you didn't—?"

"No. I thought it was you!"

"You mean it really *was* an accident?"

Curled up at the foot of their bed, Emily, the dog formerly known as Warty, sighed happily at the sound of her humans' laughter.

That last human didn't laugh when his foot made her duck squeak. He jumped back, lost his balance and fell heavily and after that, he never moved again. She certainly wouldn't want that to happen to *her* humans.

Something very like a resolution was forming in her homely, shaggy head: Never again would she leave a rubber duck where one of them might step on it.

If you can't be beautiful, then you'd better be smart.

Funny Bones, 1997
Derringer Award Nominee

No, I'm Not Jane Marple,
But Since You Ask ...

In 1990, Charlotte MacLeod proposed that members of the American Crime Writers League contribute to a fund-raising anthology to be titled First Person Sinister. *The premise was that each of us must have had a brush with crime in the past, so why not embellish those brushes and write a first person account as if we had solved the mystery? Unfortunately, so few responded that the idea had to be scrapped. (Elizabeth Peters did contribute "Liz Peters, P.I.," which can be found in Charlotte's* Christmas Stalkings*) My story is loosely based on a flasher who "plied his wares" near my college. We did indeed call the police and they did bring a suspect over to the campus that night, stand him beneath a streetlight and ask us if he were the one. That's when I realized for the first time how very unreliable the testimony of eyewitnesses can be. We all agreed that it wasn't the man's face we'd focussed on, but that was the only thing we agreed on and the police had to turn him loose.*

Nevertheless, taken with "Craquelure," above, this story does illustrate how I do research for a book.

I do appreciate your letting me come talk to you like this, Doctor. As I explained over the phone, this new book I'm researching has a character who's undergoing psychotherapy and since I've never been to a therapist, I—
Oh no, no, no, I don't mistrust the profession. Not at all. It's just that I've never needed it. Like surgery. I've never had an operation either. If you're basically sound, the need for surgeons, like the need for therapists, never arises, right?

Good! I'll try not to take too much of your time. Just meeting your receptionist and seeing the sort of books and magazines you keep in your waiting room has been a big help. What I mainly need from you now is some technical jargon to sprinkle over my book for verisimilitude, so why don't we pretend I'm a new patient. What are some reasons I might consult you?

Oh?

Oh my goodness! Really?

How do you spell that last one?

No, no, I think those are quite enough to start with. One thing, though. I don't see a couch.

No couch? But I thought therapy was always—Okay, from that smile, I'd guess you therapists have to deal with as many misconceptions as mystery writers. People usually think I'm either Miss Marple or another Jessica Fletcher. In your case, I'll bet being a woman helps. At least your patients don't expect a Freudian beard and a Viennese accent, do they?

So! If you were going to treat me, I'd come in, perhaps curl up in this really comfortable chair (such a restful shade of blue! Did you use a local decorator?) And we'd just sit here? Looking at each other and talking face-to-face? How … um … *interesting*.

Well, no, it's not that I'd be embarrassed exactly, but it's like the Catholics, isn't it? I think it's so wrong-headed of them to phase out the confessional. Not that I'm Catholic. Actually, I was brought up Southern Baptist, but I've always thought the confession booth itself was such a good idea: that you could go sit in the darkness and whisper your sins through a grill, into a priest's ear, and be absolved without ever seeing his eyes. I don't understand how any Catholics could feel comfortable sitting across the table from a priest and telling their sins in broad-open daylight. I mean, how could you look him in the eye? I've always been such an eye-contact person myself and if I were going to talk to you about *my* psychoses and neuroses—oh not that I *could*, of course. As I said before, I simply don't have any. I've always been physically and mentally healthy as a horse.

Just look at the kind of books I write.

If readers ever give much thought to the persona behind my books, they probably think I'm a nice, down-to-earth, nurturing female. I don't write violent, glitzy pornography; good is usually rewarded in my books; evil is usually punished. My way of writing may not be mean-streets graphic enough for some tastes, but it *is* very straightforward.

I hope that doesn't sound too smug? Or bland? But when I write of mayhem and murder, it's certainly not to sublimate unfulfilled appetites for color, violence, or a darker side of life. No indeed. What you see is what you get. I'm just your basic boring beige.

Well, yes, I suppose even beige occasionally has to decide whether it's going to complement black or white, and I won't say there haven't been one or two instances … okay, three maybe if you count my sophomore year in college. But I'm sure you don't want to hear—

You do?

No, that's okay; I'm used to people saying I must have the mind of a murderer. I *have* killed a lot of people. Only on paper of course. Never in real life. Although … come to think of it, that college incident might amuse you—a sort of busman's holiday?—and not just because you're a woman but because the outcome was based on an introductory psychology course that I had to take to fill my social studies requirements. The professor did a classic experiment on us that—

But maybe I should put it in context by first telling you about my roommate, Janelle Denby. Cute as a June bug and such a dear person.

As freshmen, we'd been assigned the same room by chance, but it was a lucky chance and we've remained friends ever since. We would have roomed together the whole four years if she hadn't dropped out in the middle of our sophomore year.

No, not to get married, though I admit that's what a lot of young women from my generation did. Me, for instance, but not till my junior year. No, Janelle quit because she was raped and she just couldn't seem to shake it off.

That's what they used to expect of us, if you can believe it: that rape wasn't much more serious than a broken arm; and when the body healed, the mind should forget. But I really don't think many women ever do, do they? She eventually went back and got her degree from an all-girls' school, but she could never put herself in a man's hands again, and so she never married.

Never had a child either, of course, and she used to talk about wanting four. Such a pity. She'd have been a wonderful mother. She just loved children.

Date rape's a buzz phrase for the 'nineties and it's good that women are braver today about speaking out when it happens to them; but years ago, things were different. Especially in those small Southern towns where I lived till I was twenty. You're too young to remember and Raleigh's gotten a lot more sophisticated, but back then rape was something to smirk about. And more shameful for the victim than for her attacker. Look at the callous advice we got—"*When rape is inevitable, honey, just lie back and enjoy it!*"

No woman ever said that, did she? I was really encouraged when that politician got nailed to the ballot box last spring for coming out with that awful saying. And wouldn't you know he'd be from the South? Texas, wasn't it? You could tell what era *that* good ol' boy grew up in.

Anyhow, as I started to tell you, rape in the late 'fifties was usually considered the woman's fault. She asked for it, they said. Men were subject to certain natural urges which any really *nice* girl could keep under control. If not, she must have been dressed provocatively, or she'd let him go too far to expect him to stop, or what was she doing there alone that time of night anyhow?

Even college did nothing to change that early mindset. It was part of our culture. Unless a girl came back to the dorm hysterical and bloody, it would be whispered that she only cried rape because the housemother had questioned her sternly about her disheveled appearance. (Back then housemothers took the term *in loco parentis* seriously. They literally did act like a parent.)

But Mrs. Flaxton had been making cocoa out in the kitchen that night in October when Janelle signed herself back in and got upstairs without being noticed. As sophomores, we were beginning our first year in Kirkland, an upperclass dorm.

I'd been reviewing for a quiz in that psych course with Liz Peterson, a junior who lived on the third floor, when Janelle burst through the door and immediately locked it behind her. She was a mess. No lipstick, knee socks crumpled at her ankles, her plaid cotton dress a mass of wrinkles. And she was so upset that she couldn't even tell us what had happened at first, just whimpered like a whipped puppy as she tore her clothes off and reached for her robe.

Her lips were swollen and there were bruises on her arms. I thought she'd taken a bad fall or been knocked down by a car or something, and I said, "You're hurt! I'll get Mrs. Flaxton."

"No!" she cried. "You can't! Nobody. Please, Maggie, nobody!"

She was shaking so violently that Liz pulled the cover off my bed and wrapped her in it and we held her until she'd calmed down enough to tell us that she'd been raped and Mrs. Flaxton mustn't know or she'd be kicked out of school because it was Tuesday.

Oh, I know that must sound ridiculous to you. It was ridiculous to us, too. Nevertheless, other than study dates at the library, sophomore girls (and yes, we called ourselves girls back then) weren't allowed to date except on the weekends. And going off-campus at night without signing out really was an offense that could get you suspended.

That's what Janelle had done. Between whimpers, she told us that she'd signed out to the library but had arranged to meet Buck Woodall down by the lake in a wooded park that served as a buffer between campus and the edge of town.

"Buck Woodall!" said Liz. "What on earth were you doing out with *him*?"

"I thought we were just going to walk along the lake in the moonlight," Janelle sobbed.

I was bewildered. Janelle and I had met Buck Woodall on the tennis court a few days earlier. He was a journalism major and something of a big name on campus. School paper, baseball team, student council, you name it. Incredibly good-looking with a slow bashful smile, dark sexy eyes and, yes, a reputation as a wolf with eight hands; but we forgot about that as soon as we met him because there was nothing crude or ungentlemanly about his approach. He was so smooth, a real dreamboat. I was just as smitten as Janelle, but when he put the moves on her I'd backed off and watched enviously while he turned all that charm on her.

"Oh, you poor schnook," said Liz. "Haven't you heard that he tries to get in the pants of every girl he dates? He keeps asking me out, but I wouldn't trust him for Sunday tea at the college chaplain's."

Liz was from up North and, as a junior, she was also our fount of campus wisdom, but this was the first time she'd mentioned Buck Woodall. She made up for it though in the next two hours.

It took her that long to tell us all she knew about him because Janelle went through all the classic rape responses: she locked herself in one of the two shower stalls with a douche bag and a quart of vinegar I'd stolen from the kitchen, and she stayed there with the hot water tap on full for a half-hour until our communal bathroom was a cloud of steam. When she finally came out, she threw up twice, then went back for another twenty-minute shower. And still she felt dirty. When others on the hall grumbled, I said that she was trying to steam off the beginnings of bronchitis.

In between Janelle's bolts to the bathroom, Liz told us one story after another about Buck Woodall.

I probably don't have to tell you, Doctor, how he operated. I'm sure you've had too many women sit right here in this very same chair and tell you how it began with sweet talk and gentle kisses that gradually got more urgent and then when she—or in this case, Janelle—tried to put on the brakes ...

No, the only thing new about date rape is the term itself. It may be a cliché these days, but back then—Oh God! I can't begin to tell you how frustrated and angry and helpless we felt that night.

And not just that one night. We seemed to be under constant sexual siege and there was nothing we could do about it. It was like the campus flasher.

Oh, yes, we even had one of those.

From the movie theater downtown, the most direct route back to the girls' side of campus was along Magnolia Lane, and then a right onto Longleaf. Longleaf was quiet and dimly lit. No houses. Just a lot of trees. On one side was a low stone wall backed with tall bushes where the park and lake fanned out to border the college. Stone steps led down an unlit path to the lake, and the lake was a popular place to hang out on the weekend. In fact, that's where I saw my first Frisbee.

Near the end of our freshman year, we heard rumors that a flasher had begun lying in wait at the intersection of Magnolia and Longleaf, and when he spotted any girls coming back to campus alone, he would suddenly appear under a Longleaf streetlight, expose himself, and then disappear into the bushes.

The first few times it happened, the girls reported it to the police, but they couldn't give good descriptions; and when the police rounded up some local known deviants, no one could make a positive identification. Eventually, someone in the police department must have talked to the Dean of Women, who talked to the dorm mothers, who each called a dorm meeting and explained that while men who exposed themselves were nasty perverts, they were basically harmless. As long as we never walked that route alone at night, we'd be perfectly safe.

In short, don't call the police again unless we were positive that we could pick our tormentor out of a lineup of lookalikes.

It was bad enough that the police didn't take exhibitionism very seriously, but the prevailing attitude about rape was even worse. If Janelle tried to have Buck arrested, it'd be her word against his. Too, her reputation would be forever smeared while his would actually be elevated—especially among guys who thought a woman's place was on her back anyhow. The old double standard. He's a stud; she's a tramp.

When I think how victimized we were—how—how—

Oh, thank you. A glass of water *would* be nice. No, no, I can hold the glass myself. See? My hands have almost stopped shaking.

I'm fine.

Really.

Isn't it silly of me to get so angry after all these years?

Especially since we actually got some poetic revenge. Even the way it happened was ironic.

You see, on our own, as part of a term-long research project, Liz and I'd been charting the appearances of the flasher. We tracked down rumors, found most of the girls who'd been accosted, correlated their descriptions with every known factor, from time of night to day of the month, and eventually came up with a recurring pattern that seemed to be based on the full moon. We'd actually predicted his appearance the month before and had missed him by one night. This month we were determined to nail him.

In the meantime, Liz and I'd read everything we could find about passive sexual perversion. The police had told our dorm mothers that such men never physically assaulted their victims, and the textbooks more or less backed them up. Liz and I had originally planned to go flasher-hunting alone, but after what happened to Janelle, we decided we needed more people.

That was my job. The full moon was two days away and on the evening in question, I rounded up three other girls who were willing to skip the books and go see *Gigi*.

The moon was just rising as we came out of the movie and bought ice cream cones for the walk back to campus. By the time we turned into the street that led past the park, the moon had cleared the trees. Sarah and DeeDee had seen *Gigi* the week before and were trying to remember the words to the duet between Hermione Gingold and Maurice Chevalier, while Miriam and I were debating whether we could hold out for marriage if a Louis Jourdan ever propositioned us in that sexy French accent.

Even though I made sure Miriam and I were in front of DeeDee and Sarah, I honestly didn't expect anything to actually happen, and I was as startled as they were when we suddenly noticed a man leaning against a lamp post almost a block away. DeeDee and Sarah stopped singing, and our footsteps slowed.

Everyone had described the flasher as someone young enough to be a student, and this man was certainly dressed in the campus uniform of the late 'fifties: chino slacks, madras shirt, a windbreaker draped loosely in front of him on his arm. Think Kingston Trio or early Pat Boone.

Now we didn't want to look like timid idiots in case he really was a student waiting for someone to come out of the park, so we kept walking. After all, flasher or student, he was all the way across the wide street from us, his back was half-turned, and he acted as if he barely knew we were there.

We had just decided he was okay, and were making sheepish jokes about unwarranted nervousness when he suddenly turned, moved his jacket aside, and exhibited himself to us in all his swollen glory.

Startled, we froze for a moment; Miriam gasped and DeeDee gave a nervous titter. Even though I'd spent two days going over in my mind exactly how I meant to respond, I was so shaken that it took me a moment to react. Then adrenaline kicked in, and I shook my fist at him and yelled, "You rotten creep! Who the hell do you think you are?"

"Maggie, stop!" cried Miriam as I started running across the deserted street.

"Call the police!" I shouted back over my shoulder. "This is one time we're going to have a close-up description."

The flasher was almost as startled as my friends. Evidently, no girl had ever given chase before; and after a split-second hesitation, he took off like a shot rabbit, over the low stone wall and into the bushes.

As I swung myself over the wall, I could hear him crashing through the underbrush back toward the campus. "Stop!" I yelled. "Somebody stop him!"

If it'd been the weekend, there might have been two dozen students necking on the grassy slopes to help me chase him. On that Thursday night, the woods seemed deserted. The moonlight was so bright though, that as I cut over to the paved path that led from the steps at street level down to the lake, I spotted something lying on the ground just where the path made its first turn.

A man's windbreaker.

Jubilantly, I grabbed it and raced up the steps where Miriam and DeeDee were anxiously waiting. Sarah had hurried on ahead, they said, to call the police.

"He dropped his jacket!" I said, shaking it over my head triumphantly. "But I saw who it was and you know him, too."

"Who?" they cried.

"You'll never believe it. *I* don't believe it—Buck Woodall!"

"*Really?*" DeeDee was incredulous. "He's in my journalism class. Are you sure, Maggie?"

Miriam didn't know Buck except by sight, but I saw her eyes widen as she compared our flasher's shadowed features to Buck Woodall's face by daylight.

To do the police justice, they came quickly when Sarah told them I'd gone chasing the exhibitionist. They played their flashlights over the windbreaker and, sure enough, the initials B.W. were inked onto the brand label, followed by what later proved to be his student ID number.

The campus police arrived about then. DeeDee knew that Buck lived in Cameron Hall, and both patrol cars pulled up by the door of Cameron just as Buck came strolling up the walk as if nothing had happened.

He kept insisting that nothing had, but they hauled him over to our dorm and made him stand under a streetlight while DeeDee, Miriam, Sarah and I looked him over from half a block away.

"That's him," I said.

"Gee, I don't know," said Sarah. "I thought the guy had on light chinos."

"No," I said. "Don't you remember how white his—how white he was against those dark pants? And he had on white bucks, too, even though it's October. I thought he looked familiar. When I got closer, right before he turned and ran, I definitely recognized him."

"Yeah," said DeeDee. "Buck was wearing those white shoes in class this afternoon."

"You're right, Maggie," said Miriam. "It's him, all right."

"You're willing to swear to that?" asked the city policeman.

"Yes, sir, I am," I told him.

"Me, too," said Miriam and DeeDee.

"God, I can't believe it," said Sarah. "Buck Woodall the campus flasher? And after all that Don Juan bragging he's done."

Despite Buck's denials, the police took him downtown and booked him. The story was all over campus before midnight and psych majors had a ball theorizing about his sexual neuroses. All his boasts of earlier victories suddenly seemed like lies, and several girls got their reputations back that night because people thought exhibitionists "couldn't do it" with a real girl. Anyhow, being a stud was one thing; a flasher was something else entirely.

Believe me, Buck's stud-standing couldn't have fallen any lower than if he'd suddenly been caught wearing black lace bra and panties.

Of course, he tried to say he'd been out with someone that night, but the girl he named denied it categorically.

No, it never came to trial. This *was* the South, remember? His parents hired a lawyer and got it hushed up. Well, hushed up legally. Some genies never go back in the bottle, thank God. Buck tried to finish college in another state, but enough people knew so that the story followed him there, too. His journalism career never went anywhere. Last I heard, he OD'd in some boarding house down at the beach.

You look puzzled, Doctor. What did that psych experiment I mentioned earlier have to do with this? My goodness, you *do* pay attention to every word, don't you?

It was a classic experiment, so I'm sure you're familiar with it. I forget where it was originally done, but I suspect it's still being used out there somewhere. Anyhow, the way it works is that you have a professor in the middle of a classroom lecture when suddenly the door bursts open and in rushes one person followed by another who threatens the first person with a weapon. There's a loud scuffle and they rush out again, whereupon the professor asks everyone in the classroom to write an account of what just happened: describe the victim and the assailant—which was white, which black; the weapon and was it fired; how many blows were exchanged, et cetera.

You remember how most students muddle race, dress and physical appearance? And how almost nobody ever realizes that the assailant isn't carrying a handgun? They'll describe that banana as everything from a pearl-handled automatic to a Colt .45.

Well, when my professor pulled the experiment on us, our class had to come up with one single description that all agreed with. The interesting thing was that, even though several of us started off thinking we'd seen one thing, after awhile, we found ourselves remembering it as two of our most vocal classmates described it. They were so positive and they kept reinforcing each other until the rest of us fell into line and said, Yep, that's how they were dressed, all right; that's the kind of gun he carried.

Those two were in on it with the professor, of course, and they proved to the rest of us that when several people aren't sure of something, a positive person can actually make them accept his version of an incident.

I couldn't have done it without Liz, though. She had to maneuver Buck very carefully that night so that no one saw them go down to the lake together. She had to pretend to be chilly so he'd drape his jacket over her shoulders, then drop it where I could find it, and string him along till she heard me yell.

But you know what, Doctor? Telling you this has reminded me that Janelle was in therapy for several years; so I won't take up another single minute of your time. She'll give me all the details I need for my new book. Thanks anyhow.

How do I feel about what I did? Fine. Why not? It even gave the real campus flasher such a scare that we never heard from him again.

Oh, I see what you mean: you think I might be carrying around a load of guilt because I helped wreck Buck's life? Good Lord! Didn't he ask for it? So why should I feel guilty? Besides, I told you: I'm healthy as a horse.

Physically *and* mentally.

Just read my books.

Vengeance Is Hers, 1997

The Stupid Pet Trick

At breakfast one morning, while on a book tour in Florida, I read an article in the Miami Herald *that claimed cats had active imaginations and some even seemed to enjoy playing mother to sock "kittens." My own imagination was immediately captured. I tore out the article, reread it on the train back to North Carolina and had the bones of the story in my head before we got to Georgia.*

When Dr. A. Forrest Robinson, BA, MA, PhD, unlocked the door of the Georgetown house that chilly March evening, it felt almost like stepping into one of those old domestic sitcoms—the Breadwinner Returns Home scene.

Time: 7:30 Sunday night.

Action: After a weekend business trip, enter Weary Traveler screen left. Pause to savor return and assess household. Washing machine chugs away quietly in its closet under the stairs, the smell of something savory wafts from the kitchen, the domestic sound of the vacuum cleaner aloft. Drop garment bag on 19th century deacon's bench in the hall, put briefcase on slate-topped Queen Anne side table, step to foot of stairs and call up, "Hello, honey. I'm home!"

But she wasn't Dick Van Dyke and Kevin certainly wasn't Mary Tyler Moore and he didn't come running to greet her with a radiant smile and soft murmurs of how much he'd missed her this weekend, hateful old business conference—or, in this case, academic conference—that took her away for three whole days. Nor was there a child to rush downstairs and demand to be told if she'd brought him a present.

The only one who noted her return was Mittens, a little black cat with neat white paws, who came out into the entry hall, thrupped a perfunctory welcome, watched as Amelia took off her coat and stuffed her gloves in the pocket, and then went back to whatever she was doing behind the couch in the den.

Upstairs, the vacuum cleaner continued its back-and-forth roar and now that she thought about it, Amelia looked around the ground floor in surprise.

Kevin?

Domestic?

Usually when she went away for the weekend, to a conference in Chicago or Philadelphia or to visit her only daughter in New York, she would return to find the lovely old two-story townhouse cluttered with three days' worth of dirty plates and glasses and take-out cartons, clothes strewn all over their bedroom, damp towels on the bathroom floor, Mittens' litter box reeking to high heaven. Although they had been married almost four years, she wasn't aware that Kevin even knew how to turn on the washer, much less how to program the dishwasher or run the vacuum. He was always perfectly happy to let her do it or tell her to leave it for Mrs. Ortega, their weekly cleaning woman.

Tonight the house shone as if Mrs. Ortega had just left. Fresh candles and flowers were on the dining room table where two places were set with her best china and silver. Except for a couple of mixing bowls in the sink, the kitchen was immaculate. In the den beyond, more candles sat on the Pennsylvania Dutch dower chest that served as a coffee table and two sparkling crystal goblets waited for the uncorking of a near-by bottle. He had even lit the gas logs and the flickering flames gave the room a sensuous ambiance.

She lifted the bottle in her hands and read the label of her favorite wine, feeling now like a character in *Dynasty* or the video version of a Danielle Steele novel.

Kevin's footstep sounded on the stairs and Amelia suddenly wished she'd taken time to run a comb through her graying hair and freshen her lipstick before getting out of the car. She turned almost shyly as her husband entered the den.

"Amelia! Hey, you're home early. I didn't expect you for at least another hour."

"I got away earlier and traffic was lighter than I expected," she began to explain, but he took her in his arms and kissed her long and deeply.

She hadn't realized how perfunctory their kisses had become lately until the rising passion of this one almost took her breath away.

"Ummm. Nice," she said when they came up for air. "But what's all this in aid of?"

"All what?"

"House Beautiful. Martha Stewart."

"Nothing," he said, tenderly nuzzling her neck. "You think I'm such a slob, I thought I'd surprise you for a change. If you'd waited another half hour or so, the wine would be chilled, the candles would be lit, Rachmaninoff would be playing on the CD—"

"You'd be draped on the couch in a black lace negligee?" she teased.

"Something like that," he grinned, turning her to him for another kiss.

She met his lips eagerly and with such hunger that he finally said, "Whoa! Wine and dinner first, dessert after."

Dinner was like a rerun of their first weeks together when every glance, every conversation, had erotic overtones.

A tenured professor of modern philosophy at the university, Amelia had been asked to set up an interdisciplinary seminar on popular culture and one of her graduate assistants had mentioned that there was a dishy part-time poet in the English Department who could relate Byron and Cummings through the Beatles to LL Cool J.

Amelia had never developed a taste for rap—too misogynistic for her tastes, but she recognized its significance in pop culture, and a poet who could dish the subject sounded like a good addition to her team. That he himself might be "dishy" hadn't been a factor.

Not at first, anyhow.

That was later.

After the seminar was successfully completed.

After the grad assistant became discouraged.

After he'd persuaded her that the seven-year difference in their age didn't matter.

"You wouldn't give it a second thought if you were thirty-six and I were forty-three," he'd said. "Why are you clinging to an outmoded double standard, Dr. Forrest?"

And so, to the displeasure of her daughter Elizabeth, who thought Kevin was a gold-digging bimbo ("hedonistic opportunist" were her actual words), they were married, and so he had moved into the gracious old Georgetown house she once shared with her late husband. Despite Elizabeth's assessment, he worked hard on his poetry—three chapbooks in four years. So what if he only got paid in copies of the books? So what if he still taught part-time on a nontenured line?

"It's not as if we need the money," she told Elizabeth.

"Well clearly, *he* doesn't," Elizabeth said. "Not with you supporting him."

"I don't support him. He never takes a penny from me."

"No, but does he give a penny? Does he pay anything for utilities? Taxes? Car insurance?"

"Those bills are practically the same as before we married," Amelia argued uncomfortably. "He brings me yellow roses—"

"Which he loves, too."

"—champagne and brie—"

"Which he helps you drink and eat. Face it, Mother: the only reason Kevin can afford roses and champagne and imported cheese is because he doesn't have to pay mundane living expenses."

"You could take a lesson from him," Amelia said sharply.

"Live for today? Let tomorrow take care of itself? Oh, honestly, Mother. You're starting to sound like one of those kvetching mamas on a TV sitcom, always nattering about when's the career girl going to give her grandchildren."

"I just don't want you to look up from your work someday and realize you're too old to have children."

"*You* may be sorry you didn't have a houseful, but that doesn't mean Tom and I will have any regrets."

The wine, the flickering candles, the utter relaxation of being home with Kevin after four hours behind the steering wheel were getting to Amelia. She smiled to herself as Mittens went past the doorway carrying a dark limp shape in her mouth.

Poor Mittens. Sublimating her frustrated maternal instincts by pretending that one of Kevin's socks was a kitten.

Kevin poured the last of the wine into her glass and she was just muzzy enough to smile into his eyes and say, "Are you ever sorry we didn't try to have a child together?"

For one nanosecond, there flashed across his face a look of horror identical to Elizabeth's.

"Good God, no! Whatever made you think that?"

She wasn't sure whether to feel pleased that he was satisfied with their life just as it was, or whether it was sad that he'd never experience the deep and selfless sense of completion that came when you held your own child in your arms.

"Diapers? Two a.m. feedings? Colicky crying? We're too old for that routine."

"You're not," she said quietly.

"Oh, yes, I am, my darling, even if you aren't. What I'm *not* too old for—"

He stood and blew out the candles, then took her hand and led her upstairs.

The doorbell rang while she was still marveling at the fresh linens on their bed.

"Maybe if we ignore it, they'll go away," Kevin said hopefully, as he slipped his hand inside her sweater.

The doorbell rang again with a steady insistence.

Sighing, Kevin headed downstairs.

Amelia followed to the head of the steps.

"Mr. Kevin Robinson?" asked an authoritative male voice.

"Yes?"

"Sorry to bother you, sir, but—"

"Marc?" Amelia came all the way downstairs so that she could get a clearer look at the taller of the two men in gray topcoats, who filled the doorway. "Marcus Galloway?"

"Dr. Forrest?" A genuine smile spread over the newcomer's warm brown face. "I *thought* this was where you used to live, but they told me Robinson."

"That's my name, now," she said, gesturing to Kevin. "Darling, this is one of my old students. It must be what, Marc? Nine or ten years since you took my Philosophy 4.1 seminar?"

"At least. Good to see you again, Doctor. And this is my partner." He nodded toward the white man who appeared to be a couple of years older than he. "Detective Frank Boland."

They murmured pleasantries and shook hands all around, and Amelia drew them in out of the cold night and into the warm and cozy den. She put the empty wineglasses on a nearby sideboard and relit the candles.

"Partner?" she asked, when everyone was comfortable. "You're with the District Police Department? I thought you majored in Modern Lit."

Detective Galloway grinned. "I did. And believe it or not, Kafka and Beckett and Solzhenitsyn give me a lot of insight into this job."

"A literate police officer," said Kevin. "Now there's a play against type. And what did you major in, Detective Boland?"

"*Kevin!*"

"Sorry, darling." He looked at the two detectives and gave a rueful shrug. "I apologize, gentlemen, but my wife's has been gone since Thursday and—" He broke off with another shrug and headed for the kitchen.

"Why don't I make a pot of coffee while you two catch up with old times?"

"We're the ones who should apologize," said Galloway. "Coming over late like this, interrupting your evening."

"Nonsense," Amelia said. "It's only nine-thirty and I think coffee's a great idea."

"Actually, it was Mr. Robinson we came to see," said Boland.

"Me?" Kevin turned in his tracks and came back into the den.

"Yes, sir. I'm afraid I have some bad news. One of your colleagues was killed Friday night."

"*What?* Who?"

"A Roseanne Chapman. We understand that you shared an office with her?"

Kevin nodded. "Along with three other part-timers."

"Roseanne Chapman?" asked Amelia. "*Pinkie?*"

Galloway cocked his head. "Pinkie?"

"I'm afraid that was our not very nice nickname for her," Amelia confessed. "After that famous pair of frothy English paintings. You know—*Blue Boy* and *Pinkie?* Rather insipid picture actually, and Roseanne Chapman took it a step further. She dyed her hair strawberry blond and wore nothing but pink: dusty rose in winter, pastel pink in summer. By now you must have been told that everything she owned was pink. Pink shoes, pink suits, pink coats, even pink note pads and ballpoint pens."

"Pink was her 'look,' " said Kevin.

Despite the horror of hearing that someone they knew had been murdered, Amelia couldn't help smiling at the memory she and Kevin were sharing at that moment.

They had gone up to New York to see Terrence McNally's *Master Class* on Broadway last summer. At the lines, "Everyone needs a look. You have no look. Get a look," they had turned to each other and silently mouthed, "Pinkie!"

Guiltily, Amelia pushed that unkind memory away and said, "What happened, Marc? How did she die?"

"Head wound." He spoke succinctly, as if they were caught up in an episode of *NYPD Blues.* "Someone smashed her hard and then dumped her in the Potomac, over near Roosevelt Island. Couple of joggers spotted her pink coat at the edge of the water yesterday morning. We've been questioning her friends, colleagues, the usual routine. When did you last see her, Dr. Robinson?"

Amelia looked to Kevin for help. "I can't remember if I've even seen her this semester. She was never there when I popped in to meet you."

"That's because I'm teaching a Tuesday-Thursday this semester and I think she has—*had* a Monday-Wednesday schedule," Kevin told her.

"What about you, Mr. Robinson?"

"I'm trying to remember. I did go in for a department meeting last Monday and I think she was there then, but it's such a big department and we're both part-timers, so I couldn't swear to it."

"You didn't see her since then?"

Kevin shook his head.

"Ma'am," said Boland, "if you don't mind me asking, what's that cat doing?"

Amelia leaned across Kevin to look over the end of the couch. In the open space between the couch and Boland's chair, Mittens had curled her abdomen around several cloth blobs which she alternately patted and licked.

"Damn it, Amelia!" said Kevin. "She's got my best pair of argyles again."

Automatically, Amelia leaped to Mittens' defense. "If you'd put them in the hamper instead of leaving them on the floor—"

She heard the snap in her voice and broke off with a smile at Boland. "She's playing mommy. Like a little girl playing with dolls. She steals socks and things and carries them around in her mouth as if they were kittens. She's really quite imaginative."

Kevin retrieved his argyles and gave a sour laugh. "We're thinking of trying to get her on *Dave Letterman.*"

Marcus Galloway smiled. "The stupid pet trick segment?"

Kevin nodded. "Except that she's too stupid to do it on command."

"Or too smart," Amelia said lightly.

"You could videotape her," Boland suggested. "Maybe get it on *America's Funniest Home Videos?*"

Annoyed at having two of her "babies" snatched away, Mittens trotted from the room with an ancient catnip mouse in her mouth and headed for the dining room. A moment later she sneaked back for one of Amelia's old black wool socks.

"Now she's pretending to move her kittens so we won't know where they are," said Amelia.

"My mom used to have a cat that moved her kittens every week," said Galloway. "We never knew where they were going to show up next."

He watched the little cat disappear through the doorway, then turned back to the routine questions at hand. "What about boyfriends, Mr. Robinson? Ms. Chapman was young and pretty. Did she have anything going with somebody at the University?"

"I really couldn't say. We didn't talk much, especially this semester, and when we did talk, it was about schedules or desk space, nothing personal."

"Too bad," said Boland, " 'cause she had a bun in the oven and nobody seems to know who the baker is."

"Two lives taken?" Amelia felt her heart tighten with sadness at the little pink life snuffed out before it could begin. Before it—

Sadness turned to shock as Mittens crossed her line of vision.

Instantly recognizing what it for what it was, Amelia willed herself not to gasp, but she was too late. Marcus Galloway had seen it, too, and he made an awkward grab for the pink thing that dangled from the cat's mouth. Mittens easily eluded him and scampered through the doorway.

Galloway jumped his feet but Amelia slipped past him.

"Let me," she said. "You'll only scare her."

The little cat had heaped her "babies" beneath the heart pine hunt board Amelia had inherited from her grandmother, but there was no resistance when Amelia fished out the dusty rose glove.

Numbly, Amelia found herself trying to remember the name of an old black-and-white *Twilight Zone* episode. By Ambrose Bierce she thought. "An Occurrence at Owl Creek Bridge"? Where dozens of incidents zip through the person's mind in a single brief second before the rope snaps his neck?

In that instant, with the faint smell of rose perfume arising from Roseanne Chapman's glove, Amelia saw again that tube of pink lipstick that had mysteriously fallen out of their medicine cabinet after one of her weekend conferences last autumn. Kevin told her it was a grad student and he swore it was nothing more than a casual one-night stand. Unimportant. Almost anonymous. That it would never happen again. He didn't want to lose her.

("Didn't want to lose his comfortable life." The thought was hers, but the voice was Elizabeth's.)

So this is denouement, she thought bleakly, the dramatic moment of untying all the knots that comes just before they roll the credits of a Perry Mason or a Matlock or any of a dozen Grade B detective movies. Only this wasn't a movie or television program or even a cliched he-done-me-wrong Patsy Cline song.

She thought she had made it very clear that while she might teach an occasional class in Pop Culture, she had no intention of living a life governed by pop values. Who would think that Kevin was such a slow learner? Or that he would flunk the most important test in his life?

Although it felt like a hundred years since she'd followed Mittens into the dining room, the men had barely moved when she returned.

She came no further than the doorway and she spoke only to Marcus Galloway.

"He's spent the weekend cleaning, so I don't know how much evidence you'll find in situ. But the washer has a lint filter that he probably didn't think to clean and you have my permission to take the bag that's in the vacuum cleaner. There's bound to be pink hair, pink threads, pink something."

She handed Galloway the glove and turned to go upstairs. Almost as an afterthought, she paused and added, "Oh, yes. I'd appreciate it if you would take him with you, too."

"Amelia, please!" Kevin begged. "Don't do this! I love you!"

She halted on the staircase and gave him an ironic smile. It was a *Gone With the Wind* ending and Rhett Butler's words were on her lips, but she'd be damned if she'd say them.

Besides. They wouldn't be true.

Murder They Wrote II, 1998

Roman's Holiday

When would-be mystery writer Roman Tramegra showed up in One Coffee With, *my first Sigrid Harald book, he was meant to have a small, walk-on role and then disappear along with all the other minor characters. But his irrelevant chatter, magpie curiosity and extravagant sensibilities provided Sigrid with an alternate train of thought that eventually led to the killer, and having him around to distract and annoy her proved such a useful device that I eventually let them become housemates. It occurred to me that if Roman ever actually sold a mystery novel, he would surely take his small advance and fly straight to Venice. Which meant, of course, that I had to go to Venice, too. Research. (The life of a writer is very hard.)*

*D*awn was but a gray rumor across Venice when Lt. Peter Bohr tiptoed down the stairs of the pensione, turned the heavy deadbolt of an ornate brass lock, and slipped out onto the wide promenade that bordered the lagoon.

Roman Tramegra stepped out onto the Riva degli Schiavone, gently closed the door of his pensione, and jotted a few words on a tiny pocket notebook, words that would remind him of this opening scene for his next book.

In New York yesterday morning, Tramegra had taken a crowded shuttle van over to the airport. Now, some twenty-four hours later, he stood and watched the empty *vaporetto* pull away from its stop, pass beneath a low arched bridge and turn right, toward St. Mark's Square.

A large bear-shaped man of early middle age, Roman Tramegra breathed in the familiar funky smells of damp marble and brackish water and gave a deep sigh of satisfaction. If Italy was his spiritual home (he'd actually been born in Minneapolis), Venice was his baptismal font. Until his forty-second year, he'd been a freelance writer of oddball articles which were published in travel magazines or small trade journals. Now he'd finally sold his first mystery novel, and with its modest cash advance, he'd come winging back to Venice.

Being a man given to extravagant emotions and gestures, Roman stretched his arms toward the churches that stood in stately majesty across the wide canal and murmured aloud, "*Serenissima!* I've returned to you, you *bella città.*"

As if on cue, the bells of Venice rang out across the water, a dozen or more towers chiming the morning hour in a cacophony of bronze and iron.

By midmorning, the arched bridge that faced the Bridge of Sighs would be so tightly thronged he would barely be able to pass. Here in the gray dawn however, it belonged to him alone and he stopped to take more notes of the carved white marble.

"If I use Venice as a backdrop for my next book," he'd told his housemate before he left New York, "I can call it a research trip."

"Venice as a business expense?" She had arched a skeptical eyebrow. "I guess this means that your next tax return will be a work of imagination, too?"

(Like his fictional hero, Roman's housemate was a homicide detective and Roman feared that her profession had made her cynical.)

A little further on, Lt. Bohr rounded the Doge's Palace, nodded to the golden lion upon its tall column and turned into St. Mark's Square—the most elegant drawing room in Europe, as Napoleon once termed it. "As if a Corsican peasant knew anything about elegance," thought Bohr, the son of a wealthy New York socialite and an Oxford don. But then, as always, his heart skipped a beat to behold the venerable Basilica itself, its spires and domes rising in magnificent glory against the dull sky.

As dawn's early gray gave way to brightening skies, a sleepy-looking pigeon landed at his feet and cocked an opportunistic eye for bread crumbs or corn. Soon pushcarts that sold birdfood would arrive. Soon hundreds of pigeons would be jostling each other to sit on tourist heads or outstretched hands while shutters clicked and video cameras recorded another few miles of tape.

"Sorry, *piccolino,*" he told this first harbinger of morning. "I haven't had my breakfast yet either."

He glanced at his watch. Much too early for the restaurants here on the square, but perhaps he might find an open coffee bar if he headed for the Rialto.

Accordingly, he cut across the huge empty square, toward a passageway through the arcade. As he approached though, a man and woman suddenly appeared from behind the stone columns.

Both had dark hair, half turned to gray, and both wore black twill raincoats against the cool morning air. A small brown dog with white paws strained against a long leash as it resisted being hauled away from an interesting smell behind the column.

"*Signore, per favore?*" the man asked, holding out a camera and gesturing that he wanted Roman to take their picture with the Basilica in the background.

"Ma sicuro," said Roman, but when the woman reprimanded the dog in English, he smiled and said, "Not your first trip to Venice, is it?"

The woman smiled back. "Oh, no! We honeymooned here thirty years ago. Stayed at a hotel right on the Schiavone." She gestured toward the direction from which Roman had just come.

"First trip back though. Got here yesterday and we're doing everything we did then," said the man with a slight leer as he put his arm around his wife.

"Now, Mike, behave yourself!" Her accent was pure BBC, his seemed to have a trace of Liverpool.

They smiled into the camera as Roman stepped back to get more of the Basilica in the picture.

At that instant, just as Roman snapped the shutter, a young man ran out from the arcade, tangled his foot in the dog's long leash and sprawled into the viewfinder. With a whir, the film automatically advanced and in the confusion, Roman clicked again, spoiling a second exposure.

He watched the youth jerk his foot free while the man helped him up and the woman restrained their hysterical dog. Then the young man darted across the piazza and disappeared through the columns.

"Well!" said the Englishman indignantly as the dog danced and yipped. *"That* bloke was certainly in a hurry."

Again they posed and after the picture was made, they thanked Roman for his kindness and took back their camera.

By now, sunlight caressed the golden tip of the belltower and Roman was more than ready for a caffè latte and a brioche. Bidding the couple *arrivederci,* he strolled through a covered passageway marked by an arrow that pointed toward the Rialto. Just beyond was the Bacino Orseolo where dozens of tarp-covered gondolas were moored, waiting for boatmen and tourists.

When he saw someone curled up on the white marble steps that led down into the water, Roman automatically started to pass with eyes averted. Then he remembered that this was Venice, not New York and he saw that this figure wore an expensive black warm-up suit, not the rags of a homeless beggar. A closer look revealed an elderly Japanese with blood seeping from his head onto the white marble.

Rumbling words of dismay in his deep bass voice, Roman hurried over and knelt down to help. While he tried to find a pulse, the man groaned and opened his eyes and murmured something unintelligible.

"Sorry," said Roman, who knew no Japanese. "Do you speak English? *Parla italiano?* What happened?"

"He push me." The man winced as Roman helped him sit up. "Take money and push me."

Roman pulled out his clean handkerchief and held it to the wound. "You need a doctor. Where are you staying?"

With effort, the man pointed further down the narrow street that skirted the gondola basin. "You help, please, I walk. Not far."

After introducing himself with touching politeness as Mr. Saito, the Japanese man leaned heavily on Roman's arm, barely able to walk. However, his pensione was indeed just around the next corner and when they entered, they were immediately engulfed by a concerned staff who called the man's wife, an ambulance and the police.

While they waited for the last two, Roman was struck by a sudden thought. "The man who robbed you," he said to Mr. Saito. "Young? White? Wearing a dark blue jacket?"

"*Hai, hai!*" The man nodded so emphatically that the wound, which his distressed wife had stanched, began to bleed again. "You know him? You see?"

"I'll be right back," Roman promised as he hurried to the door.

Although admittedly a few pounds overweight, Roman Tramegra was not fat. Nevertheless, there was a softness about him, as if he would feel as boneless as a cat if prodded, and he was certainly as singleminded as a cat in his pursuit of creature comforts. On the other hand, when necessary, he could move with a cat's graceful speed. Barely a minute after leaving the mugging victim, he was back at St. Mark's Square, scanning the area for the couple with the camera.

In the short time since they'd parted, the piazza had gathered more life. Flocks of pigeons swarmed around a couple of grain carts. Waiters had begun to wipe dew from the chairs and tables in front of their restaurants. At least fifty other people were now scattered down its great length and more than half of those wore black or navy coats. He walked all the way down to the Basilica which wouldn't open till ten, then back again without seeing either the couple or their little brown dog.

When Roman returned to the pensione, an ambulance boat was loading Mr. Saito for a trip to the hospital and a very disapproving uniformed policeman instantly began to scold him in broken English for disappearing so abruptly without leaving his name. A younger, thinner man in plain clothes came forward and put an end to the lecture with a quiet, "*Basta*, Sanpismo. *Signore*? I'm *Commissario* Mancini."

As the ambulance boat sped off down the canal with its siren wailing and its blue light flashing, the detective escorted Roman into the pensione's closed bar away from curious guests who had come out to watch the excitement. Violent crime was almost nonexistent in Venice. Pickpockets, yes. Shoplifting and petty thievery, of course. Outright thuggery? No. This incident would be thoroughly investigated.

"Coffee?" Mancini asked courteously.

"Yes, please, and rolls, too," Roman replied. "I haven't had a bite all morning and I'm simply famished!"

The detective spoke to his subordinate, who nodded and stepped away. Presently, a white jacketed waiter arrived bearing a tray loaded with coffee, a basket of fresh breads, and packets of butter and jams which he placed on the bar before them.

"Now then," said Mancini when coffee had been poured into the hot frothed milk and Roman had buttered his croissant. The police officer sat near them with his own coffee and a notepad, onto which he entered Roman's name and the name of Roman's pensione.

"Tramegra?" asked Mancini. "Is this an Italian name?"

Roman shook his head. "Welsh. People often confuse it for Italian. Especially with my given name. My godmother was of Italian descent. On her mother's side."

Godmother? Mancini gazed at the big American dubiously. He looked like so many other innocent tourists—middle-aged, hair going thin across the crown, well-dressed, certainly well-nourished, if not to say plump. All in all, an unlikely criminal despite Officer Sanpismo's suspicions.

"You were out very early this morning, *signore*. Before anything opened. And you were at that end of the piazza. Did you also visit the cash machine at the Banca Commerciale?"

"Cash machine? Ah," said Roman as he drew the obvious conclusion. "Of course. He must have lurked in the shadows and waited for someone to come make a withdrawal when there was no one else around."

"Not even you, *signore*?"

"Oh, no," said Roman, smearing peach jam on his roll.

The coffee was dark and flavorful, the milk thick with froth. Nectar for the gods! But he knew he shouldn't let his enjoyment of his first Venetian breakfast interfere with performing his civic duty, so he dabbed his lips on the snowy white napkin and explained how he came to be there so early. For Officer Sanpismo, he carefully described the English couple who wanted their picture taken, right down to the scarves around their necks. He also told of the rude young man who had stumbled into the viewframe and then fled across the piazza.

"Do you think you would recognize him again?" asked Mancini.

"I doubt it," Roman admitted. "He was so average—average height, black hair, and his jacket was just a dark blue zip-up."

Sanpismo rolled his eyes.

"I'm quite certain he was Mr. Saito's mugger, though. And I'm just as certain that I took at least one picture of him—maybe even two. That's why I ran back. I hoped to catch those people before they left the piazza. I was too late, but all you have to do is find them and their camera and you'll soon have your thief."

"Their names? Their hotel?"

Roman shook his head. "His wife called him Mike."

Sanpismo, who understood English much better than he spoke it, snorted scornfully and, in insultingly slow Italian, wondered aloud if *il signore* would care to guess just how many middle-aged English tourists were in Venice at the moment?

"Surely less than five with small brown dogs," Roman said haughtily.

Before Sanpismo could comment on the number of dogs in Venice, Mancini drew the interview to an end, gave Roman his card and asked him to call if he should remember anything else that would help them locate the English couple or identify the mugger. Then he and Sanpismo went out to the police cruiser they'd arrived in. By now, gondolas were streaming from the basin, each with laughing, camera-toting tourists, and they had to wait a few minutes before they could slip through an opening and motor sedately away.

Roman walked back along the route he'd come. Normally his eyes would have eagerly searched the shop windows to see what delicious new obscenity the Murano glassblowers had come up with since he'd last strolled these streets. Not today, though. Despite his plan to set a fictitious murder mystery here, he was disturbed to think that his lovely Venice might, in reality, become as violent as the rest of the world.

True, the city had been founded by violence when people of the Veneto fled to the marshes to escape looting and burning Goths. True, the ruling Doges had supplied arms and ships to competing armies, even subverting the Crusades to swell the city's coffers. They had stolen half their relics (the very bones of St. Mark were stolen from Egypt) and had bribed half the artisans of the civilized world to come adorn their city. Nevertheless, for the last two hundred years, Venice had been a peaceful—and safe—pleasure resort.

Today's mugging, thought Roman, could be an early warning of things to come unless nipped in the bud.

Now.

He straightened his shoulders. He hadn't spent a year picking his housemate's brains without learning a little something about detective work, he told himself. Would Lt. Peter Bohr turn away from this challenge? Never! Let Officer Sanpismo speak discouraging words. He would find that film. He would bring that ruffian to justice!

The first step in retrieving that film, he decided, was to think himself into the mindset of a couple who'd honeymooned here thirty years ago. That's what Peter Bohr would do.

Very well. The man had said they were doing again all that they did back then, which had amused, if somewhat embarrassed, the woman. No help there. But the woman had said that they'd stayed in a hotel on the Riva degli Schiavone. If this return to Venice was a trip down memory lane, surely they'd at least go look at their honeymoon hotel?

Dodging camcorders and souvenir stands as he left St. Mark's Square, his magpie eyes flitted across the crowds that were growing with each moment. Large dogs sat patiently while their owners examined the wares at every kiosk, and smaller dogs trotted past at the heels of housewives, but no little brown animal with neat white paws.

He began his inquiries at the Danieli, one of the largest and most expensive hotels along the water, then moved on to the others in turn. At each, he was told the same thing: No, none of their guests had dogs. Dogs were not allowed.

A block from his own pensione, Roman finally struck gold at a small hotel with a sidewalk cafe. The headwaiter remembered the couple quite well. "English? Little dog? *Si, si*! They stay here when they new marry, *si*."

Like the other hotels, this one did not allow pets either, but here on the sidewalk, no one had objected to the presence of a well-mannered dog tied to an outside chair leg while his masters ate a continental breakfast.

"You come five *minuti* more quick, you see them," the waiter said.

Five minutes? Roman looked around wildly. "Where did they go? Where are they staying?"

The waiter started to shrug, then suddenly remembered. "San Zanipolo! *Un caseggiato*."

More specific he could not be but at least Roman knew his search could now be narrowed to apartment houses near the great Gothic church Santi Giovanni e Paolo, which most Venetians shortened to "San Zanipolo."

They may have had a five-minute headstart, but surely they would pause to look in windows, perhaps stop to buy postcards or a piece of souvenir glass, maybe even treat themselves to a midmorning snack. If he got to the church square first, he could simply wait for them to pass through.

With a wistful glance at the cafe's *turistica* menu—he was ready for a mid-morning snack himself—Roman oriented himself and plunged into Venice's maze of canals and narrow streets.

To his total gratification—not to mention his total surprise, he stumbled upon the couple only three bridges away. He saw the dog first. Its small body radiated boredom as its owners stood in front of a mask shop and amiably squabbled over which mask to purchase and whose suitcase had enough room to cart it back to England without crushing it.

They greeted Roman like a long lost friend, but instantly grew frosty when he told them that he'd come for the camera that hung around the man's neck.

"Our camera?"

"Well, not the camera, just the film."

"I beg your pardon!" said the woman.

The man looked at Roman belligerently. "What are you on about, mate?"

"Not for me," Roman said hastily. "For the police."

"*Police?*"

"Remember that young man who tripped over your dog's leash just as I was taking your picture? And you remarked his big hurry?"

"Yes, and—?"

"He'd just robbed someone." Roman described how he'd found Mr. Saito bleeding on the steps of the gondola basin and how he'd tried to find them. "The police need that picture to identify the thief. If you could give the commissario a call? He speaks English quite fluently."

Roman handed him Mancini's card and pointed to the phone number.

The man exchanged a glance with his wife, then reached into the pocket of his raincoat for some lira. "Got any of more of these coins, luv?"

The woman looked alarmed. "Mike, you're not—?"

"Steady on, old girl. Got to do our duty," he said cheerfully. "Won't be a minute. Get our friend here to help you choose a mask, why don't you?"

With that, he stepped across the way to a shop that displayed a public telephone sign.

By the time she'd settled on an elegant cat mask, her husband was back. "We're to meet him by the sculpture of that big stone hand back on the Schiavone in ten minutes," he told Roman. "So it's *arrivederci* again."

As they walked away through the crowds, Roman called after them, "Isn't the stone hand over that way?"

"Not to worry, mate. I know a shortcut."

Roman spent the rest of the day in a congratulatory mood of self-satisfaction. Having, in his own mind, made Venice safe again for tourists, he sat in the bow of the Number One *vaporetto* and rode the whole length of the Grand Canal and back down again, beaming beneficently upon the palaces and churches on either side as if he were a Doge riding in a golden galley. He lunched on prosciutto and gorgonzola at a quayside cafe and, in the evening, dined on calamari at his favorite restaurant, where the headwaiter remembered him from earlier trips and brought him a complimentary cordial with his espresso.

Pleasantly tired, he strolled back to his pensione and was gratified to find a message from Mancini saying that he would phone again in the morning.

There had been more than enough time to develop the film, identify the culprit and make an arrest. *No doubt, Mancini wants to express Venice's gratitude*, thought Roman as he fell asleep to the sound of lapping wavelets beneath his open window.

He awoke with a chill rain on his face and quickly rose to shut the window. Before he could get back to sleep again, the phone rang.

It was Commissario Mancini, who apologized for waking him, but did *Signore* Tramegra remember any further details about yesterday's incident?

"Sorry," Roman said, stifling a yawn. "Couldn't you identify him from the pictures?"

"Pictures?"

"From the English couple's camera. When they brought you the film yesterday."

"*Signore*, I do not understand. I have no film from their camera."

"But he called you," Roman argued, wide awake now. "He said you were to meet him at that big stone hand on the Schiavone."

"No," said Mancini.

"No?"

"No."

Confused, Roman described how he'd tracked the couple, how the man had gone off to telephone and had come back to say a meeting was arranged. When he finished speaking, he half expected hostility or derision at his attempt to play detective. Instead, there was a short contemplative silence, then Mancini said, "San Zanipolo, eh? Thank you, *signore*. You have been most helpful, most helpful indeed."

His words did little to cheer Roman, who dressed and went down to breakfast in a mood as gloomy as the rainy day. Not that he blamed the weather, he assured the two elderly German ladies with whom he shared a table. "Only travel agents and tourists bureaus expect endless blue skies in April."

"*Ja, ja,*" they beamed approvingly. "There's no such thing as unfit weather, merely unfit clothing."

Being well provided with sturdy leather shoes, hooded raincoats and capacious umbrellas, they left him to his second cup of coffee and splashed off down the Schiavone.

An example to us all, Roman told himself as his natural optimism returned full-blown. He had found the English couple once, he could jolly well do it again. He fetched his own raincoat and folding umbrella from his room and set off for San Zanipolo. Along the way, he stopped for a handful of picture postcards and a roll of film for the small camera tucked in his pocket.

Like most squares around the city, the Campo Santi Giovanni e Paolo had an open air cafe conveniently situated to overlook the whole area. With rain pouring down, though, all the chairs and tables were stacked and chained. Roman was able to get a table by the window inside where he ordered cappucino and settled in for a morning of writing postcards and watching the *campo*.

"Dear Sigrid," he wrote on the back of a card that showed Venetians masked for Carnival season. "You laughed at my plan to write a Venetian mystery, yet here I am embroiled in one!"

Three hours later, he had written everyone who could possibly expect a card from him, without spotting the English couple or their dog. The cafe's proprietor was beginning to look askance at him so he'd ordered a sweet roll in mid-morning and knew he'd soon have to order lunch or move on.

Fortunately, the rain finally stopped and a watery sun edged through the clouds so that he could walk outside and stretch his legs with a brisk turn about the square.

As lunchtime approached, foot traffic picked up. The cafe filled with workmen from the area, tourists streamed in and out of the church.

Roman perched himself on a ledge beside the canal and watched them all.

Not for the first time, he mused upon how truly boring the work of a real detective must be. In books and television, the sleuth had but to take up his position and the quarry immediately strolled into view. Very little was ever said of the hours that could pass with nothing to show for it. He could be wasting a whole precious day of his vacation—his *working* vacation, he reminded himself—and for what? Justice? Or had it become wounded pride when the Englishman suckered him?

If he were honest, he'd also have to admit to an overwhelming curiosity. Why had the man lied? And why had his wife spoken so apprehensively? Could it be that they themselves were involved in something criminal?

The longer Roman sat there, the more certain he became. That story about a honeymoon could have been a ruse, and getting him to take their picture must have been a delaying action so he wouldn't see when Mr. Saito was robbed. Why else were they hanging around that end of the piazza? Venice was expensive and so were bank charges, so if a tourist used that ATM, the chances were very good that he'd withdraw the maximum permissible amount. And at that hour of the morning, one automatically feels safe, so what better time for thieves to lie in wait?

His speculations turned to Mr. Saito. Was he only a chance victim or had they been after him specifically? Was he really the innocent tourist he seemed or was he perhaps carrying something less innocent? Jewels? Japanese industrial secrets?

When the rain began again in the late afternoon, he unfurled his umbrella and left the square, too lost in theories to notice the workman in scruffy jacket and worn cap who had sat further back in the cafe most of the day reading a newspaper and smoking one cigarette after another. The man now pulled a cell phone from his pocket, punched in a number, then said, "He just left. Looks like he's finally giving up."

Morning found Roman implementing a new plan of action. When you sublet an apartment, he reasoned, you probably cook most of your meals, buying fresh each day as he himself had done the autumn he'd lived here years ago. Every fruit and vegetable in Italian cookery, every variety of edible marine life from the Adriatic eventually winds up in the endless stands of the Rialto Markets. Why wouldn't the English couple wind up here, too? It was an easy stroll from the San Zanipolo *campo* and it closed at noon, so even if he missed them, he still would have had an interesting morning watching Venetians shop for lettuces or select live eels wriggling like snakes beside a tray of tiny pink squid.

He bought an *ètto* of dark sweet cherries and had just popped the third one in his mouth when he saw the Englishwoman two aisles over. He almost swallowed the pit in his excitement.

The woman added fresh peas to her string bag, then strode briskly away as if finished with her shopping, but not before Roman had surreptitiously taken her picture.

This time the film's in my *camera*, he exulted to himself.

When she crossed the Rialto Bridge, he almost lost her in the crowds and after that he stayed close to her heels until they passed over the bridge at San Zanipolo. The crowds thinned as soon as she turned off the *campo* and there was no cover here in streets so narrow they were more like alleys. Worse, he knew they had a habit of dead-ending at canal edges or cul-de-sacs. Only residents or lost tourists normally came this way and he could hardly pretend to be either since she would recognize him immediately.

He hung back as she walked down a covered passageway that appeared to turn into a open courtyard, then hurried along to the end and peeked around a column.

Some ten or twelve nondescript stuccoed buildings opened onto the small square. As the woman approached one of the doors, Roman pulled out his camera, ready to document her actions. Before she could push open the door, a young dark-haired man greeted her with a laugh and held it wide for her.

Roman clicked the shutter furiously, getting off at least four clear shots before the door closed on them.

Suddenly something hard poked him in the middle of his back and he felt himself shoved forward. He smelled stale cigarette smoke and in his ear a harsh voice growled, "Keep silence and walk!"

He tried to resist, but the man's arm was like iron as it pushed him across the small square, and into another columned passageway. When the arm dropped away, Roman turned. The man wore a dirty coat and cap and he held up a warning hand as he looked back through the columns. "The husband comes," he said.

Roman looked, too, just in time to see the Englishman reel in the leash on the small brown dog before entering the same building.

"Who—?"

The scruffy "workman" grinned reassuringly and held up an identity card. "Polizia. Come with me, please."

Somehow, Roman was not surprised when they returned to the main square to see Commissario Mancini and Officer Sanpismo waiting quayside by a police launch. The undercover detective, Officer Dordoni, spoke too idiomatically for

Roman to follow all the nuances, but he did understand that Mancini was being told that Roman had passed through the square following a woman, so Dordoni had followed *il signore*. Then he'd looked back and seen the Englishman and the very dog for which he'd been watching these past two days. A very close call.

"They're all in it together!" Roman interrupted. "They were there to make sure no one entered the passageway while Mr. Saito was being robbed. If they hadn't stopped me to take their picture, I would have gone through and caught him in the act. Just his bad luck that when he came running out, he got caught up in the dog's leash."

"*Signore?*" Mancini looked puzzled.

"The thief," said Roman, patiently. "He's there. He opened the door for the woman." He tapped his camera. "And I have them both on film."

"*Permesso?*" Mancini said, holding out his hand.

Roman quickly rewound the film and handed it over with justifiable pride.

"Thank you for your help, *signore*. And now, if you would be so kind as to wait here?"

As the policemen disappeared down the narrow street, Roman sat down at one of the cafe's outside tables and ordered an espresso.

The sun shone warmly in a bright blue sky, the coffee was dark and fragrant. He raised his cup to the chap on horseback atop a nearby monument, feeling every bit as triumphant. What a graceful anecdote all this would make when Charlie Rose interviewed him someday or when Oprah recommended his book to all her viewers!

As soon as he officially identified the English couple and their accomplice for the *commissario*, the rest of the week would be his, another five days to gather material for his book and to enjoy all the wonders and pleasures of Venice in well-earned peace.

Fifteen minutes went by. Then twenty and thirty. He was beginning to get restless when at last the three police officers reappeared.

Alone.

"You didn't arrest them?" Roman asked.

Mancini told his two men to wait for him in the launch, then pulled up a chair to Roman's table.

"No, *signore*, it was not necessary."

"I don't understand. The young man—"

"Is the porter for that building," Mancini said gently. "His manager can vouch that he was there at work two mornings ago."

"But why did that Englishman lie about giving you the film?"

"It was his wife who did not wish to give it up."

"But *why?*"

Mancini smiled. "Ah, *signore*. They are reliving their honeymoon. They do silly things, things they did when they were first together alone in a bedroom."

"Oh," said Roman, beginning to comprehend. "They took naughty photographs of each other?"

"Exactly," Mancini nodded, smiling more widely now. "They did not wish to give me the whole roll. Yesterday, they took the film to be processed and this morning, he went to get the pictures. Fortunately, his camera is one that records the date and time."

Roman looked at the two pictures he had taken. The facial details were quite clear and now he could see that the mugger only vaguely resembled the porter.

"Do you recognize him?" Roman asked, embarrassed that he had so misjudged the situation.

"Oh, yes. Till now he was a pickpocket we could only slap on the wrist. But if Mr. Saito identifies him, he will soon be in jail."

Roman groaned. "I feel like such an idiot!"

Mancini leaned over and touched his arm in a consoling gesture. "No, *signore*. An idiot would not have cared. An idiot would not have spent two days of his precious vacation to bring a thief to justice. You are a catalyst, *signore*. Without you, we might not have found the English couple before they left Venice. *Mille grazie*, for what you did."

Then, with a half-salute, he was gone and the police launch roared off down the canal, leaving behind a turbulent wake that rocked the other boats moored there.

For a few moments, Roman Tramegra sat red-faced, rocked by an equally turbulent embarrassment. Then he laughed. He was a writer, wasn't he? And how could a writer exist without imagination? It *could* have happened the way he imagined.

And it *would* happen that way when he fictionalized it in his next book: *Toying with his espresso, Peter Bohr leaned back in his chair and, in flawless Italian, explained to his Venetian counterpart precisely where the commissario had misjudged the diamond smugglers.*

Roman Tramegra, he told himself. Author and catalyst.

The bells of Venice rang out in joyous affirmation.

Serenissima!

Half of Something

It is almost a given among many lawmen that a reasonably intelligent person can get away with one murder. But two?

Adam Gallardin willed himself not to look nervous or uneasy in any way.

He had thought to be out of here by noon, yet here it was almost ten after, almost as if that serious young man across the desk from him were trying to draw things out.

If he chose not to approve this loan, fine. There were other banks, other towns, although this history-laden little village on the southern coast of North Carolina was everything Adam had dreamed of when he married Marjorie back in *un*historic, landlocked Nebraska—charming streets that dead-ended at the water, friendly people with small town values, antique stores filled with beautiful pieces to satisfy an aesthetic longing that had never been satisfied, white clapboard houses that had solidly withstood coastal hurricanes and warm salt breezes for a hundred years.

The house he hoped to buy wasn't as big as the house of his dreams, but then his personal fortune wasn't as big as he'd planned either.

Half of something's better than all of nothing, he reminded himself. In the end, that's probably what swayed the jury back in Nebraska.

"If Adam Gallardin had cold-bloodedly murdered his wife for her money," his defense attorney had thundered, "would he have immediately offered her daughter half of the estate when Marjorie Gallardin had willed him everything she possessed? No, ladies and gentlemen of the jury. The Gallardin marriage was brief but happy, a marriage built on love and mutual trust. Mrs. Gallardin's fall was indeed the tragedy the D.A. has pictured, but it wasn't murder. You must not, you *cannot* convict this bereaved husband of killing the most precious person in his life."

Of course, it had also helped that Marjorie's daughter came across as a greedy, spoiled young woman when she took the witness stand. Ten minutes of Sally's nasal whine and the jury felt they knew exactly why she'd been disinherited.

"Another ten minutes," his attorney had whispered jubilantly, "and they'd have been ready to indite *her* for your wife's death."

The jury had acquitted him, but their friends—Marjorie's friends, as it turned out—were less charitable. By the time the trial was over, nearly three years had passed since her death, three years of virtual solitude.

The attorney had taken a quarter of the estate for saving his hide. Because Sally's shrill accusations had fueled his arrest in the first place, Adam felt completely justified in deducting that quarter from the half he'd originally offered her.

Even so, it left him with much less than he'd hoped. The bulk of Marjorie's investments had been in real estate and that market hadn't yet reached its fullest potential. "This area's growing," his financial advisor told him last month when Adam spoke of liquidating so he could leave Nebraska for good. "Another year, two at the most, and you can name your price. Right now, though…"

Which was why he was sitting here in South Cove's only bank to hear if he was going to be approved for a mortgage instead of purchasing the house outright. He stole another look at his watch and wondered why the delay. There was no reason for Marjorie's death or the trial to show up in his credit history, but the way computers linked in everything today, maybe this poker-faced loan officer was searching for a polite way to tell him that not only was his loan refused but the good citizens of South Cove would appreciate it if he'd get the hell out of their town.

On the other side of the desk, Chad Easling looked at his own watch, glanced through the glass door of his office, then closed the folder he'd been reading.

"I see you're a widower, Mr. Gallardin."

Here it comes, Adam thought.

"So sad," Easling said sympathetically. "Was it her heart?"

"N-No." Adam's throat was so dry he could hardly speak. "A-An accident."

"Too bad," Easling said as an attractive blonde in a turquoise sundress suddenly appeared beyond the glass door. "Still a young woman, no doubt."

Young? thought Adam as Easling held up a wait-one-minute finger to the woman at the door. Marjorie had been eight years older than he—almost fifty when she fell downstairs and broke her neck. That must mean that the bank's credit search had limited itself to only those facts with dollar signs attached.

The blonde made an impatient face and pushed open the door. Her flowing turquoise skirt swirled around slender ankles and shapely legs. As she stood there only a few feet away, Adam caught the scent of a subtle and expensive perfume.

"You said twelve sharp, Chad, and it's already ten after." Her words rebuked but her voice was music.

"Sorry, love. We're almost finished. This is Mr. Gallardin, Ruth Anne. He's going to be your neighbor, right across the street from you. I've just approved his mortgage on the Broughton house."

"Really?" asked Adam, hope rising in his heart.

"Oh, yes," said Easling with a smile that was suddenly boyish and friendly. "I'm a good judge of character, Mr. Gallardin, and I knew from the first day you applied that you'd have an excellent credit rating."

The woman looked at Adam Gallardin with interest. "The Broughton house? Oh, I'm so pleased. It's been neglected for ages. I've been dying for someone to love it."

"My big sister's an interior designer," said Easling proudly.

"Big" was clearly an affectionate phrase left over from their childhood, for she barely came up to Easling's shoulder.

"Amateur only," she demurred.

"You own that house with the elaborate widow's walk, Miss Easling?" asked Adam, impressed. The historical plaque by the front door of that three-story white house dated it at 1822, forty-five years before Nebraska even became a state.

"It's Mrs.," Easling corrected. "Mrs. Haywood."

"Don't be stuffy, Chad," she scolded, and turned back to Adam. "If we're to be neighbors, you must call me Ruth Anne."

"And I'm Adam," he said, taking the small hand she offered him.

"Why don't you join us for lunch and we can finish up the paperwork after," Chad Easling said, and his sister immediately chimed in, "Oh, yes, please do!"

They ate in a restaurant overlooking the water and Adam felt as if he'd finally come home: the ocean, soft Southern voices all around him, Ruth Anne Haywood's intelligent interest in antiques, her brother's easy charm.

By the time their bowls of she-crab soup arrived, he decided that Ruth Anne was older than her girlish slenderness had led him to believe. Faint laugh lines around her clear blue eyes and reference to a major world event "just before I started to school" confirmed his impression that she was no more than a year or two younger than his own forty-five years. By the end of lunch, he knew that she was at least ten years older than her brother, that she was twice widowed, childless, and lived alone in that antebellum jewel directly across from the house he'd soon take possession of.

"You'll have to show Adam what you've done with your place," said Easling. "Maybe give him some pointers. My big sister's a demon on historical accuracy," he told Adam. "Let her pry off a little chip of plaster from your walls and she'll not only tell you what color they were first painted, she'll take you down to the paint store and match it with the right shade."

Ruth Anne shook her head with a rueful smile. "Chad exaggerates, but it *is* exciting to help a house come back to its original beauty." She looked at him anxiously. "You *do* plan to restore, don't you? Not just remodel?"

"Absolutely," said Adam. "Maybe you could advise me. If that's not too big an imposition?"

"Deal," she said. "I love helping people spend money."

Her blue eyes sparkled like noon sunshine on the water as they shook in mock solemnity over the remains of lunch. Adam almost hated to let her hand go.

"Well, this is all fine and good for you people of leisure," said Chad, "but some of us still have to work for a living. If you want to come back to the office with me, Adam, we'll sign the papers and you can go get the keys."

He reached for the check, but Adam beat him to it.

A hour later, Adam pulled up to the curb in front of his home that would be his as soon as the real estate agent could arrange the closing. When he stepped onto the porch with the keys jingling in his hand, he found Ruth Anne sitting on a lovely old wicker swing wide enough to hold three people.

"I didn't know I had a swing," he said, delighted to be seeing her again so soon.

She laughed. "You didn't. I had my handyman hang it. A housewarming gift."

He invited her to tour the interior with him and discovered that Chad hadn't been exaggerating Ruth Anne's expertise. She knew the history of the house—who built it, which owner had boarded up the fireplaces, and where he might find antique mantles to replace the ones ripped out twenty years ago. She even promised him the phone numbers of craftsmen who could restore the plaster ceilings and put the house's pocket doors back into working order.

The sun was still high in the sky when they returned to the porch. Hoping to prolong the moment, Adam walked over to the swing. "Is it really strong enough to hold two people?"

"Absolutely," Ruth Anne said. "See how tightly the wicker is woven?"

She sat down on the swing and smoothed her skirt aside to make room for him. Huge liveoaks shaded the porch and they could look down to the end of their street and straight out into the cove, where small boats passed in the bright distance.

The chain creaked restfully as they swung back and forth. Adam took a deep breath and savored the smell of salty air overlaid with the bouquet of Ruth Anne's perfume. "All we need right now is a big glass of lemonade," he said happily.

Her laughter came like ice cubes tinkling in a tall crystal goblet. "I should have brought some over. I made a fresh pitcher this morning."

"Really? I would have thought you were more the champagne or sangria type."

"Because of my house?" She dismissed that mansion with an airy wave. "Oh, honey, it came down through my last husband's family. You should have seen the house Chad and I grew up in, a sharecropper's shack over on the Neuse River. Our dad died when Chad was three and Mama worked herself into an early grave shucking oysters at the fish house to feed and clothe us and keep us in school."

Her unpretentious candor swept him away and in the weeks that followed, he felt himself falling helplessly, hopelessly in love.

Like the house, Ruth Ann wasn't the vision he'd kept in his head during that last tedious year of Marjorie's life. She was older and less curvaceous than he'd fantasized, but their interests meshed as if they'd known each other forever. Adam discovered he'd rather spend a day with her, treasure hunting through dusty old barns and back-road flea markets, than chatting up the nubile young cuties who hung around the marina. What was nubility compared to Ruth Anne's lovely smile and delicious sense of humor?

Adam even approved of the work ethic she'd inherited from her mother. She was so competent in everything she undertook, whether it was repairing a spinning wheel or coping with the balky carburetor on her outboard motor when it conked out on them the day she took Adam fishing. She volunteered for several charities, she free-lanced as a design consultant, and she'd taken responsibility for her younger brother after their mother passed away.

She could have spoiled Chad, given him a big allowance and maybe turned him into a wastrel and idler. Instead, she persuaded her first husband to help him through college and then encouraged her second husband to start him on a fast track at the bank so that he could earn his own way.

Adam soon realized that Chad was basically lazy and relied more on charm than hard work. To his credit, although he grumbled about punching time clocks, Chad seemed equally devoted to Ruth Anne, and he appeared genuinely pleased as the relationship deepened between Adam and his sister.

"You're good for her," Chad told him. "She's been lonely too long."

Ruth Anne seldom spoke of her first two husbands except in passing, but various South Cove gossips were less reticent.

It seemed that Harry, a cardiologist, had died in a freak accident and left an estate of anywhere from a half-million to a million-five, depending upon who told the tale.

"A bad wire in the motor of his cabin cruiser sparked an explosion," said his barber. "Ruth Anne was mighty lucky that she changed her mind at the last minute 'bout going out with him that day."

"Blew him halfway to Elizabeth City," said the mailman.

Michael, who'd owned controlling interest in the bank where Chad Easling still worked, had died of carbon monoxide poisoning.

"Mr. Michael, now, he was a huge Duke fan," said his cheerful young cleaning woman, a woman who would rather dish the dirt than clean it. "That night, an ice storm knocked out the power in the first quarter of the big Duke-Carolina game, so Mr. Michael went out to the garage to listen to it on the car radio while Mr. Chad bunked down in the guestroom and Miss Ruth Anne went to bed. In the middle of the night, she woke up and went looking for him—motor was still running. They figured he musta got chilly and turned on the engine so he could run the heater and then fell asleep."

"Finding him like that near 'bout killed *her*," said his next door neighbor.

"Left her a lot to live for though," said the neighbor's more pragmatic husband. "All his bank stock, that big house, and a mighty tidy portfolio."

Six months later, with Chad's blessing, Adam proposed to Ruth Anne in an antique store in Wilmington.

"Oh, Adam, honey, I can't marry you," she'd whispered.

"But I love you. I thought you loved me back."

She sank down upon a red velvet loveseat and her blue eyes were miserable. "I do love you, oh, I *do*! But I loved Harry and Michael, too. My heart's been broken twice, Adam, and I'm too cowardly to go through that again."

Adam knelt down beside the antique loveseat and took Ruth Anne's small hand in his.

"Third time lucky," he promised.

The ceremony was private—bride and groom pledged their eternal troth before the minister of a small coastal church, with only Chad and Chad's latest tall, leggy girlfriend as witness.

"And best man," Adam insisted. "If our loan session hadn't run over into your lunch date that first day, Ruth Anne and I might never have realized how much we have in common."

"Let me not to the marriage of true minds admit impediments," Chad quoted, lifting his champagne glass in toast.

After the honeymoon, Adam moved into Ruth Anne's spacious home and for the first two months, the newlyweds seemed to float on a golden haze of connubial bliss. Half of something had become more of everything he'd dreamed of back in Nebraska.

Then the accidents began.

Somehow, the chemicals they used to clean pieces of folk art got muddled and Adam was nearly asphyxiated.

"He could have died!" Ruth Anne told Chad, who scolded them both for their carelessness.

The Tiffany lamp in their bathroom suddenly developed a short that could have electrocuted one of them if they'd touched it while standing barefooted on wet tiles. As it was, their cleaning woman got a nasty jolt.

Before renting out his own house, Adam had brought over some of the antiques Ruth Anne had helped him buy. He had hung his 1810 Sheraton tabernacle mirror over the dainty Victorian desk where she sat every morning after breakfast to return phone calls and plan her day.

A week after their near miss with the Tiffany lamp, the mirror's wire hanger somehow worked its way loose and five feet of silvered glass and gilded mahogany came crashing down on the desk, splintering the desk and shattering into a thousand sharp daggers of glass, daggers that could have ripped Ruth Anne to bloody shreds if she hadn't gone out into the kitchen to pour herself another cup of coffee two minutes earlier.

"I could have sworn those screws were too long to pop out like that," Adam said when Chad came over and saw the damage.

"Were you here when it happened?" Chad asked.

"No, I was up on the widow's walk with the telescope, watching a freighter that just pulled out from Morehead—and that reminds me, dearest. One of the railings feels a little wobbly. If you go up, do be careful," Adam said with seeming solicitation.

"I think you both ought to stay off and call your handyman right now," Chad said firmly. "No more accidents, Ruth Ann, okay?"

She patted his arm reassuringly. "No more accidents."

The next afternoon, when Chad stopped by on his way back to the bank after lunch, Ruth Anne told him that the handyman had put everything shipshape that morning. "Want to see?"

"Sure," he said and tossed his briefcase toward the nearest chair before following her upstairs.

The briefcase teetered on the edge, then flipped over onto the floor.

By then Chad was halfway up the stairs.

"I'll get it," said Adam. "And I'll bring us up some lemonade. Unless you'd like something stronger, Chad?"

From the landing above, Chad said, "Better not. I have to get back to work."

As Adam lifted the briefcase, the top fell open and a couple of faxes slid out. Horrified, he realized they were copies of Nebraska newspapers. The top headline read *Woman Accuses Stepfather of Murder*.

He quickly riffled through the other sheets till he came to the smaller story headlined *Jury Acquits in Gallardin Trial*.

The chemical fumes, the electrical short, the smashed mirror—they must have triggered Chad's suspicions about Marjorie's accidental death.

Before their wedding, he'd told Ruth Anne about Marjorie—the same version he'd told the jury—and Ruth Anne had wept for him, attributing to him the grief she'd twice endured. Of course, *she* hadn't been accused of murder and he hadn't thought she needed to hear about that small difference in their circumstances. He'd been too afraid of her reaction. And now Chad was probably up there giving her all the gory details. Would she feel betrayed? These last few months had been the happiest in his life. Money was wonderful but in his heart of hearts, he knew that he could live content in a rented room if Ruth Anne were there beside him. How could he bear to see her sweet look of love turn to horror?

He didn't realize long he'd been standing there until he glanced up and saw a white-faced Chad looking down at him. Too late to pretend, he crammed the papers back inside the briefcase and held it out to Chad.

"Did you tell her?"

Chad shook his head grimly.

"Chad, I swear to you—"

"Don't bother saying it, Adam. I honestly don't care whether your first wife's death was purely accidental or not, but if Ruth Anne so much as sprains her ankle from here on out, these papers are going straight to the District Attorney. You won't find North Carolina juries as understanding as Nebraska's." He looked Adam straight in the eye and said softly, "Cherish her, okay?"

"I will," Adam promised, almost weeping with gratitude. "I do."

His brother-in-law snapped the briefcase closed, straightened his tie, and headed for the front door.

"Well, back to the salt mines," he said with a semblance of his old cheerfulness. "Ruth Anne stayed up to watch a huge sailing yacht put in at the marina. She thought you'd want to see it, too."

Emotionally drained, yet with a lighter heart than he'd have thought possible five minutes ago, Adam stepped out onto the widow's walk balancing a tray with a pitcher of lemonade and two glasses. It took a moment for everything to register.

The newly-mended railing had pulled away from the post and Ruth Anne was nowhere to be seen.

The tray fell from his nerveless fingers. Pitcher and glasses spun away as he rushed over to the gap.

Three stories down, one of the glasses hit the stone patio beside Ruth Anne's crumpled body and smashed into diamond-sized bits that caught the sunlight and mocked him with their bright sparkle.

"No!" Adam whimpered, knowing in that instant that his whole life was now as thoroughly smashed as that glass. No one would believe this was an accident. It would all come out about Marjorie's death and they'd say he married Ruth Anne for her money, too, and then killed for it. Another trial, another public pillorying, and for what?

Even if they didn't send him to the gas chamber, what did it matter? They would certainly give him life in prison and what good was life without Ruth Anne?

"No!" he moaned again and stepped up onto the coping. He gazed out over the water with tear-blurred eyes and in that instant between launching himself into oblivion and oblivion itself, it suddenly pierced his numb brain that those faxes had been dated the day before his first meeting with Ruth Anne.

And there were no huge yachts anywhere in the cove.

Growth Marks

This is another not-really-a-crime story by my definition of crime stories—no murder, no theft, only the secrets of a grief-stricken mother's heart—but it was enough of a domestic puzzler that Nancy Pickard selected it for her last anthology.

*S*un., Feb. 9th—*Ted & Abby have finally left. It's 90 min. by the interstate back to Winston & I persuaded them to leave early so I wouldn't worry about them slipping & sliding on dark icy roads.*

Not that she would, thought Grace Currin as she re-read what she had just written in her journal. Ted approached driving like everything else in life: safely, cautiously. That was a terrible thing to say about one's own son and Grace knew she should be down on her knees giving thanks for his thoughtfulness. On the other hand, he didn't have to come running down here today as if one day without hot water would trigger a massive heart attack or something.

Just because her heart had started giving a couple of irregular stutters in the last year didn't mean she wasn't perfectly capable of managing till tomorrow when her usual fixit man could come. Nevertheless, as soon as Ted called that morning and she mentioned the problem, nothing would do but he and Abby had to drive down with his plumbing tools and spend the afternoon tearing out the innards of her water heater.

Just like Hank used to be, she thought. Couldn't stand to let things go unfixed five minutes.

Abby didn't seem to mind helping him either. Grace *knew* she should be grateful for their solicitude but it had meant running out in the rain to the grocery store so her refrigerator wouldn't look as if she didn't eat properly and then hurrying back to freshen up the whole downstairs so they wouldn't know that she spent most of these short winter days either in the kitchen or holed up in her bedroom.

So of course that had left her a little breathless, which meant she'd had to listen to yet another round of how the house was too much work and much too big for one woman alone. Never did have an ounce of imagination, Ted. Not like Will, who—

"Oh, no, you don't, Grace Currin!" she scolded herself out loud. "Stop whining for what you've lost and be grateful for what you still have."

Quickly, almost superstitiously, she counted her blessings: a sensible solid son and pleasant daughter-in-law who seemed to love each other, adequate income, good friends—though Sally was remarried and involved with step-grandchildren and Jan had moved to Florida—and, above everything else, reasonably good health (if you don't count the arrhythmia, and I don't, thought Grace) which allowed her to continue living on her own.

So the house calls up lonesome memories sometimes, she thought. So what? "You should be glad you've had people, things, a whole *life* worth feeling lonesome for," she told herself sternly.

When she and Hank first moved in and began restoring the house themselves, the inside was scarcely habitable: crumbling plaster, rotten roof, bare lightbulbs dangling at the end of frayed cords—what the classifieds used to call a real Handyman's Special. Will was three, Ted eighteen months, and she was blissfully pregnant again. (Even though they'd gotten a late start, she and Hank were going for four.)

Hank always blamed the paint-remover fumes for her miscarriage and it nearly broke their hearts at first when the doctor said there would be no more babies, but Will and Ted kept them hopping: Cub Scouts, Little League, swimming lessons, the big house filled with friends and family.

Even now, all these years later, when she wandered through the wide halls and spacious rooms, she could still hear echoes of running sneakers, doors slamming, boyish laughter. She could pass the scarred newel post and remember how Will's baseball bat always banged it as he swung around the corner and took the stairs two at a time. Forever in a hurry. As if he'd known that he—

"There you go again!" Grace fumed, annoyed that she was letting old memories overwhelm her. "If you can't write a proper journal entry without turning into Poor Pitiful Pearl, then you should clean up the kitchen, read a book, or go watch a rerun of *Murder, She Wrote* up in your bedroom."

Sat. March 6th—I could absolutely spit! That mouthy Sally Massengill. Spends so much time minding Martins's puling grandbabies that her brain's turned to mush. After I specifically swore her to secrecy, what's the first thing she says to Ted when she sees him out pruning the shrubs that have overgrown my driveway?

(I'd come back in to stir up a Brunswick stew so Abby won't have to cook tomorrow. She

didn't feel well enough to come this morning. Nothing serious, T. says; just that she's been
working hard lately & can't seem to catch up on her sleep.)

Anyhow, soon as S. got through breaking her solemn word & had pushed that baby
stroller on down the sidewalk, T. burst into the kitchen, all excited because some idiot with
more money than brains made that ridiculous offer for my house last week. Now that this
neighborhood's been designated a historical section, we get more sightseers driving through &
the minute that man saw the eight-sided corner turret, the porch & eaves dripping with
ginger-bread, & the leaded glass windows on either side of the front door, he'd slammed on
his brakes & marched right up to ring my bell.

"Did he really offer you that much money?" asked Ted.

"What price dreams?" Grace asked tartly, adding a dash of red pepper to
the savory stew.

Ted looked puzzled.

"He said when he was a poor boy growing up in Buffalo, there was an old
Victorian house near his school and he promised himself he'd have one just
like it someday."

Despite barging in on her like that, the man from Buffalo had been charming. She'd given him a cup of coffee, a slice of her apple pie and, because his
story had disarmed her, a tour of the house.

"Great!" said Ted. "I was afraid this place might be a white elephant."

No imagination at all, thought Grace. Ted and Abby and their friends
moaned about mortgages, but they really did think suburban new was worth
more than restored urban old. Against her better judgment, she told him what
Jan and Bill got for their 1922 brick house on its quarter-acre corner lot when
they moved to Florida last August.

Ted's first reaction was shock, his second was to ask how soon her lawyer
could draw up the papers.

"You forget," Grace said crisply. "When your father and I were living over
our first store in Boylan Heights, this was *our* dream house, too."

Tues. March 22nd—Like it or not, it seems I'm going to give the man from Buffalo exactly
what he wants.

After Hank's death, Grace had resumed her girlhood habit of keeping a
journal. It was company somehow, a way of coping with loss and a hedge
against loneliness now that the last store was sold and she was officially retired
these past two years. She didn't write in it every day, only as the mood took
her, which was usually of an evening after looking back over the last few days
or week. But today, she was still so shaken that as soon as Abby left, she found

herself needing to set down the words that had flown between them.

Abby had taken off from work at lunch for a doctor's appointment and afterwards had driven straight over to tell what Grace knew she probably should have guessed two weeks ago—finally there was to be a baby.

Abby blurted it out as soon as Grace opened the door. Downstairs was so chilly that Grace had bundled her right up to the bedroom and tucked her into a blue velvet chaise lounge with the fleecy white afghan Hank's mother crocheted many long Christmases ago. With hot water bubbling over an old-fashioned spirit lamp, Grace soon had her daughter-in-law's hands around a steaming cup of tea.

Abby had never been inside that room unannounced and Grace was embarrassed by its untidiness: the heaped up pillows on the bed, her robe draped across the foot; newspapers and murder mysteries piled on the night stand; yarn spilling around the rocking chair before the fireplace where gas logs flamed warmly beneath a mantle cluttered with family pictures. (Grace hadn't the patience to become an expert knitter, but it seemed to keep the arthritis in her fingers at bay so she made herself do it while she watched the evening news every night.) On a tray beside the door, used teacups waited to be carried back to the kitchen. A jug of spent pussy willows dropped pollen on the wide window ledge, but she'd always had good luck forcing spring bulbs so crocuses bloomed brightly in their shallow bowls and a dozen hyacinths made the room smell like springtime.

Abby took it all in with interest and before Grace could apologize for the mess, she snuggled deeper into the woolly afghan. "What a cozy hobbit-hole. I don't blame you for wanting to stay."

Grace smiled warily, pushed the knitting out of the rocker, and sat down with her own cup of milky tea. "Maybe now that Ted's going to have you and a baby to worry about, he'll quit trying to make me leave."

"If you really think that, then you don't know Ted very well," Abby said, more bluntly than she'd ever spoken to Grace in the six years she and Ted been married.

It was good to discover Abby had some backbone but Grace was so surprised to have it jabbed at her that she could only stare at the younger woman with her mouth open.

"Ted's afraid that your heart—"

"My heart's perfectly fine," Grace said stiffly. "Dr. Lemmon says as long as I take my pills and don't overdo, I can live with it stuttering along like this for another twenty years. Ted knows that."

"Just the same, he feels responsible for taking care of you," Abby said.

"Nobody asked him to," she snapped impatiently.

"Hank did." Abby's voice was quiet. "A month before he died."

I should have known, thought Grace, and abruptly lifted the cup to her lips to mask her sudden emotion.

Dear steady Hank! Hers might be the flair and imagination that attracted customers to their three office supply stores, but his was the service and reliability that kept them coming back. And Ted was his child, just as Will was always hers; so of course he'd absorbed that sense of responsibility. As children, Will was totally enchanted by helium balloons and sparklers, but ephemeral wonders brought Ted little joy. He was usually so worried that the string might break or that a hot wire might burn someone that he seldom lost himself in rapture.

"Poor Ted," she sighed.

"I know you think he's dull and stodgy—"

"I've never said that!" Grace protested, guilt sharpening her tone. "I adore Ted."

"Not as much as you adored Will." Abby set her empty cup down on the low table between them so hard that her teaspoon rattled on the saucer.

"That's not true!" Rattled herself, Grace filled the teapot with more hot water but Abby waved away her offer of another cup.

"You never met Will," Grace said defensively. "I didn't love him more. Just differently."

"Ted thinks you wish he'd died instead of Will."

Grace was so stricken by that accusation that she couldn't reply.

At least Abby was perceptive enough to recognize genuine shock. She reached across the table and, in a rare gesture between them, clasped her mother-in-law's hand. "I thought he was wrong," she said. "I told him he was, but he's always blamed himself, you know."

"Yes." Being Ted, how could he not? Grace thought, anguished. It was never Ted's fault though. Will was older and should have realized the danger. Diving into the moon he called it, forgetting how dry the summer had been, not noticing in the moonlight how low the lake level had fallen beneath the rock they used for a diving platform.

"Anyhow," said Abby, "Ted worries about you. Your heart, this house. That's not going to change, Grace. And I don't want him to change," she added fiercely.

"No," Grace agreed, still shaken.

"So it looks like we have two options." She spoke bravely enough, but

Grace could hear the tremor beneath her bravado. "Ted and I can give up our jobs in Winston and move here near you, or you can sell this place and move to Winston, because once the baby comes, I'm not going to watch Ted keep tearing himself apart racing back and forth on the interstate every weekend and feeling guilty because he can't give his mother and his child equal time."

"My dear, don't give it another thought," Grace told her briskly. "Of *course* I'll sell now that there's a real reason to. I wouldn't miss the opportunity to babysit with my very first grandchild for all the houses in the world. Now what are you hoping for? A boy or a girl?"

Perceptive though she might be, Abby was too newly pregnant not to be diverted by Grace's questions; and if she were a little puzzled by her easy victory, she didn't risk losing it by asking any questions.

Numbly, Grace uncapped her pen and continued writing.

Part of me dies every time I think of what I've agreed to, but fair is fair. I owe Ted this, if nothing else, if I really did let him see—Not that I ever thought it again after that first wild grief. I didn't! I swear I didn't.

Mon. Apr. 18th—We signed the papers this morning. I've agreed to vacate by the first of June. My last spring to see in bloom the dogwoods & azaleas we planted, the drift of daffodils on the west lawn, Aunt E.'s yellow jasmine twining through the pines at the back of the lot. I'll be gone before my hydrangea blooms beside the kitchen door.

Will and Ted had given it to her for Mother's Day the year they were ten and eight, proudly lugging it up to her bedroom in a foil-wrapped pot that was top-heavy with two huge blue pompons.

"Will says they're the same color as your eyes," said Ted as he crawled into bed with Hank and Grace and put his solemn little face up to hers for a closer look.

"Why, so they are," Hank had said, looking from the flowers to her eyes to confirm the claim.

But Will had known without needing to compare, thought Grace, and her heart was sliced anew by his senseless death.

Fri. May 13th—For a while there, began to think I'd have to put everything in storage & camp in on Ted & Abby.

With the first of June hurtling down on them, Grace had diligently read the classifieds, listed herself with two different real estate agencies and trotted in and out of dozens of condos, townhouses and duplexes without finding any- thing remotely suitable until three days ago. The ad appeared in a biweekly newspaper published in a small town outside Winston, only seven minutes by back roads from Ted and Abby:

Starter home. 2 bdrms, 1 bath, din.rm, fireplc, mod.kit, nice garden, many extras. Reasonably priced.

Their idea of reasonable certainly wasn't Grace's and the many extras seem to include a quick-stop convenience store at one end of the street and a volunteer fire department at the other end. The floors needed refinishing, the master bedroom was currently papered in nursery rhymes and Ted thought both the roof and the heating system would probably have to be replaced in the next three or four years; but after some of the places Grace had seen those past few weeks, this "starter home" was a house she could end in and she had signed the papers that day.

Anyhow, it's a location I've bought, she wrote in her journal, *not a home, so what difference does it make?*

At least Ted was pleased.

Sun. May 29th—The movers will come on Tues. Ted & Abby both volunteered to come back & help pack the smaller, special things tomorrow, but Sally & I did most of them today. They seem a little shocked by how much I'm willing to part with.

After Grace had tagged all the furniture she planned to take with her and told the children to keep or sell whatever was left, she realized that Ted had begun to feel guilty because she wouldn't be able to fit ten rooms of furnishings into the new house. As if that mattered! Thirty years old, she thought impatiently, and he still didn't understand that things in and of themselves had never meant much to her.

Silver, crystal, porcelain, even the few valuable antiques that had come to her through the years had always been treasured more or less in direct proportion to their personal associations. The cane-bottom rocking chair her grandfather made with his own two hands was infinitely dearer than a period Sheraton drop-leaf table bought to fill a troublesome space in the front parlor, so the rocker would go in her new bedroom while Abby and Ted were given the table. Her nieces were delighted to get the Bavarian crystal chandelier and the mahogany breakfront they'd always admired; but Grace kept the ceramic lamp her sister Meg had made in her first pottery class.

"Oh Grace, are you sure?" squealed Sally when Grace took over a dozen brass candlesticks to add to Sally's own collection.

"We use things, we enjoy them, and then we let them go," Grace told her. "Why make complications out of something so simple?"

What wasn't simple were the things she could neither keep nor give away, the instances where she had no choice. She would not let herself get morbid about it, but there was a certain slant of light across her bedroom ceiling that always woke her early on summer mornings, the satin smoothness of the bannister as she pulled herself around the top step, an autumnal winelike fragrance that drifted over from Sally and Martin's yard when their scuppernongs ripened, the patterns cast by the full moon when she visited her hibernating garden on a chill winter night.

Dry-eyed she watched the Goodwill people cart away Hank's den: the old rug worn threadbare beneath his desk, the rumpsprung leather couch where he used to stretch out to watch ball games, the boys piled on top of him like two puppies. The man from Buffalo had four young children and she did not flinch when they pulled from the garage outgrown bicycles, skateboards with missing wheels, and other relics of her sons' separate pasts. Those were only things.

The only time it got really tricky was when Abby and Ted were helping her clear the kitchen and she opened the pantry door and saw the growth marks. She wondered if many houses still had them? Her grandparents' house had, and all her aunts and uncles'. "Oh my! Look how you've grown!" they'd exclaim; and before the visit was over, they would make pull off her shoes and stand up as straight as she could while someone laid a pencil on her head, drew a short line on the inside jamb of the pantry door, then labeled it *Grace, 51/2; Grace, 14 yrs.*

The lowest mark on her own pantry door jamb belonged to her brother's first grandchild, just five months old at the time. (The last time they measured him, he was still a fraction under six feet.) The oldest mark, though, was Will's, caught in mid-flight as he darted through the unfamiliar rooms joyfully exploring every new cubbyhole. It was neatly labeled the day they moved in. Next day, feeling vaguely historical, she and Hank solemnly measured each other and Ted, too.

Through the years it became almost a logbook as visiting relatives, close friends, the boys' first girlfriends removed their shoes and stood up tall to be measured, each mark identified by name and date. Tipsy with New Year's Eve champagne, someone would herd the whole party out to the kitchen. "Let's see if anybody's grown this year!"

Abby's mark was dated the night she and Ted announced their engagement.

No matter how many times she and Hank redecorated, that inner door jamb was left unpainted, and part of each birthday celebration was the ritual measuring: Will at 9, Ted at 7; Will at 14, Ted 12; Will at 19—after that, Ted's marks went on alone, passing Will's, passing his father. Grace remembered how proud he was the day he caught up to Hank. Proud and yet a little anxious, too, not to hurt Hank's own pride.

Soon the man from Buffalo would send the painters through, she thought. Two layers of fresh white enamel and it would be as if none of them had ever stood there flushed with laughter, self-conscious, barefooted.

Ted paused behind her on his way out to the hall with a carton of dishes. "Something wrong, Mom?"

"No, no," she said brightly. "Why in the world do you suppose I accumulated so many cans of mushroom soup? Packing canned goods is such a bore. Why don't we just leave this pantry for the movers?"

Sat. Aug. 20th—While looking through my knitting bag for some patterns (I'm going to try my hand at a fancy crib blanket for the baby as soon as the weather turns cooler), I unearthed this journal. Couldn't think where in the world I'd stuck it in all the last-minute confusion of packing.

To catch up: The man we'd hired to paint & re-paper here at the new house turned out to be slower than molasses & it took an extra week before the place was ready.

Grace leaned back in her chair, remembering how the movers had agreed to hold the furniture and how, rather than make a further nuisance of herself with Ted and Abby, she had decided it would be just as easy for her to drive down to Wilmington with the things she wanted her sister to have as it would be to box and ship them.

Her brother's wife said she'd drive up from Charleston and at that point, two Atlanta cousins said well, if it was a party, they'd come, too. There were things Grace wanted each of them to have, so in the end she'd driven off into the sunrise feeling like a gypsy peddler with her car jammed full and a small rental trailer tagging along behind.

That week at the beach was just exactly what she'd needed. The five women had known each other since infancy, through childbirths and deaths, and now with sagging breasts, flat-heeled shoes, hearing aids and the first walking cane. They talked and laughed and talked and cried and then talked some more until Grace finally felt that she was in control of her life again.

The movers had already delivered her things under Ted and Abby's supervision the Saturday morning that she returned, and Abby had gone out for sandwiches so that Ted was there alone when she pulled into the drive.

The first thing she noticed as she went up the walk to the open front door was her hydrangea bush, drastically pruned and a little wilted around the edges, but not bad considering all it had recently gone through.

"I know June's a bad month to transplant things," said Ted from the doorway, "but I think I cut it back enough to make up for root loss and I've watered it every night. We can plant it somewhere else if you'd rather."

"No, this is perfect," Grace said, absurdly pleased to see that scraggly bush again and picturing how pretty it would look once it regained its full spread. "How on earth did you sweet-talk the man from Buffalo—?"

"Mr. Heit," said Ted, looking almost as happy as the day he'd helped Will lug that pot of blue flowers up to her bedroom. "He's going to build a brick terrace at the kitchen door, so he was glad for me to take it."

Her old furniture looked strange in their new positions but as Grace walked through the little house, she knew time would soon make everything familiar.

Ted followed her out to the kitchen where he and Abby had been unpacking pots and pans and all those cans of mushroom soup. Without a pantry, the new cabinets were going to be hopelessly crammed, but Grace assured Ted that everything was fine, just fine.

"We did your bedroom first," he told her, "so if you'd like to lie down for a few minutes—"

Grace sharply reminded him that she was only sixty-four, not ninety-four, and certainly not in need of a morning nap after a mere three-hour drive.

The cheerfulness faded from his face. "Okay," he said and went back to unpacking dishes while she stepped into the bathroom to freshen up and give herself a good scolding in the mirror.

She decided it was all the newness that had set her nerves on edge. Everything sparkled and gleamed and the very air smelled of new paint, new paper, new grout. Once she'd been eager for new experiences, but this house had no history, this house—

It's because Hank was never here, Grace told herself bleakly. And there was no mark on any ceiling where Will once bounced a ball too hard, no chip missing from the sink where he dropped his first bottle of aftershave lotion, no lingering echo of his excited "Hey, Mom! Guess what?"

She splashed cold water on her face, took a deep breath, and opened the door in time to see Ted shut the closet at the end of the hall. He had a guilty expression on his face.

"I wondered if you were all right," he said.

Will could always look her in the eye and spin the most outrageous and totally believable lies. Poor Ted couldn't shade the truth by a hair without giving himself away.

Grace walked down the hall. For such a small house, the closet was rather large: four feet deep with wide shelves above the clothes pole and narrow shelves running from floor to ceiling on the left wall. Two storage bags hung from the pole and boxes of Christmas ornaments had been stacked above. Nothing to make a grown man apprehensive.

Puzzled, she started to close the door and then she saw the marks pencilled on the freshly painted inner jamb, marks that began less than two feet from the floor and stair-stepped up past six feet, each neatly labeled with a familiar name and a date.

"I traced them off on tissue paper," Ted said. "You don't mind, do you? I know you're not sentimental, but with the baby coming, I thought it'd be fun to watch—" He hesitated. "And besides, it was like bringing along something of Will."

Even as a small boy, he'd always saved the real truth for last.

"Mom?"

Blindly she turned to him—the sturdy son she had loved yet never properly valued—and at the sight of her face, his crumpled, too.

They held each other wordlessly for a long moment, then Grace heard Ted's choked voice say, "I *did* try to stop him, Mom. Honest I did."

"Shh, honey," she murmured brokenly. "I know you did. It wasn't your fault, Ted. I've never blamed you for Will's death. Never."

She looked him straight in the eyes and said it again and this time, unlike thirteen years ago, she saw that he finally believed her.

How stupid and selfish of me, she thought, and, yes, how unimaginative, too, to think I was the only one with grief still green after all these years.

Well, that was June and this is August. I won't say there aren't things I still miss but the library's within walking distance, the fire engines add excitement, & now that I'm practically living in his pocket, Ted's quit worrying about me so much & spends more time worrying about Abby. He'll always be a worrier, I guess. "Just like his father," I tell Abby.

"If I'm as lucky as you," she says.

Mom, Apple Pie, and Murder, 1999

Virgo in Sapphires

For our wedding anniversary, my husband gave me a necklace with the traditionally appropriate gemstone. The day after our anniversary, I received a note from the clerk who had sold it to him, congratulating us and wishing me much enjoyment from the necklace. Being a mystery writer, I immediately thought, "What if the note had arrived day before yesterday and I did not get a necklace yesterday?"

When Laura Hart opened the door that Saturday morning in early September, she found the postman busily stuffing their mailbox. Car keys in one hand, an expensive flat leather purse in the other, she gave a quick glance at her small gold wristwatch and saw that she had plenty of time to chat a moment before meeting her friend Sylvia for lunch. Laura believed in kindness and courtesy.

"Looks like someone's having a birthday," the postman said, handing over a thick sheaf of mail. A bright pink envelope decorated with summer flowers slipped to the ground and he quickly retrieved it.

"Me," Laura smiled. "Tomorrow."

Thirty. One of life's major milestones. A time to take stock of the past and take charge of the future.

All week, cards had been arriving from far-flung friends and relatives. Her sister had sent one bordered in black, mock sympathy for growing so old; and her parents and in-laws had sent sweetly sentimental congratulations. Most of the other cards were funny variations on the ageing theme. She thanked the postman for his good wishes that she have a happy birthday, inquired about the arthritis in his knee, and listened to his answer with what appeared to be genuine interest. Then when he moved on to the next house, she laid the bills and junk mail on the hall table and tucked the rest in her purse beside several other cards she had planned to share with Sylvia over lunch.

Her friend could use a good laugh, thought Laura, as she drove the short distance from her home in an old historic district of Raleigh to their favorite restaurant, just off Glenwood Avenue. Although Sylvia swore that nothing was wrong, she had seemed so edgy lately that Laura wondered if she were starting to realize that divorcing Simon might have been a mistake. All last year, it had been "Virgos should never marry Sagittarians." "Sagittarians are grasshoppers, feckless and irresponsible." "Sagittarians promise you diamonds, then give you rhinestones." And throughout the legal proceedings, she'd been as giddy as a girl in love at the thought of regaining her freedom, of putting order back into her life, of being accountable to no one.

These last few weeks, however, she had begun to speak wistfully of the little things she missed now that there was no husband of her own around any more, Sagittarian or no Sagittarian.

Like Laura, Sylvia was a Virgo, too, with a twenty-seventh birthday of her own, just five days later. Unlike Laura, Sylvia took their daily horoscopes very seriously. She and Simon had bickered for ages, but to say that they should have divorced—or never even have married—simply because Simon had been born in December?

How silly, thought Laura.

"What about Will and me?" she'd teased. "According to you, Gemini and Virgo are just as badly matched, yet look at us. Married five years and couldn't be happier."

Sylvia had shrugged. "Only because he was born on the cusp of Cancer, Virgo's perfect mate. Simon and I are flat in the middle of our signs."

The calendar might read September, but the sun was as hot as July and the air still held August's sticky humidity. Laura was glad to enter the restaurant's air-conditioned coolness. Sylvia was already there, sleek and beautiful in a sleeveless green linen dress, her long blonde hair tied back with a matching silk scarf to set off her pearl earrings. Even though Sylvia was one of her closest friends, Laura couldn't help noting a slight softening in the other woman's upper arms, a hint of sag above the elbow. Complacently, she knew that her own upper arms were as firm as daily workouts could make them and her plum-colored dress was also sleeveless.

Virgos were supposed to be detail-oriented, she thought with a sudden touch of bitchiness, and wondered when Sylvia would realize she wouldn't be able to go bare-armed much longer.

"I love that color," Sylvia sighed as Laura joined her at the table, "but purple makes me look so washed out."

"They say blondes have more fun," Laura said, "so it's only fair that brunettes should get to wear purple."

The restaurant wasn't too crowded at the moment and their waiter came right away to take their order. Over glasses of Chardonnay, as the two women waited for their food, Laura used her butter knife to slit open the bright-colored envelopes and soon they were laughing at some of the more risque birthday cards with their bawdy suggestions for how to celebrate. One card even held a long sausage-shaped, flesh-colored balloon with such extremely graphic instructions that Laura turned red and hastily hid it in her purse while Sylvia laughed out loud.

Eventually, Laura opened a small square card. Her smile turned to puzzlement and she looked more carefully at the ivory-toned envelope, turning it in her hand to seek a return address. There was only a dark blue Gothic F imprinted in on the flap.

"What is it?" asked Sylvia.

"I'm not sure. I thought it was another birthday card. Now I see it's addressed to Mr. and Mrs. William Hart, but the note itself is to Will. It's—oh, my stars!" she exclaimed as her eyes raced through the short message. "Listen to this, Syl. 'Dear Mr. Hart, I thoroughly enjoyed meeting you and assisting with the jewelry selection. The sapphire earrings are perfectly beautiful. I do hope Mrs. Hart is pleased with her birthday present. She's a very lucky woman. Thank you so much for shopping with us and I look forward to serving you again. Sincerely Susan Dunsel, Fitchett's Jewelers.'"

Sylvia's blue eyes widened. "Fitchett's? That's the most expensive store in Raleigh."

Laura was reexamining the envelope. "The postmark's smudged, but it seems to have been mailed yesterday afternoon. She must have thought it wouldn't arrive till Monday, after my birthday was past."

A happy glow suffused her face and she shook her head in rueful amusement. "Sapphire earrings? That dear, sneaky man! All month he's been saying that his sales were down and commissions were off. I thought tomorrow was going to be nothing more exciting than breakfast in bed and maybe a dozen roses."

Knowing how much Sylvia loved earrings, especially earrings set with precious gemstones, Laura wasn't surprised to glance up and find naked envy in Sylvia's pale blue eyes. Envy and something else. Anger? Sylvia was notorious for her hot temper.

She leaned across the table and said, "Listen, Syl, promise me that you'll never tell Will, okay? He must be planning a really special day and he'd be so disappointed if he ever learns I knew about it ahead of time."

"As if I'd have a chance," Sylvia said sarcastically. "I got custody of you; Simon got custody of Will, remember?"

Laura nodded. That was another awkward result of divorce. Spouses couldn't help taking sides. After Simon and Sylvia split, Will said he just didn't feel comfortable spending any time with her. Not that he seemed to spend much time with Simon either—their friendship had been quite casual, occasioned more by their wives than by mutual interests. But Laura assumed his distaste for Sylvia was due to male solidarity and she hadn't questioned his stand. Fortunately, Sylvia usually chose to make a joke of it, likening it to another division of marital property, as if Laura were a set of cookware and Will the microwave oven.

All winter, Laura had felt bad about not inviting Sylvia over to the house when Will was there, but her friend had just shrugged. "Simon's probably convinced Will that the divorce was all my idea."

It wouldn't have taken much convincing. Sylvia clearly wanted out the marriage much more than the bewildered Simon had. And Laura had picked up on enough clues to realize that the divorce wasn't merely a conflict of celestial signs. Syl was too radiant and usually too busy to meet with any of her women friends for lunch or to make their weekly gym dates after work.

Clearly there was a man involved, moreover a man she expected to marry or move in with as soon as she dumped Simon.

"*This* Virgo's not meant to live alone," she said cryptically.

Unfortunately, it did not seem to be happening. The decree was final two months ago, yet Syl wouldn't admit she was seeing anyone special. Moreover, her kitten-in-cream radiance had dimmed in the last couple of weeks. She was brittle and more short-tempered than usual, for all the world like a woman who suspects she's about to be dumped herself.

Their food arrived, polenta with portabella mushrooms and smoked mozzarella on a bed of leafy greens. Laura put away her birthday cards and spent the rest of their meal trying to dispel the gray cloud that suddenly hovered over their table. Sylvia's mercurial mood swings were legendary among her friends. She could be sunny, charming and amusing one minute, stormy and vindictive the next. For some reason, her earlier good humor had now vanished. She drank three glasses of wine in rapid succession, snarled at the waiter and rudely asked the people at the next table what they were staring at.

Laura braced herself for the worst and it came as they were leaving. She heard a crash behind her and turned to see that their hapless waiter had somehow upset a tray of cold potato soup into the laps of those same people. Sylvia herself did not look back. With chin held high, she seemed oblivious to the chaos behind her.

Only the satisfied little smile on her lips betrayed her.

As they parted outside the restaurant, she again wished Laura a happy birthday, then spoiled it by sending sarcastic regards to "the world's most perfect husband."

On Monday, Sylvia called Laura at work. She had spent a lonely weekend wracked by jealousy. Lucky Laura was going to be wined and dined and given sapphire earrings and probably bedded by her very sexy husband.

What would her own birthday bring? Her horoscope promised "something special in the air" but Sylvia couldn't bring herself to believe it. Her lover had promised to come Friday night, but could she believe *him* any more than her horoscope? They used to spend every free moment together. He couldn't seem to get enough of her. Lately though, he claimed to be working longer hours. But was he really working?

She knew that hearing Laura chirp and burble about Will's extravagant gift would make her even more jealous, nevertheless she still called and asked, "So how was your birthday?"

"Awful!" Laura moaned. "The worst in my whole life."

Apprehensively, Sylvia said, "What's wrong?"

"I can't talk about it now. I'll start crying again. Could you meet me at the gym after work?"

By the time Sylvia got to the gym and changed into the shorts and tank top she wore when working out, she found a grim-eyed Laura pumping furiously on the stationary bike. Her face was already shiny with perspiration and her dark hair curled in damp ringlets across her forehead.

"Whoa!" said Sylvia, sliding onto the neighboring bike. "Slow down before you have a heart attack. What happened?"

"My birthday happened," Laura said tightly. She paused long enough to wipe her face on the towel draped over her bike handles. "Breakfast in bed in the morning, dinner at Antonio's last night."

"And?" her friend prompted.

"And thirty-five roses in between. A pink one for every year of my life plus five red ones in the middle for every wonderful year we've been married. Isn't that romantic as hell?" She resumed her furious pedaling.

Sylvia's blue eyes widened. "No sapphire earrings?"

"No sapphire earrings."

"But I don't understand," said Sylvia, pedaling slowly. "What did he say when you asked him?"

"I didn't."

"But—?"

"You, my family, all our friends—everyone thinks Will and I have the perfect marriage. And it should be perfect. But you know how Will is."

Sylvia shook her head.

"He's a salesman," Laura said impatiently. "Charm is part of his stock in trade. That's why he's so good at his job. That's why he can afford to buy sapphires for his new mistress," she added bitterly.

"*What?*"

"You've seen the way he flirts with my friends at parties. It's almost enough to make me take your nonsense about horoscopes seriously. 'Gemini: amorous, impulsive, adolescent when it comes to women.' That's what you said the first time I told you Will's birth date. Remember? It's so automatic, I don't think he even realizes it himself. Half the women we know would knock me over to get at him if they thought they had a chance. You're the only one he never made a dent in. Look at that note from Fitchett's. You could almost feel the heat coming off the page: '*I look forward to serving you again.*' I just bet she does. In her bed, no doubt."

"Oh, Laura," Sylvia said sympathetically. "Don't torture yourself. Do you really think that he's ever been unfaithful?"

"I'm not a fool, Sylvia. I can read the signs."

"But you don't know for sure."

"No?" Laura signaled to the attendant, who came over with bottles of chilled water for both of them. She pressed the cold bottle to her hot cheek. "Then who did he buy those earrings for?"

"You, of course," said Sylvia as she uncapped the plastic bottle and took a sip. "But maybe he changed his mind. Decided he couldn't afford them after all and took them back. Didn't he tell you his sales were off?"

"I don't know that I can believe him any more." Laura set the water bottle on the floor beside her and began to pedal again. "He's been traveling so much this year, I was sure he was seeing someone out of town. It's not all that unusual for men to have a final fling before they really settle down for good, is it? The old seven-year itch? Except in his case, it's a five-year itch. I didn't say anything because I thought if I kept quiet, he'd get over her. And he did. I'm *sure* he did. These last few weeks have been absolute heaven. He hasn't traveled as much, he's been home early more nights. But now he's starting with some-one new. I can feel it, Syl. He was only going through the motions with me yesterday. We didn't even make love."

"You're probably imagining things," Sylvia said briskly. "If he didn't return the earrings, maybe he's saving them for your anniversary."

"Our anniversary's not till March."

"Well, Christmas then."

Laura scowled. "The note from Fitchett's said birthday."

"True," Sylvia said slowly.

Laura began her cool-down and gave a fatalistic sigh. "Well, whatever hap-pens, happens. I guess I'll just have to tough it out. Thanks for giving me a shoulder to cry on, Syl."

Sylvia wiped her face with the sweatband on her wrist and smiled. "That's what friends are for."

"Want to come over Friday night and celebrate your own birthday? Will has to fly to Chicago for a Saturday morning sales conference. We could invite Liz and Marta, open champagne, have a pajama party."

Sylvia shook her head "Sorry, but I've already made plans. In fact, my horoscope says this is going to be an extra-special birthday this year."

"Really?" Laura looked at her a long considering moment. "You have that kitten-in-cream glow on your face again. All I can say is good luck, kid. Hope your birthday turns out better than mine."

Sylvia held up two crossed fingers. "Me, too!"

Sylvia held that thought all through the long week that followed. Waiting for Friday night had been almost like waiting for Christmas morning, but it was finally here.

She had let the housework slide a little since Simon moved out, but this week, she had cleaned every night till the house fairly sparkled. Two places were set at the gleaming dining table. Candlelight bounced off her best china and crystal and was reflected in the silver ice bucket where a bottle of chilled champagne waited to toast her birthday.

Attention to details, she thought happily as she laid the carving knife beside the walnut carving board where he would slice the Châteaubriand as soon as it came from the broiler. She wasn't much of a meat eater, but for him, the bloodier the better.

Virgos delight in making everything special for the ones they love, Sylvia told herself, and she gave the bedroom a final inspection. Cool perfumed sheets awaited their hot passion. Already she could feel her body begin to soften, feel herself melting as she thought of where the evening would end. Surely this would be the night that he finally said the words she'd been waiting all these months to hear—that he wanted her as his wife.

She was wearing his favorite dress and nothing underneath except a lacy garter belt and stockings. Her long blonde hair fell loosely around her face, just the way he liked her to wear it.

She heard his key in her lock and rushed to the door, eager for that first greedy kiss after all these days they had been apart. She was too excited to analyze whether his embrace was equally passionate, whether his lips met hers as eagerly as in the beginning. She'd been so afraid their affair was cooling, yet here he was in her arms again, tall and handsome and desirable as ever.

"Happy birthday, honey!" Will said when their lingering kiss had ended and he could finally speak. He handed her a small flat box wrapped in silver paper and tied so tightly with silver ribbons that her eager fingers couldn't undo the bows.

"It's so small," she cooed. "So light! What on earth could it be?"

"Just a little something I picked up last week to add to your collection."

She laughed in delight and kissed him again. Men were so funny. As if her jewelry box were full of real gemstones. These would be her first sapphires. She should have known Will was buying them for *her* birthday, not Laura's.

"Let me get something to cut the ribbons before I break a nail," she said.

Will followed her into the dining room and nuzzled the back of her neck while she slipped the knife beneath the ribbons and tore off the paper.

"You smell good," he said huskily as his hand slid inside the front of her dress. "Why don't we skip dinner and go straight to dessert?"

"Ah, you silly darling," she said fondly. Yet her body arched in pleasure beneath his hand and for a moment she almost forgot about his gift.

Then the silver paper fell away, Sylvia lifted the box lid and stared blankly. Instead of sapphire earrings, it was a small ornately engraved silver fork with two flared tines.

"What—?"

"It's a lemon fork," he said proudly. "The antique dealer said it was probably 1860 to 1870. I know you've showed me your collection a dozen times, but I couldn't remember. You don't already have one, do you?"

Collection, she thought dully. My collection of whimsical Victorian silver serving pieces.

"It's as cute as you are," Will said as his fingers cupped her breast.

She heard Laura's voice in her head, *"But now he's starting with someone new. I can feel it."*

Angrily, she slapped his hand away and whirled on him. "You give me a lemon fork? And who gets the earrings, Will?"

"Earrings?"

"Sapphire earrings. From Fitchett's. I know all about them."

"Then you know more than I do," he said with matching anger.

She was in a rage now, remembering her week of loneliness, the nights when he'd told her he was away on business, treating her as if she were Laura—someone he could take for granted, could lie to, could cheat on. Well, she wasn't meek little if-I-don't-ask-questions-he'll-come-back-to-me Laura.

"What was tonight?" she screamed, her fury fueled by humiliation at how he planned to use her. "One last time before you move on to greener pastures? Who else are you sleeping with?"

"You're crazy," he blustered, but his guilt was so glaringly obvious that even he recognized it.

"Ah, the hell with this!" he snarled. "I've had it with your temper tantrums and your jealousy. Who needs it?"

He had taken only one step away from her when he felt a stunning blow on his back, then such pain as he had never known. Something held him, clawing at his lungs. He pulled away, glanced back and saw the gory knife in her hands, his own life's blood dripping from its deadly point.

It was the last thing he ever saw.

The police officers were gentle. They hated having to come and tell the widows, but this one seemed to have her emotions in check now that the initial shock was wearing off.

"Poor Will," she said sadly. "Sylvia wasn't his first affair and she wouldn't have been his last. But she was the one with the hottest temper. All the others seemed to have gone quietly."

"She keeps screaming about a pair of sapphire earrings, Mrs. Hart. That he'd bought them for someone else, not her."

"Earrings?" asked Laura, looking up at the officers as if bewildered.

"Yes, ma'am. Said you thought they were for his new mistress and this time you were right."

Laura shook her head. "I'm sorry. I honestly don't know what she's talking about."

She answered the officers' other questions with stoic bravery, but when they were gone, she went into the bedroom and found the card still stuck in her purse with her birthday cards. She smiled as she looked at it a final time. Wonderful what you could do with computers and a good printer these days. As if Fitchett's—*Fitchett's!*—would ever hire the sort of salesperson who would write such a gushy indiscreet note. The slightly smudged postmark she'd created for the envelope had been a lovely touch and she was sorry Sylvia hadn't bothered to look at it.

So much for Virgo's vaunted attention to detail, she thought scornfully.

All that Zodiac nonsense and where had it gotten Sylvia?

Sitting in jail and facing trial for murder.

She, on the other hand, was now a widow, well-rid of a cheating spouse and a traitorous friend.

In fact, she was now a very well-to-do widow indeed, Laura thought, suddenly remembering the hefty insurance policy on Will's life, his company's generous retirement plan, the stocks and CDs they'd acquired together.

All hers now.

She had hoped Sylvia would make a scene in a restaurant when he didn't produce that non-existent pair of sapphire earrings for her birthday. She had thought that maybe Sylvia would publically embarrass Will, perhaps even smash him over the head with a wine bottle and put him in the hospital with a concussion.

She had only meant to punish the two of them a little before suing Will for divorce. It truly had not occurred to her that things could turn out this well.

She shredded the counterfeit Fitchett's card and flushed away the pieces.

Fitchett's.

Such an excellent store. Once the estate was settled, maybe she would pay them a visit. Buy something tasteful for herself. In emeralds perhaps.

Or rubies.

She had never really cared much for sapphires.

Eiskalte Jungfrauen, 2000
Edgar, Anthony, Agatha Nominee

The Third Element

The law of self-defense really is defined by the three conditions, i.e. elements, that I've listed here.

"It's all Douglas Woodall's fault," Miss Eula declared as she waved away the plate of homemade cookies Aunt Zell was offering for dessert. "How *could* he be so mean as to prosecute Kyle?"

Aunt Zell passed the plate to me. "Well, Kyle did sort of shoot that Wentworth boy," she said, trying to be fair.

(Which was putting it as tactfully as possible since Miss Eula's grandson had done a lot more than "sort of" shoot Hux Wentworth. Kyle Benson had actually emptied all nine rounds of a 9mm automatic into Hux's back while Hux lay wounded on the floor.)

"But it was self-defense," Miss Eula insisted, as Kyle himself had insisted ever since it happened last fall. "Are you supposed to let yourself be beaten to a bloody pulp before you can defend yourself? You're a judge, Deborah. Is that really what the law says?"

"Not exactly," I answered, speaking around one of Aunt Zell's lemon crisps. As a district court judge who will never hear a murder case of any sort, I could take the academic view. "You can use force to defend yourself, but the third element of self-defense, the one that says you can use deadly force, means that you have to be afraid for your life. Doug Woodall's saying that once Wentworth was down and wounded, Kyle and Brinley could have escaped without killing him. Their lives were no longer in danger and Kyle shouldn't have kept shooting."

Actually, considering how many bullet holes they found in Hux Wentworth's back and considering the previous history between those two, Miss Eula's grandson was lucky that our DA hadn't asked the grand jury to hand down an indictment for second-degree murder rather than voluntary manslaughter.

And despite Miss Eula's huffing, Doug had considerately waited till after Kyle graduated from Carolina this past June instead of pushing to calendar the case months earlier.

Now it was July and the whole Benson clan was camped out in the courtroom while the prosecution and defense went through the tedious and time-consuming process of picking a jury.

Miss Eula is their matriarch and she's also the oldest living member of Bethel Baptist Church out in the country where Mother and Aunt Zell often visited when they were growing up. Mindful of her advanced age and the thirty-minute drive to and from Dobbs, Aunt Zell had invited Miss Eula to come for lunch every day and then to lie down for a little rest afterwards before going back over to the courtroom.

Miss Eula's will is strong, but her body's frail so she'd made only token demurrals before accepting, although she still blamed Doug Woodall for all the inconvenience. "See if any of us ever contribute to his campaign again," she said darkly.

Poor Doug. He was between a rock and a hard place on this one.

Elections are usually a cake walk for our District Attorney, but this time around, he has serious opposition and he's been accused of going easy on people of substance (which the Bensons are) and of not going after a killer as vigorously when the victim is of a lesser social class (which Hux Wentworth certainly was).

While it's true that Doug doesn't exactly bust his budget when one migrant worker kills another over a bottle of Richard's Wild Irish Rose and then flees the state, he does care when residents get themselves killed, even when that resident is somebody as sorry and no good as Hux Wentworth.

The Wentworths were always a violent family, root and stock. Hux's brother is sitting in State Prison right now for murder and Hux himself had served a short term up in Raleigh for armed robbery. But he was big and handsome and could turn on a rough sort of charm when he chose to.

Having danced with the devil a time or three myself, I can understand how a nice girl like Brinley Davis could let herself be blindsided by a bad boy "misunderstood" by everyone else. Unfortunately, she had to learn by experience that if you're gonna pick up trash, you're gonna get your hands dirty before you can turn it loose.

Hux Wentworth wasn't a piece of mud to be scraped off the heel of a summer sandal. He was bubblegum, twice as messy, twice as sticky, and when Brinley tried to tell him that she was interested in someone else—Kyle Benson, in this case, Hux's first reaction was threaten to beat the living-you-know-what out of Kyle. Since Kyle is built like a wiry tennis player and Hux had the bulk of a linebacker, it was lucky that Kyle was back in Chapel Hill by the time

Brinley told him this or it might be Hux standing trial for Kyle's death instead of the other way around.

Actually, if you could believe Brinley and Kyle, that's nearly the way it was.

I had heard their story from Miss Eula. I'd heard it from Sheriff's Deputy Dwight Bryant, who was first detective on the scene. I'd also heard it from just about anybody else who could get me to stand still long enough to speculate about Kyle's guilt or innocence with them, including Portland Brewer, my cousin-by-marriage and Kyle's attorney. At this point, everybody in the whole damn county had heard it. The main facts were not in dispute:

a) Brinley Davis had told Hux Wentworth she didn't want to see him again.

b) Hux Wentworth said he'd kill Kyle Benson and Brinley, too, if she tried to go out with Kyle.

c) At fall break, Brinley stayed home while her parents drove out to the mountains to see the leaves. (Portland's eyebrows had arched slyly when she told me, "Brinley said she'd seen leaves before.") Her parents probably hadn't even cleared the Dobbs town limits before Brinley called Kyle and told him she was nervous about being all alone in that big house. (So okay, little Brinley's not a pure-as-the-driven-snow-princess. Who is, these days?)

d) Brinley and Kyle were snuggled on a couch in the den watching a video when Hux crashed through the french doors.

Literally. Without even trying the knob.

Unfortunately for him, French doors are built more sturdily than he realized and while he stood there, momentarily dazed and bleeding from a dozen superficial cuts, Brinley and Kyle took off like a pair of terrified rabbits.

According to Dwight, Hux left a trail of blood and glass as he tracked the two through the house, up the broad staircase, along the hall, to the master bedroom where Brinley remembered that her daddy kept a loaded automatic pistol in the night stand. She hastily dug it out of the drawer, thrust it into Kyle's hands, then dragged him into her parents' bathroom, locking the door behind them.

That door was even stronger than the french doors, but Hux kicked it open with a mighty roar.

At this point, depending on who's telling it, the tale splits. According to Brinley and Kyle, they were in fear of their lives.

"Shoot, Kyle, shoot!" Brinley screamed, whereupon Kyle Benson emptied the gun, all nine slugs, into Hux Wentworth.

Seven of those slugs hit him in the back—as he was trying to flee, said our District Attorney—and it was on the basis of those seven extra shots, two of them fired while Hux was lying face-down on the bathroom tiles that Kyle had been charged with voluntary manslaughter.

Now it was going to be up to twelve citizens of Colleton County to decide.

"So how did your jury shape up?" I asked Portland when we met for an early supper two evenings later at a local steak and ale place that overlooks the river. With her husband out of town and my guy a hundred miles away, we were both at loose ends.

"Who knows?" she shrugged wearily. Jury selection had finished that morning and opening arguments had begun that afternoon with nothing more than a lunch break.

Ned O'Donnell, the superior court judge who was hearing this case, runs a tight ship. He is very solicitous of jurors and keeps things moving so they aren't inconvenienced a minute longer than necessary.

Voir dire (questioning prospective jurors) is always tiring and Portland looked drained as she ticked the results off on her fingers.

"We wound up with five middle-aged white women—schoolteacher, beautician, social worker, file clerk and daycare worker, and one elderly black woman who used to keep house for the governor's great aunt. Judge O'Donnell offered to let her off because of her age, but she said she wanted to do her civic duty. Two black men—an orderly from the hospital and a retired black postal worker, and four white men—two farmers, a sheet rocker, and a driver for Ferncliff Sausage who has tattoos from his wrists to his shoulders."

"Like Hux Wentworth?" I asked, drizzling a little olive oil over my salad of mixed summer greens.

"Exactly like," Portland nodded. "But he didn't give me any grounds to challenge for cause and I didn't want to use up my last peremptory challenge in case the next person was worse."

"Maybe he'll scare some of the women enough to let them sympathize with Kyle," I said, offering what comfort I could.

She laughed and took a sip of her beer. "Want to split a steak?"

"Sure," I said. We've been splitting food since grade school.

"Another beer for y'all?" asked the waitress even though our glasses were still more than half full. We shook our heads and she went off with our order.

We spoke of this and that, but Portland kept circling back to Doug Woodall's eloquent opening argument.

"Oh, Doug," I said dismissively. "He has to put on a strong case, but you're not really worried, are you?"

"I don't know, Deborah, and that's a fact. We've got a great expert witness, an ME who can explain those shots in the back—"

"He can?"

"She."

"Uh-oh. Mistake right there," I warned. "A woman disputing the word of a male expert in front of a Colleton County jury?"

"Don't try to teach your grandma how to suck eggs," Portland said smugly. "The state's ME is a woman, too."

She held up her hand to illustrate Wentworth's torso and her expert witness's interpretation of the angles of penetration.

"The first slug hit him in the hand. The next one in the shoulder. The force of the first two bullets spun him around—" She twisted her hand and slowly bent it back. "—so that the next seven caught him across the back as he was going down. Kyle didn't shoot him on the floor, it's just that the angle changed as Hux was falling away from them."

"Okay," I conceded, playing devil's advocate, "but Kyle grew up with guns. He knows what one bullet can do. How you going to explain away nine of them?"

"That's what Doug argued."

"And your response?"

"Yes, ladies and gentlemen of the jury, Kyle Benson did indeed grow up with rifles, shotguns and an old-fashioned revolver, *but*—" She paused dramatically. "—he'd never fired an automatic before."

Our steak and two plates arrived and I divided the filet right down the middle while Portland did the same with our single baked potato. We'd forgone the Texas toast and made the waitress take the sour cream and butter back to the kitchen so that neither of us would yield to temptation in the middle of swimsuit season. The steak was grilled just the way we like it— almost crusty black on the outside, bright red on the inside—and that first bite awakened the carnivore that slumbers deep in my taste buds. Much as I adore fruits and vegetables, every once in a while I take a truly sensuous pleasure in red meat.

"Mmmm!" Portland murmured happily, echoing my own enjoyment.

"You ever fire an automatic?" she asked, unable to keep her mind off the case.

I nodded. From my own days as a trial lawyer, I remembered this obsession to keep going over and over the facts.

"Well, then, you know that once you pull on that trigger, it'll keep firing till you release the pressure. The gun's empty almost as soon as you start. And don't forget our ear witnesses."

"Ah, yes, the McCormacks."

I've met them and wasn't particularly taken with either. They're from Connecticut. He's upper management in one of the high-tech corporations over in the Research Triangle. Very fond of the sound of his own voice. She's a listener. Reminds me a little of the way Nancy Reagan used to listen adoringly whenever Ronnie spoke.

The McCormacks live next door to the Davises if you can call houses set squarely in the middle of acre lots and surrounded by lots of mature trees and shrubbery "next door." The McCormacks planned to host a large brunch on their patio the next morning so they were outside, making last minute preparations, wiping down the patio furniture, setting up the extra tables on the edge of the back lawn.

When Kyle and Brinley fled her house that night, they had headed straight for the bright lights of the McCormacks' patio.

"Doug's opening statement kept stressing that there was no way Kyle didn't know that those first two shots hit Hux and put him on the floor," Portland told me. "He's going to try to get McCormack to say that Kyle and Brinley were exaggerating their fear, but he can't get around the fact that McCormack heard all the shots and that he's positive there wasn't a break between them."

She gave me an ironic smile. "Unlike Fred Bissell."

I smiled, too, remembering a client my cousin John Claude had defended last year. Mr. Bissell claimed he shot both his wife and the man she was in bed with in the heat of the moment. Unfortunately, three neighbors swore there was a long pause between the first two shots and the last two—one bullet for the wife, three for her lover. He's currently serving a nineteen-to-thirty—not what Portland had in mind for young Kyle Benson.

"What about Mrs. McCormack?" I asked.

Portland shrugged. "She just echoes what her husband says. And you know how Judge O'Donnell feels about superfluous witnesses who don't bring anything new to the table."

Indeed. Doesn't matter if it's prosecution or defense, Ned never hesitates to apologize to the jury for having their time wasted by either side. Doesn't take much to have a jury turn against you.

"What's really worrying me is the way Doug's harping on that old Little League accident," said Portland. "Trying to make it sound as if Kyle and Hux had such a blood feud going that Kyle took this opportunity to deliberately get rid of a lifelong enemy. Hell! They were kids. Kyle barely remembers it."

"He might not," I said reluctantly, "but from what I hear, Hux Wentworth did."

My nephew Reese had been playing the night it happened and half my family were there to cheer him on. It was his and Hux's last year of Little League and Kyle's first. Kyle was small but he had an arm and the beginning of a good fast ball. His team was so far behind the coach decided to put him in for a little seasoning and Kyle was told to go out and pitch as hard as he could.

First up was Hux Wentworth, who had a tendency to crowd the plate. Kyle's first pitch was over Hux's head. His second was dead on the money. It would have been a called strike except that it slammed into Hux's hand gripping the bat directly over the inside corner of the plate. Broke the index and middle fingers of his right hand.

Outraged, Hux had stormed the pitcher's mound. It took both coaches, the umpire and my nephew Reese to stop him and in the melee, the fingers were so badly hurt that by the time Hux's mother figured her home remedies weren't working and carried him to a doctor, there was irreparable nerve damage.

According to Reese, Hux forever after blamed Kyle for ruining his potential baseball career. The hand still functioned well enough for most things, but Hux could no longer control his slider, his "money pitch," as he called it.

"Did he really have that much potential?" I'd asked Reese back when the shooting occurred last fall and that old Little League story had resurfaced.

"Nah," Reese had said scornfully. "His slider that he keeps bitching about? It was an okay pitch, but it was all he had and I guess it got to seem like more the older we got. It was like, here was Kyle with his rich family, that new car they gave him, finishing college and all, and that pissed Hux big time 'cause he won't going nowhere. Didn't even finish high school. Like he'd've had all that stuff, too, if Kyle didn't break his fingers? Yeah. Right."

This from my nephew who barely scraped through high school himself, drives a pickup and seems perfectly content to go on working off my brother's electrician's license for the rest of his life.

"And then when Brinley Davis dumped him, I heard Hux was like, 'He took my slider and now he's taking my girl? I'll cut off his effing balls.' And I guess he would've if Kyle didn't shoot him. They say he had a knife with him that night."

"No knife," Portland said regretfully, when I repeated Reese's words. "And Doug's subpoenaed Brinley as a hostile witness. Going to try to make her admit that she'd told Kyle that Hux was bearing a grudge and that Kyle was taking it seriously."

"Hard to prove a negative," I said, quoting one of our law professors at Carolina.

Even though we're practically the same age, Portland kept her life on track back then and graduated from law school three years ahead of me. Despite the time difference, we'd taken courses from many of the same professors.

"Dr. Gaustaad." She pinched her nose to imitate his distinctive pedantic twang. "'Never ask a question you don't know the answer to.'"

I pinched my own nose and chanted, "'Always interview your witnesses at least three times.'"

We were laughing so hard I almost choked on my last swallow of steak. The waitress came by and tried to offer us dessert, but we were good and ordered cups of plain black coffee.

"Did you?" I asked.

"Did I what?" Portland asked, looking wistful as the dessert cart, with its generous portions of bourbon-pecan pie and double chocolate brownies, rolled away from us.

"Interview all your witnesses at least three times?"

"Sure."

"Really?"

"Well, all but Bill McCormack," she admitted. "He's so full of himself. I interviewed him twice and read the transcript of the deposition Doug Woodall's staff took and he didn't change a word of his story."

"All the same," I said, "if Doug's going to try to show Kyle's state of mind with McCormack's testimony …"

With her very short, very curly black hair, Portland always reminds me of Julia Lee's poodle. At the moment, she was looking like a rather worried poodle.

Here in July, it wasn't quite dark outside at this hour, but it would have been pitch black in October.

"You interviewed him in the daylight, right?" I said.

She nodded.

"Why don't you go back and interview him now, when it's dark? Get him to take you out on the patio, turn on the lights and recreate the scene. Maybe it'll spark just that one detail that'll make a difference."

"On the other hand," Portland said dubiously, "it might spark a detail I don't want to hear."

"Better to hear it tonight than on the witness stand next week," I told her. Reluctantly, she reached for her cell phone.

"Come with me?"

The McCormack home was just as I'd expected from meeting the owners: pretentiously tasteful fieldstone, modern without being modernistic, landscaped for ostentatious privacy.

"I understand your reasoning," said Bill McCormack after Portland reintroduced us all around, "but I've already told you and the D.A. both what happened that night and walking through it again isn't going to change anything."

Nevertheless, he led us through the house, into the "great" room, and out a set of sliding glass doors onto a broad flagstone patio. Concealed floodlights washed the area in brilliant light.

While Portland went over the events of that October evening once more with McCormack, I engaged his wife in conversation. She seemed a bit surprised that I wanted to talk to her when her husband was holding forth, but I was curious about an exotic-looking stand of daylilies beside the patio and it turned out that they were that were hybrids she had bred herself.

"A hobby of mine," she said shyly. "I'm trying to breed a pure red with the stamina of those old orange ditch lilies but with a longer bloom time."

She flipped another switch to illumine a border of more lilies at the far edge of the closely clipped grass. "I have sixteen different varieties here. They start blooming in May and go till frost."

"Really?" As a new homeowner still fumbling along with no clear idea of how I wanted my yard to look, I was intrigued by an ever blooming border that wouldn't take much care.

"Yes, I was so worried when Brinley and her friend came running through it last fall. It was the first year my Alyson Ripley lily had bloomed and I was afraid they'd trample it to pieces."

"The Davis house is over there?" For some reason, I'd thought it was on the opposite side.

"Beyond the crepe myrtles," said Mrs. McCormack with a nod. "They always lose their leaves early and that's how Brinley saw our lights so easily." She shook her head. "Such a terrible experience. They were so scared they didn't look where they were going. Right through my lilies. And the way they kept looking back over their shoulders, I thought I was going to see a pack of dogs at their heels and my border would be wrecked for sure."

"That's my Frances," McCormack said genially as he and Portland came up behind us. "More worried about a few flowers than a man getting shot next door."

He gestured toward the trees. "But this is the way they came all right. First we heard the shots all bunched together, and then while we were trying to decide if we'd really heard shots, they came running through here, across her flower bed and up to where we were standing on the patio. The girl was screaming blue murder and he was yelling, 'Call 911.' You don't have to worry about my story, Ms. Brewer," he said magisterially. "I'm quite sure they weren't acting."

"See?" said Portland when we were back in her car and driving away. "What did I tell you? Daylight, moonlight, his story doesn't change."

I couldn't believe what I was hearing. "You're not still going to call *him* as your witness, are you?"

"I don't have to. Doug'll do it."

"But didn't you hear what Mrs. McCormack said?" I demanded.

"About her flower bed getting trampled?"

"What are the three essential elements of justifiable homicide?" I asked, pinching my nose à la Professor Gaustaad.

She stuck out her tongue but decided to humor me. "First, that the defendant must be free from fault, must not have said or done anything for the purpose of provoking the victim."

"Was Kyle at fault? Did he provoke? No," I said, answering my own rhetorical questions. "He was an invited guest in the Davis home, minding his own business when Hux Wentworth burst through the door. The second element?"

"There must be no convenient mode of escape by retreat or by declining combat," Portland parroted as she put on her turn signal to make a left back to the steakhouse and my own car. "And he did try to retreat but Hux followed and broke through a second locked door."

"And the third element, if you please, Ms. Brewer?"

"There must be a present impending peril, either real or apparent, so as to create in the defendant a reasonable belief of existing necessity. Well, that's what exactly what Kyle believed, but how do we prove it?" Portland said with exasperation. "How's Mrs. McCormack's lily bed going to convince a jury he really truly believed it?"

"Okay, look," I told her, spelling it out. "Hux Wentworth is built like Man Mountain, right? He crashes through a glass door like it was paper. He's bleeding all over, yet he barely notices his cuts. He chases them through the house and crashes through the bathroom door without even breaking a sweat. Kyle pulls the trigger on an unfamiliar gun and as soon as Hux goes down, he and Brinley are out of there. You heard McCormack. They were still trying to figure out what the shots were when those two kids ran into his yard. *And they were looking back over their shoulders.* Why were they looking back, Por?"

"My God," she exclaimed as she pulled into the steakhouse parking lot and stopped beside my car. "Did they really think Hux could still be chasing them after all that?"

"Why not?" I said. "He'd come through glass, he'd come through solid oak. In their state of panic, why wouldn't they think he could come through bullets?"

A week later, I adjourned my own court early so I could hear Portland's closing argument.

"In their state of panic," Portland said, "why wouldn't they think he could come through bullets, too? You have heard Mrs. McCormick state that when they first stumbled into her yard, only moments after the sound of gunshots died away, they kept glancing back over their shoulders. Why? Would you look back if you knew your attacker was lying dead? No, ladies and gentlemen of the jury. They looked back because they were afraid that Hux Wentworth was still coming after them and they were terrified that he would catch them."

Doug Woodall made a game attempt to persuade the jury that Kyle and Brinley were play-acting, but it didn't work. They were only out long enough to pick a foreman before returning with a not guilty verdict. Ten minutes max.

Ned O'Donnell thanked the jury and then thanked both sides for an expeditious trial. "Not a single superfluous witness," he said approvingly.

Smugly I waited for Portland to finish hugging Kyle and to come thank me, but as soon as we were alone, she said, "I'm writing Professor Gaustaad to thank him for advising at least three interviews."

"Gaustaad?" I was indignant. "Hey, *I* was the one that made you go back a third time."

"I know," she grinned. "I'm going to thank him for hammering it into your head."

A Confederacy of Crime, 2000

What's in a Name?

This story is another example of reaching into my cluttered mind and pulling out an oddball fact that a horse-loving friend told me years ago. According to Paula Carlton, dogs and horses both recognize their names, so if you're going to change it, life will be easier on both of you if the new name sounds like the old one.

It was a *Romeo and Juliet* love story.

Literally.

The Possum Creek Players staged a farcical version of Shakespeare's classic play last year—and yes, I agree that Shakespeare shouldn't be subjected to the desecrations of modern slang and modern levels of morality, but this was a very witty adaptation written to celebrate the four hundredth anniversary of the play's original performance. Although the first half was played for laughs, the direction was such that by the end, we had segued fully into the original version, language and all. The audience, which had come for the laughs, found themselves totally involved, and there wasn't a dry eye in the house when Juliet, arising from her drugged "death" to find that Romeo has killed himself, commits suicide herself.

No laughs. Pure Shakespeare.

Romeo and Juliet were played by a couple of semi-professionals with Equity cards, but the rest of the cast was drawn from stagestruck amateurs around the area. I myself played Lady Capulet, and before you picture me in gray wig and greasepaint wrinkles, remember that she was only fourteen when Juliet was born if you can believe the lines Shakespeare has her speak. Friar Laurence was played by Paul Archdale, a Dobbs attorney with a thick shock of white hair; and Marian Wilder, who owns a boarding stable between Dobbs and Cotton Grove, played Juliet's nurse.

It was lust at first sight.

But this *is* the Bible Belt and while the belt may have loosened a bit over the last few years, single women still can't let it all hang out. Not when they give riding lessons to impressionable children with straitlaced mothers. Nevertheless, courthouse gossip had Marian's little green pickup nosed under his carport, flank to flank with his silver BMW, six nights out of seven. His golden retriever immediately bonded with her fox terrier and the two dogs could be seen riding in her truck or romping together in the pasture almost every day.

Paul's taste usually runs to entry-level paralegals in flowery dresses, but he seemed to enjoy the novelty of a roll in the hay with someone who pitches hay for a living and who was his own age for a change.

Marian Wilder is widowed and childless and a lovely earthy woman with a heart as big as one of her horses. She wears her dark wavy hair clipped short and is letting it go gray. Her strong chin and determined nose are softened by deep blue eyes rimmed in long sooty lashes. Her laugh bubbles up in her throat like a brook that chuckles over smooth stones. It was clear to me what Paul saw in her, but I couldn't understand what she saw in him. He's a showboating egotist who never met a mirror he didn't love. It's impossible for him to pass any reflective surface without checking to see that his silk tie is perfectly knotted or to smooth his prematurely white hair with a beautifully manicured hand.

Marian cuts her own hair, probably hasn't had a manicure in twenty years, and prefers denim to silk.

With Paul's short attention span and voracious appetite, I expected the novelty to wear off before we finished rehearsals. But no, a month after we closed the play, I heard that he had been seen pricing diamonds at the Jewel Chest on North Main. My friend Portland, whose law offices are in the same building as Paul's, said he'd even asked her where she and Avery went on their honeymoon.

"You think it's possible Paul Archdale could love somebody besides himself?" she asked doubtfully.

"Do pigs fly?" I said. "Get real."

It came as no surprise when I heard that the affair had ended scarcely three months after it began. What *was* a surprise—and much snickered over behind Paul's well-tailored back—is that Marian was the one who did the dumping. It was a first for Paul, and not something he was treating as a life-enhancing learning experience, according to my sources (any resemblance between said sources and partners in his own firm being purely coincidental.)

None of this would have concerned me personally except that shortly after the breakup, Marian Wilder appeared in my courtroom before the first case was called. When I gave her permission to approach the bench, she came up, leaned in so that we wouldn't be overheard and begged me to sign a restraining order against Paul.

"He hurt you?" I asked, keeping my own voice low. "Threatened to kill you?"

"Not me," she said and her deep blue eyes filled with sudden tears. "Junebug."

The only Junebug in my memory banks was my brother Herman's granddaughter, born in the month of June and a real cutie, hence the nickname. I hardly thought Paul Archdale was any danger to a four-year-old living in Charlotte.

"His golden retriever," Marian explained. "He's going to have her put down."

"You want me to restrain him from having his own dog put to sleep?"

"He knows how much I love her and this is his way of getting back at me for ditching him."

It was too early in the morning and I'd had only two cups of coffee. "Let me get this straight. Paul's mad at you, so he's going to kill his own dog for revenge?"

"He doesn't give a flying flip about her." Marian spoke so sharply that my clerk looked up curiously from her computer screen and a couple of lawyers sitting in the jury box paused in their whispered conversation. She glared at them and they immediately dropped their eyes.

"She was a legacy from on old lady that he conned the same way he conned me."

In passionate whispers, Marian explained that Junebug had originally belonged to an elderly client, to whom Paul was assigned when she outlived the senior partner in his firm. She and her late husband had met at Duke and the bulk of their fortune was in trust to the university, but as she grew older, the interest accumulated faster than she could spend it and she found herself with a spare hundred thousand or so that wasn't already earmarked. Widowed and childless, she had poured all her love into her pets, a couple of ancient cats and a golden retriever puppy; and when she developed congestive heart failure, it had distressed her that they might be left homeless. Enter Paul, who shared her distress and guess what? Damned if he didn't seem to love her pets almost as much as she did.

"I think Paul hoped she'd leave him a bundle outright, but instead, she made him their guardian and left him six thousand a year for as long as they lived. The two cats died before she did, but Junie was still a pup."

"He's going to put her down and give up six thousand a year?"

"He says that's just chump change for him these days. The real reason he's doing it is because he knows how much it'll hurt me. When he was begging me not to leave him, I made the mistake of saying that I'd already stayed two weeks longer than I would have because of Junie. She loves me more right now than she ever loved him. And why not? I took her out of that fenced-in yard. I let her romp all over my pastures and bridle trails. She and my dog are like litter mates. You can't let him kill her! Please?"

Her eyes filled again and a tear spilled over onto her neat blue chambray shirt.

"I'm surprised he found a vet that'll put a healthy dog down for no real reason." I said as I clicked on my laptop computer and started looking for case law and precedents.

"He says Junie bit him. That's the only way he can get Gene to agree to this."

"Gene Adams?" Dr. Gene Adams takes care of Hambone, my Aunt Zell's beagle and had, despite his basic shyness, played the Prince of Verona in our production of *Romeo and Juliet*.

Marian nodded. "I told Gene he had to be lying. Everybody knows how sweet-tempered goldens are. No way she's a biter, but Gene says there's nothing he can do about it. He says that if he won't put her to sleep, Paul's threatened to just shoot Junie himself. They're going to do it at four this afternoon."

I pulled up the text to North Carolina's cruelty to animals statute and rapidly scrolled through, skim-reading as I went. The gist was that should any person "maliciously torture, mutilate, maim, cruelly beat, disfigure, poison, or kill" an animal, that person would be guilty of a Class I felony. The word "maliciously" was defined as "an act committed intentionally and with malice or bad motive." Marian could swear on the Bible that these words exactly described Paul's true motive for killing his dog. Unfortunately, the law had several exemptions and one of them allowed "the lawful destruction of any animal for the purposes of protecting the public, other animals, property, or the public health."

Paul didn't have to prove that the dog had bitten him. His word was enough. The law doesn't try to understand *why* a dog bites; it only assigns liability when it does.

"I'm sorry," I told Marian. "Unless there's something in the original owner's will, there's no legal way to restrain him."

"The will?" she breathed, hope spreading across her face.

"If she was a resident of Colleton County, it'll be on file here at the courthouse," I said.

Marian gave me the woman's name and I told her I'd look it up during my lunch break.

"If there's nothing there, could you just talk to him?" she implored. "He respects you. I saw how he went out of his way to be nice to you during the play."

I was amused. For such a competent business woman, Marian Wilder could be extremely naive. Of course Paul Archdale was nice to me. Most attorneys are. Judges are supposed to be objective, their decisions unaffected by personalities. But judges are also human, and when a ruling for your client could literally go either way, best not to have been rude or disrespectful to the judge.

If Paul's dog were a pit bull or rottweiler, I might not have interfered. But this was a golden, for pete's sake, probably the least prone to biting in the whole canine family. Against my will, I heard myself say, "Okay. I'll talk to him."

Easier said than done as it turned out. Paul was supposed to try a case in front of me later that morning, but the charges against his client had been dropped and the hearing canceled.

Down in the county clerk's office, I found Louisa Ripley Ferncliff's emended will with no trouble and was bemused to see that she must have been smarter than Paul could have wished because she'd figured out a dog's average life expectancy and put a sunset clause into the bequest. It expired this very year. How nice for him. Put a guilt trip on Marian when he was probably going to dump the dog anyway now that she was no longer worth six thousand a year to him.

I called over to his office and was told that he'd be out for the rest of the day. A machine answered his home phone. I left a message, but wasn't hopeful he'd get it in time.

Court finished at 3:40 and Marian was waiting for me in chambers.

"Was there anything in the will to stop him?" she asked.

"Sorry," I said.

"Well, what did he say when you talked to him?"

"I didn't," I told her. "I couldn't get in touch with him."

She looked aghast. "And they're going to do it in twenty minutes! You've got to come with me to Gene's. Talk him out it. Please?"

It was only six minutes across the river to Gene Adams' clinic. Marian was so agitated, I made her follow my car instead of tearing over through red lights. When we got there, Paul and Junebug were the only ones in the waiting room. As soon as she spotted Marian, that beautiful animal stood up and started wagging her tail happily. Paul had to double his hold on her leash to keep her from rushing over. Marian immediately knelt down beside her and started petting the dog, who nuzzled her with touching enthusiasm.

Paul seemed surprised to see me.

"You here to pick up an animal, Judge?" he asked, reaching out to shake my hand.

"Not exactly." I kept his hand in mine and said in my most coaxing tones, "I came to ask you to rethink what you're about to do. Is it really necessary to put this dog to sleep? I read Mrs. Ferncliff's will and I know the dog's annuity expires this year, so couldn't you just give her to Marian? Let her go live at the stable?"

"And maybe have her bite one of the children who go to ride there?" he asked with matching earnestness. "I'd have it on my conscience for life if one of those kids had to have stitches in its face."

"Goldens aren't natural biters," I argued. "Surely it was an aberration."

He hesitated. After all, I *am* a judge and he's an ambitious attorney.

Unfortunately, Marian picked that minute to look up from the dog. "Liar! She never bit you. You're only doing this because I dumped you."

Paul's lips tightened and he gave Junebug's leash a vicious tug just as Gene Adams opened the door to his examining room.

The dog yelped and looked at Paul reproachfully but he didn't notice.

"Sorry, Judge," he said. "But the only thing to do with a biter is put it down."

Oblivious to its fate, the condemned dog had gone back to nuzzling Marian's hand, tail thumping happily against the tiled floor. Marian was openly weeping now and Gene was clearly distressed by her unhappiness, yet was too shy to offer a consoling hug. Paul tried to look sad but I could see malice in his eyes when Gene said, "Are you sure this is really necessary, Paul?"

"The damn dog bit me. It's my public duty."

So he had read the statute, too.

"What are you going to do with her?" Marian asked. "Afterwards, I mean."

That was clearly something Paul hadn't given thought to.

"I can dispose of the body, if you wish," Gene offered. His words were for Paul, but his eyes were on Marian and I suddenly realized that Paul wasn't the only one who'd fallen for her during the run of our play.

"No!" Marian said fiercely. "Let me bury her out at the stable. She was so happy there. Please, Paul! You can't say no to this."

Actually, he probably would have had I not been standing there.

"If that's what you want, then of course," he said, as if bestowing an enormous favor.

The injection wasn't something I wanted to watch, but Marian dragged me inside. Gene rummaged through his file cabinet and came up empty-handed.

"I don't know where my secretary keeps the releases," he told Paul. "But here." He quickly scribbled some phrases onto a pad. "Just sign and date this and we'll get started."

Paul signed impatiently without reading, then stood back as Gene lifted Junebug onto a table and weighed her so he could compute the correct dosage.

While Marian scratched her ears and whispered sweet sad words of goodbye, he filled a syringe with pentobarbitol and inserted the needle so gently that Junebug didn't flinch. A few moments later, the dog gave a big sigh and lay down. Her eyes closed, her body relaxed, her breathing slowed. Quicker than I expected, Gene covered the dog's body with a disposable paper sheet.

"So how much do I owe you?" Paul asked, reaching for his wallet and bringing it back to a commercial transaction.

"Nothing," Gene answered brusquely. "I don't charge for putting an animal to sleep like this."

"Well, okay, then," said Paul. "Thanks."

There was a moment of awkwardness as he tried to figure out the protocol of leave-taking after an execution.

Gene ignored his outstretched hand. "One more thing, Archdale."

"Yeah?"

"If you decide to get another animal, find yourself a different vet."

Except for the lines Shakespeare had provided, none of us had ever heard this big shy man speak so forcefully. Paul glowered and left in a huff, but Marian reached out her hand and squeezed his.

"Thank you, Gene."

He turned bright pink and said, "I'll carry her out for you."

I followed them to the truck and Marian had him lay the body on the passenger seat in the cab.

As he closed the door, Gene gathered his nerve and said, "I'm finished here for the day. How about I come on out and dig her grave for you."

"You don't have to do that," Marian said.

"I want to."

"Okay, then. Thanks. And thank you, too, Deborah, for trying." With tears stinging her eyes again, she gave us both impulsive hugs and drove off toward her stable.

Well, I thought, looking at Gene's face, one good thing might yet come out of this unhappy little episode.

Less than a week passed before I heard that Gene had located another female golden for Marian through one of the breed's rescue shelters. Once again her terrier had someone to romp with and people began to wonder—okay, *I* wondered—if there might be wedding bells in their future.

"In the fall," Gene admitted shyly when I carried Aunt Zell's beagle in for its booster shots a month after I'd watched him euthanize Junebug. "I guess Archdale did us a favor after all."

"It was good of you to go help her bury the dog," I said, imagining the bittersweetness of the moment. Digging the grave. Laying that poor animal to rest. "Where did y'all put her? In the pasture?" Then I remembered that Marian had a small pet cemetery where her first pony was buried. "Or down by the paddock?"

Hambone yelped as the needle went in and it was a moment before Gene answered. "Under that oak tree at the top of her pasture. We like to ride up there."

"That's a beautiful view," I said, thinking that it was also a romantic view— rolling green pasture that sloped down to thick woods.

A week later, I found myself enjoying the same view while seated atop one of Marian's mares. I'd driven over that afternoon to ask what she charged for jumping lessons. One of my nieces wanted to learn the proper form and, since her birthday was coming up soon, I thought it might make a great present.

Marian was fuming because all the horses hadn't been exercised and when I showed up in jeans and sneakers, she soon had me booted and in the saddle of a sturdy little dun-colored mare named Cornelia.

She didn't look at all like my idea of a stately Roman matron.

"Her name was Cornmeal when I bought her," said Marian. "Horses and dogs. They know their names and if you want to change it, you have to pick something that sounds similar. Cornelia's maybe a little too elegant but Cornmeal was too much of a put-down."

We spent the next half-hour galloping briskly around the pasture. Tuggle, the fox terrier and Juliet, the new golden retriever tagged along till Marian blew on a dog whistle strung around her neck and with a gesture of her arm, sent them to wait for us on the crest of the hill.

"Juliet?" I teased when we pulled up beside them under that big shady oak. "Because the play was where Gene fell for you?"

"And I was so stupid I never noticed him for Paul."

"Don't beat up on yourself," I said. "You weren't the first, you won't be the last."

I glanced around, half expecting to see a stone marker, but the grass was smooth here under the tree. Nor was there any sign of recent digging.

"Where did you and Gene bury Junebug?" I asked.

"Down by the paddock," she said. "Next to Starfire."

I suddenly found myself remembering the apocryphal story of Susannah and the lying elders.

"We saw her sin under a mastic tree," the first one told Daniel when questioned separately.

"Under an evergreen oak," said the other.

Marian and Gene really needed to get their stories straight.

"Ready for another gallop?" Marian asked, gathering up her reins

"Not just yet." I hadn't quite finished working it all out, but when I did, I laughed out loud, wondering just what sort of release Gene had maneuvered Paul into signing.

"What?" she asked.

"*What's in a name?*" I quoted happily. "*That which we call a rose, by any other name would smell as sweet*, right, Junebug?"

The golden retriever perked up her ears.

Marian gave me a wary look and her horse moved uneasily beneath her. "What are you talking about?"

"Shakespeare, of course. Juliet took a sleeping potion that, how does it go? ... *wrought on her the form of death*? Gene gave the dog just enough sedative to put her in a deep sleep and keep her asleep till he could be here with you when she woke up.

Her face paled beneath its tan. "He couldn't bear to let an animal be killed for spite. You're not going to tell Paul, are you?"

"Tell him what? That you have a new dog? When everyone's heard how much trouble Gene took to find you a dog as near like Junebug as he could?"

She relaxed visibly into the saddle. "Thanks, Deborah."

Down at the stables, an old blue Volvo wagon had pulled into the drive. Both dogs went streaking down the slope, racing to get to Gene Adams first.

Marian cantered after them, her face aglow with quiet happiness.

I chucked Cornelia's reins and we followed more slowly so that Marian would have time to warn Gene that I knew and to assure him their secret was safe with me.

Except that it wasn't.

The very next day, Paul Archdale waylaid me after court. He stormed into the office I was using and acted ill as a cat with a tail full of sandspurs.

"I guess you and those two lovebirds think all golden retrievers look alike to me," he snarled. He was too angry to accord me the usual courtesy of my robe.

I closed the door and looked at him coldly. "I don't know what you're talking about."

"Marian was in town today and my dog was riding in the back of her truck. Adams never put it down, did he? And you were in on that little farce, too, weren't you? Begging to save it when you knew damn well Adams was just going through the motions to fool me."

"I believe you signed a paper giving him the right to treat the dog as he saw fit," I said, hedging for time.

A worthless ploy. No attorney worth his salt would let a little technicality like that deter him.

"He deliberately misled me." Paul's face was almost beet red beneath his thick white hair. There was nothing handsome about his mouth, now twisted with fury. "By God, I'll have his license and I'll have you up on ethics and I'll damn well see my dog with a bullet through its head before this day's out."

I could only stare at him impotently. While I could truthfully say that I thought Junebug was dead when Gene put her body on the seat of Marian's truck, there was no way I could put my hand on a Bible and swear I still thought she was dead.

Paul was almost bouncing on the balls of his feet in malicious triumph. "Thought you could fool me. Thought I wouldn't know my own dog!"

Well, as a matter of fact, yes. To most people, one golden retriever *does* look pretty much like another. Who'd have guessed that Paul Archdale had taken that much notice of a dog he'd never bonded with?

I thought of Gene Adams hauled up before a professional board of ethics. I pictured the very real possibility of getting censured myself.

And poor old Junebug. Finally free to romp and race and—

Hey, wait a minute here!

"I'm afraid you've made a mistake," I said. "It's not your dog."

"Like hell it's not!"

"No, no," I said, giving him my sweetest smile. "I read the will, remember? You and I are probably the only ones who realize it was probated seventeen years ago. There's no way that's the same dog that old Mrs. Ferncliff left in your care seventeen years ago. Marian's dog can't be more than three or four years old. But we'll get an opinion from an outside vet if you like. They can approximate an animal's age. An eighteen-year-old dog would barely be able to hobble across a room. It certainly wouldn't have the stamina to chase after horses all day. I'm sure the trustees over at Duke would be interested in learning just how long the original Junebug's actually been dead. Is this her first replacement or maybe the second or third? If we subpoena your financial records, will we find check stubs or credit card listings for the kennel where you bought them?"

I watched the color drain from his face as our roles reversed and he realized that he was awfully close to starring in his own ethics hearing. Not to mention a possible criminal trial if the Duke trustees did get wind of it and pushed for prosecution. I could almost see him multiplying six thousand dollars a year by eighteen years.

With compound interest.

I myself would need a calculator, but even without one, I knew it wasn't, to use his phrase, chump change.

"You're right," he said at last. "I was mistaken. It's not my dog." The words almost choked him. "I apologize."

As I watched Paul Archdale slink away like the villain in a Possum Creek melodrama, I couldn't help thinking of good old Shakespeare. An apt phrase for every situation.

Like, *all's well that ends well.*

The Mysterious Press Anniversary Anthology, 2001

Mixed Blessings

As soon as I saw a newspaper picture of a modern day pilgrim lugging a wooden cross up and down the eastern seaboard, I knew such a man was going to have to show up in Deborah Knott's courtroom. (Alert readers will spot Carolyn Hart's Annie Darling, who just happens to be a friend of Deborah's.)

The first time I saw it was two years ago. I was driving back from Broward's Rock, an upscale resort island down near the South Carolina-Georgia border. Not a place I could normally afford to vacation in, but my friend Annie owns a bookstore there and had invited me for a long weekend. As the daughter of an ex-bootlegger and someone who grew up sweating through my share of the farmwork, I'm always interested in seeing how the other half live and play.

Anyhow, I had left the island and was heading west on a little two-lane road. Fortunately, the sun had already set, but there was still a blazing gold-and-red afterglow in the western sky. A few miles before I reached I-95, a reddish light appeared on the right shoulder up ahead. It was as if a ragged patch of glowing sky had dropped onto the roadside and was bobbing along eastward. The car ahead of me slowed to a crawl and I tapped my brakes, too, to warn the car behind.

To my bemusement, it was a full-size plastic cross, illuminated from within so that it gleamed bright red in the twilight. In the brief moment it took me to drive past, I only had time to note that it rode on the back of a sturdily built man with dark hair and ragged beard and a determined look on his face.

A large lighted plastic cross was not the oddest sight I'd ever seen along southern roads—after all, this *is* the Bible Belt—but it tickled me to picture him lugging it onto the ferry to Broward's Rock. The tiny town at the ferry landing is open to anyone but what about the gated communities that take up most of the island? Would the guards at those gatehouses turn him back or look the other way as he passed? And if he made it through, what would all those wealthy vacationing golfers from up north or the midwest make of him?

I made a mental note to call Annie when I got home and ask, but like so many of my mental notes, it faded before I reached the North Carolina line where Pancho's South of the Border, the ultimate in tacky rest stops, gave me a whole new set of absurdities to contemplate.

The next time I saw that cross was in the last place I could have imagined: my own church, the First Baptist Church of Dobbs.

Our minister, the Reverend Carlyle Yelvington is a thoughtful, dignified intellectual, as befits the pastor of the oldest and wealthiest Baptist church in Colleton County. He entreats his congregation to lead a moral life by gentle appeals to logic and ethics. Charismatic techniques horrify him and he would never get down and mud-wrestle someone into salvation, but he's smart enough to know that a good rousing fire-and-brimstone sermon can act like a bracing spring tonic for the Baptist soul. Accordingly, he has a carefully screened roster of more dynamic preachers whom he invites to come and witness to us five or six times a year when he has to be away.

Unfortunately, the more dynamic preacher he'd invited this Sunday was himself called away at the last minute, and instead of consulting with Mr. Yelvington's secretary, he took it upon himself to send a substitute of his own choosing, which is how we wound up with Brother Reuben in the pulpit shouting out a message of damnation and redemption, "yea, even to those amongst you to whom much has been given without you giving back to the Lord who's blessed you with so many worldly goods, who's set you on such a high horse that you think you got in the saddle all by yourself."

In ringing tones, Brother Reuben explained how, only last week, a man of God had appeared in the doorway of his poor little mission down in Fayetteville, laboring under a heavy burden, "a burden put on him by the Lord Jesus Christ himself, a burden to go out into the highways and byways and preach the word of God. Well, my friends, that's what he's done all week down there in Fayetteville and when I got the call Thursday night to come here this morning, I knew that the Lord had laid a blessing on you and that He wanted Brother Buck to come on up here to Dobbs, to bring his burden into this fine and stately house of worship and preach His word right here."

With that, he turned to the double doors that led back to classrooms and robing room and church offices and shouted, "Brother Buck, in the name of our Lord Jesus Christ, come forth!"

The doors swung open and there was that same bright red cross that I'd first seen in South Carolina, riding on the shoulders of the same dark-bearded man. I now saw that he was older than my brief impression, probably late forties or early fifties. He wore a blue T-shirt imprinted with the words, "I am a soldier of the Cross," and his face and muscular arms were deeply tanned. I also saw that cross was ten feet tall and constructed of bright red Plexiglass, crimson as the blood of Christ. Two little hard-rubber wheels, the kind you see on push mowers, were mounted on an axle through the base of the cross to make it easier to carry, but the thing still must have weighed a ton. When Brother Buck mounted the dais and stood beside Brother Reuben, it towered another four feet above their heads.

Wilma Carter, Mr. Yelvington's elderly secretary, sat in appalled silence in the pew ahead of mine, but my friend Portland Brewer was cracking up beside me.

"Friends," said Brother Reuben, "this is Brother Buck Collins and he's got a message you should open your hearts and hear. Tell 'em, Brother Buck!"

Buck Collins' testimony began with a certain predictability: the dissipated youth, the drugs, the gambling, the drunken nights of wenching and whoring.

Okay, every word might have been true, but over the years I've noticed that reformed sinners tend to—well, not lie exactly, but more like "enhance" the darkness of their sinfulness in order to dramatize the extent of their reformation and redemption.

Anyhow, five years ago, in the depth of his degradation, his sister persuaded him to go to church with her one Sunday morning. The preacher seemed to speak directly to his heart.

"And I went out of that house with my soul on fire, tormented by the flames of hell. That very same night, friends, our Savior appeared to me in a dream, saying 'Go out into the highways and hedges, and compel them to come in, that my house may be filled.' Well, friends, two days later, I set out on my journey with nothing but a back pack and my new faith in the Lord, who promised to provide my daily needs. Even the poorest man is rich when the Lord looks after him."

However, he'd no sooner set out, than he met an evangelist carrying a small cross of two poles lashed together. "As soon as I saw it, I knew immediately that Jesus wanted me to bear His cross, too, so I went back home and got this one built."

("A classic case of penance envy," Portland whispered in my ear.)

He had been on the road ever since, traveling from church to church, mission to mission, spreading the word of redemption and salvation to all he met along the highways and back roads.

"Amen, Jesus!" said Brother Reuben when the testimony ended. "And now I'm gonna ask the choir to lead us in singing *The Old Rugged Cross.*"

The choir, which had planned a joyous Purcell anthem, had to scramble for their hymnals and that lugubrious dirge.

Two mornings later, I saw the cross yet again. It was leaning sideways on its base and crosspiece in the hallway outside Major Dwight Bryant's door. Dwight and I have known each other since I was in diapers and he was a lanky kid in and out of our house like one of my eleven older brothers. Since I'm a district court judge now and he's second in command under Sheriff Bowman "Bo" Poole with offices here in the Colleton County Courthouse, we still see each other almost every day; and I often take my lunchbag down to his office while he eats a sandwich at his desk.

Today's was an enormous BLT made with tomatoes from my daddy's garden that I'd brought him the day before. I love BLT's, too, but I'm not six-three, which is why I was eating peach yogurt.

"Don't tell me Brother Buck's in jail here," I said, settling into the chair across from him.

"Change the subject," he told me.

"Why?" I asked indignantly. And then it dawned on me.

"Don't you read your calendar?" he teased.

Well, I do, of course—mostly to see if any of my friends or neighbors are going to be standing in front of me, which happens more often than I'd really like. But my eyes had slid right over the name of Buck Collins, who would be the subject of a probable cause hearing this afternoon. So quite properly, Dwight and I couldn't talk about it, even though I was dying of curiosity.

When his name was called, Buck Collins walked down from the jury box where the jailer had seated all his prisoners. Like the rest of them, Collins was dressed in an orange polyester jump suit. He took his place behind the defendants' table and I asked if he were represented by an attorney.

"No, ma'am," he answered softly.

I explained his right to one should he so desire and how the state would pay the costs if he couldn't afford it. When he shook his head again, I asked him to sign the waiver in front of him that would affirm his decision and to hand it to my clerk.

As he started to write, a man stood up three rows back and said, "Your Honor, can I hire him a lawyer?"

I could have gaveled him out of order, but I like to allow a little leeway, especially since I recognized Brother Reuben and what were probably several of the Fayetteville mission regulars seated in the same row as the stranger.

"Your name, sir?" I asked, motioning him forward.

"Jack Marcom, ma'am. From Brunswick, Georgia."

He was neatly dressed in pressed chinos and blue plaid shirt with a button-down collar. A pair of wire-rimmed sunglasses dangled from his shirt pocket. He held a blue canvas pork pie hat in his hands and the top of his head was nearly bald, making his long face look even longer. Mid-forties, I'd say. A couple of years younger than Buck Collins, but not quite as muscular.

"What's your relationship to Mr. Collins?" I asked, motioning him forward.

"He's my wife's brother and I can get a lawyer for him if—

"No," said Collins, who had stood stolidly till then, not looking around when Marcom spoke. "I hold myself accountable and I don't want a lawyer, so let's just get this over with. Please, ma'am?"

"We will," I said. "But you're accused of a serious crime and I'd advise you to consider Mr. Marcom's offer."

"C'mon, Buck," his brother-in-law entreated. "Let me do this."

Collins finished signing the paper, gave it to my clerk and returned to the defendants' table, all without acknowledging the other man's presence.

"Can't I get him one anyhow?" Marcom asked me.

"No!" said Collins.

"Be seated, Mr. Marcom," I said. "Mr. Collins is the only one who can make that decision and if he chooses not to be represented, that's his right. Go ahead, Mr. Nance."

"This is a misdemeanor possession of stolen property, Your Honor," said Chester Nance, the ADA who was prosecuting today's calendar. "Also misdemeanor breaking and entering. Call Officer Walker to the stand."

The Dobbs police officer took the stand, was sworn in and stated his name and rank.

"Describe to the court what you observed last night around ten-fifteen," said Chester Nance.

In careful pedantic legalese, Officer Walker described how he was patrolling the town last night when he saw a man walking alone on the sidewalk outside First Baptist. Since downtown still rolls up the sidewalks at nine o'clock on a Monday night (my words, not Walker's), a pedestrian was unusual enough that he kept the man in sight in his rearview mirror.

"Then I saw him turn into the walk that goes around to the offices at the rear of the church. I drove around the corner, parked my cruiser, and came up through those bushes back there. I heard what sounded like breaking glass and arrived just in time to see the defendant reach through the door window, unlock the door from inside and turn the knob."

"And what did you do at that point?" asked Nance.

"I identified myself and placed him under arrest. Upon being searched, it was discovered that he had four credit cards which we ascertain to belong to four members of the church choir."

Nance held up a plastic bag with the multicolored cards, which he wished to place in evidence.

I took the bag and could read the names through the plastic. All were prominent, well-to-do women. I myself have never seen the point of having more than one credit card, but these women probably had stacks and wouldn't have noticed one missing card for days if Collins hadn't been caught. They were trusting souls to leave their purses in the robing room where anyone could get at them. Still, the only one I've ever seen carry a pocketbook with her choir robe is Miss Nora McBride, an elderly spinster who has an estimated worth of three million dollars and a soprano voice that soars like an angel.

I handed the bag back to Chester Nance, who said, "No further questions, Your Honor."

I looked at the defendant. This close, I could see the flecks of gray in his beard and hair, the weathering of his skin. His eyes met mine, then dropped, as if in shame.

"Do you have any questions for this witness?" I asked him.

"No, ma'am. I just want to plead guilty and start serving my time."

I excused the witness. "Any priors, Mr. Nance?"

"Not in the state of North Carolina," said the ADA. "At least, not under this name. We haven't heard back from Georgia yet, and I have a feeling we're gonna find he's done this before."

At that point, Brother Reuben stood and raised his hand, "Ma'am? Judge? Can I speak on Brother Buck's behalf?"

"Very well. Step forward."

The preacher came up to the bar railing and said, "Judge, I know it looks bad, but this is a good man sitting here. Weren't you in that church Sunday morning?"

I nodded.

"I thought I remembered you," he said happily. "Well, if you were there, then you must a seen the goodness in his face, the sincerity in his voice—"

"But not the credit cards in his pocket," jibed Chester Nance.

"Now, I don't know how the devil managed to tempt Brother Buck," said Brother Reuben slipping deeper into earnestness, "but I do believe God told him it was wrong and I do believe God sent him there last night to put back that which he had stolen."

I looked at Collins. "Is that the way it happened?"

He nodded. "But I don't expect you to believe me and it doesn't really matter because I wasn't thinking straight. I see that now. I was trying to get away from this sin without paying the price."

Something about his mock-meek humility goaded me. "Tell me something," I said. "Just how many times have you done this before?"

"Done what?"

"Used men like Brother Reuben here to take you into affluent churches where you can find opportunities to steal? When they trace back on you, are they going to find a trail of missing credit cards or other items?"

He tried to meet my eyes and failed miserably. I was ready to give Collins the maximum sentence then and there, but the reality was that whether or not he got any jail time would depend on whether he had any prior convictions.

"Will two days give you enough time to hear from Georgia?" I asked Nance. He nodded.

"Then bring him back in two days and I'll hear his plea and set the sentence."

"Could we post a bond for him?" asked Brother Reuben.

I looked at Nance, who shrugged. "I've got no problem with that."

"Very well," I said. "Bond is set at five hundred dollars. See the clerk downstairs."

Buck Collins was the last case on my docket and I signed a couple of forms for my clerk, looked over the calendar for tomorrow, read through some pending files, then called it a day.

As I came down the steps at the rear of the courthouse on my way to the parking lot, I found Collins's brother-in-law loading the Plexiglass cross into the back of a ten-year-old white Chevy pickup. With sunglasses covering the lines around his eyes and that blue canvas hat covering his bald spot, he looked ten years younger than he had in court. Lettering on the truck door let me know that Jack Marcom was the owner of Marcom's Cabinet Shop in Brunswick, Georgia—*Cabinets and Bookcases Our Specialty.* Not all that prosperous, if you could judge by the age of the truck. I noted that his only jewelry was a cheap wristwatch and a plain gold wedding band. The men who were helping him tie the cross down had the pasty faces of recovering alcoholics.

In front of the truck was a shabby old Buick station wagon with two more men leaning against it, probably waiting for Brother Reuben to finish up with the bail bondsman and paperwork that would get Collins released from jail.

Marcom recognized me even though I was no longer wearing my black robe and he tipped his hat. "I want to thank you, ma'am, for letting Buck out on bail. It'd near 'bout kill my wife to hear her brother had to stay in jail."

"Is she up here with you?" I asked.

"No, ma'am. I was coming up to Florence, South Carolina this weekend to see about some walnut trees that blew down during that last hurricane. Good walnut's hard to come by. And Bonnie, that's my wife, Buck's sister? Anyhow, Bonnie said long as I was this far north, how 'bout I come on up and check on him. Make sure he's okay. She worries about him out on the road, so whenever I get the chance, I bring him some fresh clothes, new shoes, some of Bonnie's homemade fudge. She was hoping now that winter's coming on, maybe he's walked far enough north, that maybe I could swing him around, get him to walk south for a change."

"How did you know where to find him?"

"Oh, he called Friday morning. Calls collect most times. He's the only family Bonnie's got. Besides me and the kids, of course. She told him to call her every week even if he didn't have the money and he's pretty good about it."

Marcom's matter-of-factness took me aback. As a child of a cynical culture, I was both amused and offended by Brother Buck Collins's wacky zeal, a zeal that was probably sincere despite his thieving. But clearly Jack Marcom saw him as the much-loved brother of his much-loved wife and took his ministry very seriously.

I walked over to get a closer look at the bright red cross. "You know, I saw Mr. Collins a couple of years ago when I was in South Carolina," I said. "It was almost dark, but the cross was all lit up. Does it still have a light inside?"

"Here, let me show you," he said, with almost proprietary pride.

He tugged at a section just beneath the crossbar and it popped right off. I saw that it had been held in place by strip magnets glued to the inner surface and to the plastic section itself. Inside was a small lightbulb wired to some flashlight batteries. A slotted section just below that held a thick packet of the inspirational leaflets and Bible tracts that Brother Buck had distributed at our church on Sunday. I suppose since the cross was hollow, he could have used it as a rolling suitcase except that clothes would have blocked the light. As it was, the light couldn't reach the very bottom of the cross because of the section that housed the wheels. That's why it had seemed to float on Collins' shoulders and off the ground when I first saw it in the twilight.

Now that I was up close, I marveled at the workmanship that went into that cross. Instead of just butting the pieces together so that the raw edges were exposed, someone had carefully beveled all the edges so that the joints were almost invisible.

"Before he went on the road," I said, "was Brother Buck a cabinet-maker, too?"

Marcom gave a rueful laugh and shoved his blue hat to the back of his head. "Buck's a good man, Judge. Out here doing good for the Lord as the Lord leads him, but you give him any kind of a power tool and you're just asking for trouble."

"So you're really the one who built this?"

"Well, we all have to use the talents we have where we can, don't you think? Bonnie, she said it was the least we could do to help his mission. And it's been real educational, some of the places he's been, the people he's met. Why, Jimmy Carter stopped along the road one time and talked and prayed with him for over an hour. Can you imagine that? A president of the whole United States? And when Buck came through Pinehurst a couple of months ago, some millionaire let us stay in his guesthouse right on the golf course." Awe and modest pride were in his voice. "Treated us like we were just as good as anybody else, which is what the Bible tells us, of course, but some people—"

I didn't get to hear the rest of his story because I saw Brother Reuben and Buck Collins push open the courthouse door and start down the steps toward us. Talking to Jack Marcom about the cross was one thing, socializing with someone I'd soon be passing judgment on was quite another. As I moved away, I asked Marcom if he'd be in court on Friday.

He nodded. "With a lawyer, if Buck'll let me."

I stopped by Aunt Zell's to pick up a pair of slacks she'd hemmed for me. She and Uncle Ash were on their way out to supper and they invited me to join them, but I wanted to get home before dark and work on the perennial flower border I'd planted beside my new porch. The weeds were about to take it.

As I drove out of Dobbs, I was not surprised to come upon that cross again. Highway 48 leads not only to my house, but on to Fayetteville as well. What did surprise me was that the cross was now lashed to the top of Brother Reuben's battered old station wagon and Buck Collins was in the front seat. Trailing along behind was Jack Marcom in his pickup, accompanied by a couple of the mission derelicts. Why wasn't Collins riding with him?

On Thursday morning, while signing some forms for ADA Chester Nance, I asked if the state of Georgia had come through with anything on Buck Collins.

"Nope. South Carolina says they detained him briefly on a misdemeanor theft, but had to turn him loose for lack of evidence."

"That wouldn't have been at Broward's Rock, by any chance, would it?" I asked.

"Nope," said Chester. "Charleston."

I knew it would be a major and thoroughly unlikely coincidence and it was certainly a hair or two out of line as presiding judge. Nevertheless, at lunchtime, I called my friend Annie and caught her at her bookstore. She remembered Buck Collins and his red Plexiglass cross perfectly.

"That's when Laurel's diamond earrings went missing from the choir room."

Annie's mother-in-law is a true eccentric who's prone to sudden enthusiasms, but I'd never heard that singing in a church choir was one of them.

"Oh, yes," Annie said grimly. "Two contraltos were out that morning and Laurel insisted on filling in for both of them. At the last minute, she decided that diamonds didn't go with her robe and she just pulled them off and put them in her purse and never once thought that the purse might not be safe there."

"Was Brother Buck in the choir room?"

"Yes, and we'd already had opening prayer and the first hymn before he joined the services. Laurel didn't notice her earrings were missing till we were on our way to Sunday brunch. We raced right back to the church and searched it thoroughly, but no luck. They weren't insured, either. That's when she noticed one of her credit cards was missing. We called some of the other choir members and they had missing credit cards, too."

The upshot was, Annie told me, that her husband Max rounded up their local police chief and took a speed boat across the channel. "When they got off the ferry, Max and the chief were waiting for them."

"Them?"

"His brother was with him that morning. I think he'd brought Buck Collins some new shoes. The old ones were worn out."

"So did they find anything?"

"Not a thing. The earrings were a matched pair of flawless diamonds, one carat each, but small enough to be hidden somewhere maybe, but what with the credit cards, too …" Her voice trailed off uncertainly. "Collins insisted that they do a strip search on both of them and the Chief complied. He even checked to see that the heels of their shoes weren't hollowed out. And Max searched the cross himself. Did you know it's hollow and has a light inside?"

I told her I did.

"You know, Deborah, our church gets a lot of summer visitors and I didn't like wondering if one of them was the thief, but Buck Collins struck me as a very sincere man. I'd hate to think I was such a bad judge of character. And speaking of summer visitors, when are you coming back to see us? Laurel's talking about taking the LSATs and applying to law school."

I laughed and told her to wish her mother-in-law good luck for me.

But after I hung up, I had to shake my head at Annie's trusting nature. She always thought the best of everyone. Buck Collins might have radiated innocence and sincerity to her; to me, he just looked guilty and ashamed.

And well he should. I'm always a little cynical about reformed sinners who parade their redemption so publically. Bragging that the Lord provided for all his daily needs.

Right.

With a little help from whatever his sticky fingers could pick up. Even if they were fenced for only ten percent of their actual value, two carats of flawless diamonds would pay for a lot of flashlight batteries. They would print a lot of Bible tracts. No to mention a few religious T-shirts.

I thought of his sister down there in Brunswick. Another trusting soul, who helped the Lord provide, sending him shoes and homemade fudge. Least he could have done was give her a little credit.

Fudge? Shoes? Buck Collins had been on the road five years he said. That added up to a whole bunch of shoes. And probably warm jackets for the winter, not to mention underwear and jeans. Of course, the missions he stayed at could have provided some of his clothing, but I was willing to bet that every time he called home (and called collect, let us not forget), sister Bonnie was in his ear with "What do you need?" and "What can I send you?" then sending her patient and loving husband out five or six times a year to find him.

It was a wonder the poor man had time to keep his business going. And not going too well if I could judge by his old truck, his simple clothes, and the fact that his only jewelry was a cheap wristwatch and a plain gold band.

So maybe Buck Collins was right. The Lord had indeed provided by providing him with a devoted sister and generous brother-in-law.

But here in Colleton County was where this Buck stopped, I thought grimly. If Chester Nance turned up any prior convictions—and one count of littering was all it would take—then the most I could do would be to hit him with a hefty fine and put him on probation with some community service thrown in. Either way though, this conviction would show up the next time things went missing from a church robing room.

I sat in court that afternoon dispensing justice. Or trying to. The B+ student on his second marijuana possession. The two migrant laborers who'd tried to knife each other but now claimed to be the best of friends. The relentless woman who kept calling her neighbor at three in the morning just because his dog barked a little. ("A little?" the woman screamed. "A *little?* Let me tell you—")

And all through it, like a refrain—shoes and fudge, fudge and shoes. I found myself thinking about love and wondering if it went both ways.

At the break, I sent a note to Chester Nance, asking him to make sure the cross was in my courtroom the next morning.

So there it was, a fourth—and I hoped final—time. My bailiff propped it in the jury box, which was pretty appropriate. Brother Reuben and Jack Marcom were there once again to lend moral support as Buck Collins took his place at the defendant's table. Today's T-shirt was dark green with a scattering of flowers and the words, "Consider the lilies of the field."

"You haven't changed your mind about an attorney?" I asked, when Chester Nance finished reporting that he could find no prior convictions of any misdemeanor or felony on Collins.

"No, ma'am."

"Mr. Collins," I said, "you are not under oath, but it's my job to ascertain the truth and I hope you will give it."

He looked at me warily.

"Did you take those credit cards?"

"I do plead guilty, Your Honor."

"That's not what I asked, Mr. Collins. Did you personally take those cards out of their purses Sunday morning?"

"It was a temptation too strong to resist. I *am* guilty."

I had to admire his wiliness. In another time, another place, he might have made a great trial lawyer.

"Yes or no, Mr. Collins. Did you take those cards?"

"Yes!" he said, almost exploding. "Yes, I took them, okay? There's a place I know that buys credit cards if you can get them there within twelve hours."

"Which you were prepared to do?"

"Yes, ma'am."

"And this isn't really the first time, either, is it? You took a pair of diamond earrings down in South Carolina, didn't you?"

"They searched me," he said. Behind the neatly trimmed beard, his face blazed red with embarrassment. "They didn't find them."

"Because you'd hidden them in the cross?" I asked.

"They looked there, too."

"Did they look in the secret compartment?"

He gaped at me. "How do you know about that?"

I directed the bailiff to bring the cross to him.

"It's in the wheel housing, isn't it?" I said. "You want to show me?"

With a sigh, Collins pulled off the magnetized strip of red plastic that allowed access to the wheel axle. Then he pulled at the inner plate that appeared to separate the housing from the hollow interior so that the leaflets couldn't fall down into the wheels and jam them. Instead the real separator, a rectangle of white plastic that didn't match the rest, was another four inches higher up, forming a neat little cubby hole plenty big enough to hold earrings or credit cards or maybe even a small kitchen sink.

"This is where I hid them," said Collins.

"You built it specifically to have a place to stash stolen goods?" I asked.

"Yes, ma'am."

"Oh, shoot, Buck!" said Jack Marcom on the front row behind him. "I already told her you barely know which way's up on circular saw. She knows you didn't build that."

"You be quiet, Jack!" He whirled around and shook his finger in his brother-in-law's face. "You just be quiet, you hear?"

He turned back to me. "I said I was guilty. What more do you need?"

"The truth, Mr. Collins. And in your case, the truth will set you free. As Mr. Marcom says, I have heard about your incompetence with tools. And this place that buys credit cards if you get them there within twelve hours? Carrying a cross, you could barely get out of Colleton County in twelve hours.

"You call home every Friday and tell your sister where you are and what you'll be doing. And if it's hanging out in someone's guesthouse by the eighth green or preaching to the well-to-do, then your brother-in-law shows up with fresh clothes, new shoes or food, doesn't he?"

"Bonnie and Jack, they believe in what I'm doing," said Collins.

"Did you ever think how expensive it must get for them?" I asked. "All those collect calls? How many children do your sister and Mr. Marcom have?"

He sighed. "Four."

I looked over at Marcom. "Four children to feed and clothe on top of helping your wife's brother, Mr. Marcom. When did you add that little box over the wheel housing and when did Mr. Collins finally stumble on it? Monday? Did he catch you retrieving those credit cards he tried to return that night?"

"He didn't know anything about it," Collins said stubbornly. "I had somebody in Charleston fix it for me."

Jack Marcom stood up, twisting his hat in his hands. "Your Honor—"

"You be quiet, Jack!" Collins roared. Then his voice softened. "You think about Bonnie and those little children depending on you and you just be quiet, you hear me?"

Marcom sat back down and Collins faced me resolutely.

"So what did you do?" Dwight asked me as we waited for the microwave popcorn to finish before sticking a video of *Stage Door* in my VCR.

(The ending's a little too schmaltzy for both of us, but we like seeing Lucille Ball before she became Lucy, and watching Katharine Hepburn come to terms with "the calla lilies are in bloom again" is always fun.).

"What *could* I do?" I said. "Without any priors, the law only allows a fine and community service."

I tore open the popcorn bag. The buttery aroma immediately filled the kitchen.

"But what about his brother-in-law? He might've been stealing from the rich to give to the poor, but he was still a thief and you let him off?"

"*I* didn't let him off," I said, nettled. "Collins let him off by swearing he did it all by himself. My only consolation is that if there's a next time, this will show up on his record."

"*If* there's a next time?" Dwight asked cynically.

"If," I said firmly. "I have a feeling Brother Buck had his eyes opened this week and that he really is going to trust the Lord to provide from now on, instead of his sister and brother-in-law."

"A fully reformed, reformed sinner," Dwight teased. "And all because of you."

I was still uncomfortable with the whole situation—punishing the technically innocent while the technically guilty went free? And yet, there was a certain rough justice at work here, though I never would have admitted it. And Brother Buck and Jack Marcom had each received a lesson in sacrificial love. All the same ...

"This isn't the way it should have turned out," I mourned.

Dwight patted my shoulder. "Well, now, you don't know that, Deborah. The Bible does say that the Lord works in mysterious ways."

"Maybe," I said. "I just wish He wouldn't do it in my courtroom."

Women Before the Bench, 2001

Till 3:45

Girl children have a wider choice of crime-fighting role models these days. It's not all Nancy Drew any more. I've never met Wendelin Van Draanen, but I admire her Sammy Keyes books.

From nine in the morning until three every afternoon, Mara Wolfe was a diligent worker, moving papers from her In-basket to her Outgoing with care and efficiency. She was patient on the telephone, even-tempered with her co-workers, and did not grumble when yet another task was added to her workload. As the hands of the little clock on her desk edged past three, however, her concentration faltered and callers were cut short or put on hold as soon as her other line lit up to signal a second incoming call.

3:10. 3:15. Mara had timed her daughter's walk through lower Manhattan. Fourth grade let out at 3 p.m. From the schoolyard gate to the door of their small apartment over a used book store was precisely fourteen and a half minutes.

Add five minutes for giggling with her friends at the corner, then another thirty seconds for checking that no one loitered in their building's communal vestibule before Gwen pulled out the brass latchkey she wore on a ribbon around her neck.

Allow four more minutes in case she had to scurry to the bathroom— "Sometimes I can't wait," Gwen had said rebelliously—and that made 3:24 the absolute earliest Mara could reasonably expect her daughter to call.

The telephone rang and Mara scooped it to her ear.

Business. Aware of her supervisor's considering glance, Mara managed to keep a smile in her voice as she answered the client's question.

The light on her second line remained dark.

3:27, 3:30 and her imagination began to picture all the grim things that could happen in this city to a wiry little ten-year-old with short brown curls, a chipped front tooth, and a trusting nature.

After her ex-husband ran to another state to avoid paying child support,

Mara couldn't afford their heavily mortgaged West Side condo and she'd moved downtown to be near her only living relative. As long as Aunt May could keep Gwen after school, everything was manageable, an adventure even; but after her aunt moved to Florida, reliable day care strained their slender budget to its limits and Gwen hated it.

"They're all babies," she grumbled. "Nobody else in my class goes to day care. I'm big enough to take care of myself."

As was bound to happen sooner or later, Gwen woke up sneezing and sniffling on the same winter morning Mara was scheduled for a business meeting she simply couldn't afford to miss. There was no other choice. She left Gwen tucked into bed with telephone, tissues and orange juice on the night stand; the television on her dresser; a half-brave, half-excited expression on her face; and Mr. Ed, their big horse-faced tomcat, snuggled at her feet.

Old Mrs. Bersisky in the next apartment grudgingly gave permission for Gwen to call her in an emergency ("A real emergency, mind you, and not just because she's bored"), and the bookstore owner downstairs said, sure, he'd keep an ear out for any unusual crashes overhead.

In the three years Mara and Gwen had lived there, the shop directly beneath them had changed hands several times. In fact, Mr. Ed was a legacy of the first tenant, a frail and kindly old gentleman whose musty stock of organic herbs and spices seemed to attract a surprisingly large clientele right up to the day an undercover narcotics agent arrested him for selling peyote and other more exotic hallucinogens.

Organic Herbs had been succeeded by Citizens for a Caring Congress, Mason's Used Furniture, and the Pearl Too Co-op.

Mara still regretted that last. Used furniture had meant a strong smell of paint thinner and hot glue wafting up the stairs and she had been terrified of the fire hazard, but the co-op brought a stream of friendly knitters who placed their sweaters and scarves on consignment at ridiculously low prices.

Unfortunately, Mara and Mrs. Bersisky seemed to be their only customers and the business melted away entirely in last June's heat wave.

The latest venture had opened in November. Rechristened the Murder for Money Bookstore, it stocked nothing but used murder mysteries, detective and spy stories, and thrillers; and it seemed to draw as varied a clientele as had the old herb and spice shop.

Mara didn't approve of the store. Or its proprietor. Dayton McGuire was a tall loose-knit man who appeared to be five or six years older than she. He wore glasses and his shaggy brown head even showed a few responsible gray hairs, but Mara was not convinced. His eyes were vague and preoccupied behind those glasses and he had a very casual attitude toward business. He took anybody's personal check without asking for three IDs, kept his bills and receipts wadded together in an old shoebox beside the cash register, and never answered the telephone if someone else was nearer.

Mr. Ed seemed to like him though. Something about used books must have excited old memories of herbs and spices because when Mara or Gwen unlocked the door, the big yellow cat would often sneak between their feet, shoot down the stairs, and lurk at the bottom until someone opened the door to the vestibule where Murder for Money's door was usually open.

"Hey, no problem," Dayton McGuire had said when Mara retrieved their pet with profuse apologies the first time.

The second time they missed the cat, Mara and Gwen found him purring atop a stack of Mike Hammer mysteries. "Come on down, Mr. Ed," Gwen coaxed.

The third time, Mr. McGuire said, "I think his real name's Edward Macavity."

Gwen giggled at the silly sounding name, but Mara was suspicious. "Macavity?"

"T.S. Eliot," their new neighbor grinned. "One of his poems was about Macavity the Mystery Cat. Or, in Mr. Ed's case, the mystery lover."

"I doubt it." Mara stood on tiptoes to reach their truant animal, unaware that Dayton McGuire was regarding her long slender legs with an appreciation usually reserved for a first edition of an early Rex Stout.

"You don't approve of murder mysteries?" he asked mildly.

"Not really." She held Mr. Ed in a firm grip. "They seem a waste of time, although I suppose there are people who enjoy that sort of thing."

McGuire nodded in solemn agreement and his eyes behind those wire-rimmed glasses were very blue. "Yeah, mystery fans are a lazy lot of time wasters: presidents, scientists, philosophers."

Really, his eyes were the most astonishing blue, thought Mara. Then, as his words penetrated, she realized that those same blue eyes were also mocking her. She flushed to the roots of her honey-blonde hair and left with as much dignity as she could muster while clutching a squirming cat.

Except for Gwen's bad cold a few days later, Mara might never have spoken to him again, but she couldn't leave her daughter alone upstairs without covering as many contingencies as possible even though Dayton McGuire struck her as flip and irresponsible when she finally got him on the phone after the store opened.

As it was, that whole day proved the most anxious in Mara's life. She telephoned as soon as she got to the office and again whenever she had a free moment until Gwen complained at lunchtime, "Mom, you woke me up *again!*"

When she got home, Mara found that Gwen had passed the afternoon very amusingly. "Day brought me an Encyclopedia Brown book and I figured out nearly all the answers."

"Mr. McGuire," Mara corrected automatically.

"He said for me to," Gwen argued. "He said if I could call a cat mister, we ought to call misters by their first names."

It would have been churlish not to go down and thank him for his kindness, but Mr. McGuire brushed off Mara's thanks.

"Part of my strategy," he said. "Hook 'em while they're young and they're customers for life."

Gwen rapidly progressed from Encyclopedia Brown to Nancy Drew, the Hardy Boys and Wendelin Van Draanen's street-smart Sammy Keyes; and when her cold cleared up, she dug in her heels about returning to the after-school center. As far as she was concerned, she'd proved she could take care of herself.

Mara felt guilty about letting her daughter become a latchkey kid, but there was no denying that her salary would go further without daycare fees. Gwen promised that she'd come straight home after school and call as soon as she was safely in, that she would stay inside and keep the door locked, and that she would not play with matches nor turn on the stove.

During the icy slushy months of February and March, Gwen had kept her promises. She fed Mr. Ed, tidied her room, did her homework, worked on her Girl Scout badges, and then watched television or read steadily through the books Mr. McGuire lent her. With the coming of spring though, the novelty of looking after herself started to wear thin and of late she'd begun to dawdle with her friends on the way home from school.

It was not enough to call outright disobedience, just enough to keep Mara on edge as she watched the hands on her desk clock move past 3:35.

Gwen shifted the weight of her pink nylon bookbag to her other shoulder as she climbed the steep stairs and wondered if old Mrs. Bersisky would come out of the other apartment today to ask if the mail had come. Mrs. Bersisky rarely had a smile on her thin lips, was quick to find fault, and had made it quite clear that she was nobody's surrogate grandmother.

"And I won't put up with childish racket," she'd said when Gwen and her mother first moved in. "No running on the stairs. No banging doors. You hear?"

Gwen was scared of the crotchety, arthritic woman and she rather thought her mother was, too. But Mom expected her to be polite to all adults. Even cranky ones. "It's probably because she never had any children of her own," she'd said.

Fortunately, Mrs. Bersisky wasn't there today as Gwen unlocked the apartment door.

For the past four days, the old woman had been leaning on her walking stick and standing in the doorway of her own apartment when the child came home and Gwen had been surprised by her smile of sudden friendliness.

The first day, she'd thrust a small key into Gwen's hand and croaked in what was probably meant to sound like a friendly chirrup, "Now don't dawdle, little girl. I'm expecting an important letter."

Startled, Gwen had dropped her bookbag on the landing and headed back downstairs with the key to the mailbox next to hers and Mom's. The postman usually came around the time she was getting home and she'd offered several times to fetch Mrs. Bersisky's mail, only to be refused.

"I may have arthritis, but I can still climb stairs." She had eyed Gwen's scout uniform sharply that last day. "And I'm not your good deed, miss!"

Which had made Gwen flush because that really was the only reason she'd kept offering.

But if Mrs. Bersisky wanted to be nice now, that was fine with Gwen and she had emptied the box quickly without trying to read the envelopes. All junk mail though, she was pretty sure.

"Thank you, little girl," Mrs. Bersisky had simpered "and here's your dime for saving me all those steps."

Before Gwen could say that she didn't want to be paid, Mrs. Bersisky had shut the door in her face.

The same thing happened the next day and the next: Mrs. Bersisky in her open doorway, the key, a couple of circulars addressed to occupant, the dime, the closed door—all as if they'd been doing this for months.

Yesterday was different again though. No sign of Mrs. Bersisky. But just as Gwen was taking the key out of the lock, the woman's door opened and Mr. Ed, who had been winding around Gwen's ankles, scampered across the landing and into Mrs. Bersisky's apartment.

Appalled, Gwen had dropped her book bag and darted after him, apologizing frantically.

Inside, the apartment was both brighter and less cluttered than she'd imagined except for a row of potted plants in the sunny front window. No sign of her cat though. She turned and almost jumped out of her skin. Immediately behind the door stood a tall dark-haired young woman who held the cat in her arms as she scratched under his chin.

"He's a real lover, isn't he?" she asked with a friendly smile.

"Not usually," Gwen said, confused. She didn't know Mrs. Bersisky ever had company and while Mr. Ed liked to be petted, he didn't usually let strangers actually pick him up.

"So you're the nice little girl who gets Granny's mail for her every day." The woman smiled. "She's been telling me all about you. Why don't I hold on to Mr. Ed while you go check her box?"

"Okay," said Gwen.

The box held a magazine, a circular and a long thin envelope with the name of a bank on it. Through the window of the envelope Gwen saw Mrs. Bersisky's name printed on a pale green background. The young woman took the envelope from her with a happy smile. "Here's the first one, Granny!"

Mrs. Bersisky's shoulders seemed to slump as she handed Gwen a dime.

Today, Gwen was so distracted by Mrs. Bersisky's unexpected absence after four days of being there that she forgot to call her mother and began to fix herself a snack. A new Nancy Drew book lay on the table and as Gwen spread peanut butter on some crackers, half her mind was on the plot, the other half on why Mrs. Bersisky's granddaughter had stood behind the door yesterday while the older woman handed over the mailbox key. Had she been there every day?

But if Mrs. Bersisky never had any children, how could she have a granddaughter?

Absentmindedly, Gwen let Mr. Ed lick a smear of peanut butter from her fingers.

And that was another thing. How did she know their cat's name?

Maybe, thought Gwen, she used to live in the neighborhood. There *was* something familiar about her.

And then Gwen remembered. Someone else used to work in the store downstairs when they first moved here three years ago.

"I was just a little kid, then," she told Mr. Ed, "but I remember that old man who used to have you. And there was a girl. Purple hair. She had a ring through her lip, one through her nose, another one through her eyebrow, and even one in her belly button. Her hair's black now and she doesn't have any rings except in her ears, but it's the same person, isn't it, Mr. Ed? That's why you let her pick you up, isn't it?"

Mom said the old man had gone to jail for selling drugs. Did the girl go to jail, too?

"I bet she's not really Mrs. B's granddaughter," Gwen told her cat.

Mr. Ed no longer listened. Instead, he'd gone over to sniff at the apartment door. As Gwen followed, she heard a noise outside on the landing and pressed her eye to the peephole.

Across the landing, Mrs. B's granddaughter, if that's who she was, pulled the door to and headed for the stairs with something in her hand. The mailbox key!

Gwen quietly eased the door open and slipped across to Mrs. Bersisky's door, Mr. Ed at her heels. As she suspected, it wasn't latched and she pushed it open and let the cat run inside again, half expecting to get yelled at. Instead, she was shocked to see her elderly neighbor seated upright in a heavy wooden chair, her arms bound behind her with a pair of pantyhose and a gag in her mouth.

The old woman's eyes rolled frantically as she tried to speak.

"Is she coming right back?" Gwen whispered fearfully.

Mrs. Bersisky nodded emphatically just as the vestibule door banged at the foot of the stairs.

With no time to get away, Gwen dived behind the couch under the front windows and lay on her stomach so she could see past the fringe that didn't quite brush the floor.

A moment later, the young woman came through the door waving two long narrow envelopes over her head. "Payday, Granny! Just like I thought."

Checks, thought Gwen, remembering the envelopes Aunt May and Uncle Pete used to get every month.

The young woman ripped these two open and her eyes widened as she read the figures. "Why, Granny, what big dividends you have!"

To Gwen's dismay, Mr. Ed chose that precise moment to come wandering out of the bedroom and rub against the woman's ankle.

"What're you doing here, Ed?" Her eyes narrowed suspiciously as she looked around the living room. "I pulled the door shut, so how did you—? The little girl!" She gave Mrs. Bersisky's white hair a vicious tug. "Is she in there, old lady? You don't tell me, I'm gonna—"

Mrs. Bersisky closed her eyes stubbornly.

The woman picked up Mrs. Bersisky's stout walking stick and headed for the bedroom.

As soon as she'd passed the couch, Gwen eeled out and hurried toward the door, but before she'd taken three steps, the walking stick caught her a blow on the shoulder so hard that it knocked the breath out of her and she felt herself falling.

3:44. 3:45.

Gwen had never been this late.

Ignoring her supervisor, Mara dialed her apartment. After ten rings, she broke the connection and looked up the number of the Murder for Money Bookstore. Her fingers were unsteady as she dialed because she was half angry that Gwen might be carelessly breaking the rules and more than half terrified that something serious had happened.

The bookstore telephone rang and rang and rang. It was maddening the way Dayton McGuire could ignore the phone if he were shelving books or talking to a customer about the differences between Dashiell Hammett and Ross Macdonald.

"If it bothers you, answer it and take the message," he'd said more than once when she'd practically shrieked at him that his phone was ringing.

Her other line lit up and Mara eagerly switched over. Instead of Gwen, it was a long-winded client who seemed to take forever to state his needs. By the time both lines were free, it was almost four o'clock. She called her apartment again. No answer.

She tried Mrs. Bersisky's number. Busy.

Whimpering with pain, Gwen rolled away as the woman grabbed for her and rushed back to the front windows. "Help!" she cried trying to tug one open. "Help!"

The young woman gave a bitter laugh. "Scream your head off, kid. This is New York. Nobody comes when you yell for help in this town."

Remembering all the things she'd read, Gwen knew she was right. She tugged harder at the window. It wouldn't budge and one of Mrs. Bersisky's potted plants crashed to the floor.

"Get away from that window!" snarled the woman, flourishing the walking stick. As she swung at Gwen again, she caught the telephone instead and sent it flying.

The telephone! Gwen felt like kicking herself. Instead of hiding like a jerk, why didn't she dial 911 as soon as she saw Mrs. B. tied up? Stupid, stupid, stupid! She snatched up another of Mrs. B.'s potted plants.

The woman laughed. "Put it down, kid, and I won't hurt you. I'll just tie you up while Granny and me go cash these checks at the bank. Soon as I get the money, I'll let her go. Promise."

As Gwen hesitated, the woman moved closer. The child was trapped between the couch and windows and she screamed again as the woman lifted the heavy cane to smash her head.

4:05 and Mara held the receiver to her ear, grimly determined to let it ring a hundred times if that's what it took to make Dayton McGuire answer his phone. She wished there were some way she could turn up the volume and make it ring even louder at his end.

Eventually someone picked up and a lackadaisical male voice said, "Hello?"

"Mr. McGuire?" (He had never invited *her* to call him Day and they remained Mr. McGuire and Mrs. Wolfe.)

"No."

"Is he there?"

"No."

"Well, who's minding the shop?"

"I am, I guess," the voice admitted. "They left in such a hurry—"

"Who did?" she asked impatiently.

"Him and that little girl from upstairs. When the ambulance was taking too long, Professor Martin said he could drive them to the hospital in his car but Day would have to go along and—"

Mara's heart seemed to stop in mid-beat. "Which hospital? What happened? Is she hurt?"

"She was breathing again when they got her in the car. I don't know what hospital. Look, I gotta go. You call back when Day's here, okay?" And ignoring Mara's pleas for information, he hung up.

Her supervisor came over. "Is something wrong?" she asked, concerned by Mara's suddenly bloodless face.

"I don't *know!*" Mara cried, reaching for her purse. "They've taken Gwen to a hospital and I don't know which one. Or why. Please, I have to go!"

"Of course you do." The woman pulled a twenty-dollar bill from her pocket. "Take a cab. It'll be quicker. And call me as soon as you learn anything."

"Oh, thank you!" Mara exclaimed and dashed from the office.

"*She was breathing again*," the man had said.

Did that mean Gwen had *stopped* breathing? Why? A fall? An electrical shock? Had she choked on something? Had someone hurt her?

A thousand images of her daughter's thin little face rigid with pain or limp with death rushed through Mara's mind as the cab slipped in and out of traffic lanes, strained at red lights and squeezed the yellows. Her thoughts were an anguished blur but one thing she knew: If the worst had happened, she'd never *ever* forgive herself.

Day McGuire thought she was too uptight with Gwen, set too many rules, kept her too closely penned after school.

"Why don't you let her play downstairs?" he'd asked when Mara stopped in to pay him for that last batch of Nancy Drews on Friday. "She ought to be out in the fresh spring air, not cooped up reading every afternoon."

"Don't you read the newspaper?" Mara had asked. "Don't you even read your own books? Here you are surrounded by thousands of books on murder and mayhem and you ask why I don't let a little ten-year-old girl play on the sidewalk?"

"I could keep an eye out."

"Oh, sure," she'd said sarcastically. "Right up to the moment someone asked you how many cases Lord Peter What's-his-name solved."

As the cab swung into her street, Mara strained forward on the edge of her seat until she spotted her building. Everything looked normal in the afternoon sunshine, even prosaic. There were no milling crowds beneath the tree outside the bookstore, no police questioning witnesses, no yellow tape, no television cameras.

She gratefully doubled the cabbie's tip because he'd brought her home so quickly and hurried across the sidewalk.

The bookstore was unlocked but completely deserted. Mara raced upstairs to the apartment. Gwen's bookbag was by the door and the makings of a snack cluttered the table, but no sign of her daughter. And no sign of Mr. Ed either. She darted across the landing to ring and pound on Mrs. Bersisky's door, but no one responded.

A terror so thick she could almost touch it settled onto Mara's heart as she hurried back to her own apartment and called the nearest hospital. She willed her voice to steadiness while asking about a ten-year-old, Gwen Wolfe, who might have been brought in within the last hour or so.

They switched her to the Emergency Room and the harried nurse who answered assured her that no little girl had been treated there that afternoon. No one remembered a Dayton McGuire or a Professor Martin either.

It was the same at the second nearest hospital and at two others further away.

The police! she thought, and phoned the local precinct. The desk officer was solicitous but he knew nothing about any young girl at that address.

Frustrated, Mara tried to call Mrs. Bersisky again and found the line still busy. Once more she pounded on the woman's door and even put her ear against the cool panel to listen. No sounds.

There were two more apartments upstairs. Mara knew both couples worked all day, yet she could not quit without trying them, too.

Nothing.

She was halfway down the stairs when her own telephone rang, but by the time she could rush back, the ringing had stopped. Too late to wish she'd squeezed their budget for an answering machine.

Blocked at every turn, Mara wanted to put her head down and howl for the first time since her divorce. Until 3:45 this afternoon, she had felt that she and Gwen were living an adventure of sorts. Not that everything was perfect, but at least she was in control, making her own choices. Now the future stretched ahead bleakly and she missed her aunt desperately. If only there were a shoulder to cry on or someone to put arms around her and tell her everything was going to be all right.

Wrapped in a numb fatalism, she went downstairs to the bookstore where she found Mr. Ed asleep on a carton of books. Whatever happened to Gwen had probably happened over an hour ago and there was nothing she could do to change it. Day McGuire and one of his customers had taken Gwen somewhere for help. Sooner or later he would have to come back and then she would know. Until then she had no choice but to wait.

There were two people browsing through back shelves when she entered the store and several more soon arrived. She took their money, gave them receipts, and began straightening out some of McGuire's clutter behind the sales counter.

She was sorting through a sheaf of cancelled checks when the bell over the door tinkled again. She looked up automatically and the sales counter seemed to sway and tilt as Day McGuire held the door open for Gwen, who bounced in, looked surprised, and exclaimed, "Mom! Where have you been? We've been calling *everywhere!*"

The next thing Mara knew, she was lying on the floor behind the sales counter and McGuire's warm deep voice was reassuring Gwen, "She just blacked out for a minute. See? She's already coming around."

He lifted Mara's head. "Okay now?"

Mara felt the room steady and pushed herself into a sitting position. Gwen was kneeling beside her and Mara put her arms around the child, held her tight, and began to cry.

Gwen squirmed with embarrassment. "Don't cry, Mom. Everything's okay."

"I thought you were hurt," said Mara. "Someone said you'd stopped breathing."

"Not me," said Gwen. "Mrs. Bersisky. After her phony granddaughter ran away—"

"Phony granddaughter?"

"Used to sell drugs out of this store," McGuire explained. "She's running from a parole violation and planned to steal Mrs. Bersisky's annuity checks to finance her getaway. Gwen put a stop to that."

Gwen quickly described the events that led up to this afternoon. "Mrs. B. told her I always got the mail for her and that I'd be suspicious if she quit letting me. She was hoping to slip me a note or something but she never had the chance."

When Gwen told about getting hit by the walking stick, Mara felt a rage she'd never experienced before.

"Oh, honey." She gently stroked Gwen's bruised arm. "How did you get away?"

"She said nobody would come if I yelled for help," Gwen said proudly, "so I threw a flower pot through the front window and yelled 'Fire!' as loud as I could."

"Almost beaned my best paying customer," Day McGuire grinned, "but it sure got our attention. We went charging upstairs with a fire extinguisher."

"The woman ran away but while they were chasing her, Mrs. Bersisky quit breathing so I gave her CPR just like we learned in Scouts."

"Probably saved her life," said McGuire. "Gwen did CPR till Mrs. Bersisky started breathing again, then got an aspirin down her and we took her to the hospital. The doctor thinks she had a mild heart attack, but thanks to your daughter here, she'll probably be all right."

"I just tried to think what Sammy Keyes would do," Gwen said. Then, remembering her previous grievance, she scowled at Mara. "But where were you?"

"That's right," said McGuire. "Gwen did all the responsible things, but what about you? We tried to get you at your office but your boss said you'd gone charging out a half-hour earlier, so we called you at home and first the line stayed busy and then you wouldn't answer. No message where you were going, no thought of how worried Gwen would be."

There was nothing vague or preoccupied about the book seller's manner now and he sounded almost angry as he hauled Mara to her feet. "This is the last place I'd have thought to find you."

Something about the tone of his voice made Mara swallow the sarcastic retort she normally would have made.

8:46. All the excitement had been talked out and things were almost back to normal. Mr. Ed was asleep on the windowsill. Gwen had finished her homework, had taken her bath, and was helping Mara make sugar cookies for tomorrow's Scout meeting when Mr. McGuire knocked at their door with a stack of used books in his arms.

"Sherlock Holmes for you," he told Gwen, "Dorothy L. Sayers for your mother. Along with a proposal."

Mara was startled, but his next words dispelled whatever she might have thought he meant.

"I need somebody to keep my shelves in alphabetical order, so I thought I'd hire Gwen if that's okay with you? An hour and a half a day, five days a week for, let's say, a dollar an hour?"

Gwen's eyes were shining as she quickly calculated her weekly take. "Can I, Mom? Please?"

"That's very generous of you, Mr. McGuire," Mara began, when the oven timer rang and the smell of well-done sugar cookies called them to the kitchen.

Day McGuire trailed along after them and Mara automatically poured him a glass of milk, too, as he accepted a cookie.

"I thought we could trade," he said. "You do my bookkeeping and I'll watch Gwen. You've already made a good start on straightening out my system."

"That shoebox is a system?" Mara asked dryly. Her smile agreed to his plan though and Gwen was ecstatic. Nevertheless, Mara couldn't quite quash a small twinge of disappointment when the tall man stood to leave. She should have known he was only being neighborly.

As she held the door for him, he said, "Read the books I gave you in order. There'll be a test at the end of *Gaudy Night*."

Mara was puzzled.

"That's the book where Lord Peter finally proposed to Harriet Vane," he explained diffidently.

His sudden shyness made Mara's heart begin to beat absurdly fast. "Did she accept?"

"Why don't we talk about it over dinner this weekend?" he asked, and something more than neighborliness gleamed behind the laughter in his eyes.

Love and Death, 2001

The Choice

The trigger for this story was a déjà vu experience similar to the one the protagonist here experiences.

Kate?"

She whirled around, the blood draining from her face, then returning so rapidly that she flushed like a guilty schoolchild.

"I'm sorry," Sam said. "I didn't mean to startle you. I thought you heard me when I came in."

He peered over his wife's slender shoulder through the tall narrow window slit that gave light to the stair landing and realized suddenly that this was not the first time he'd found her here.

"What do you see out there?" he asked.

He himself saw nothing except bright sunlight playing on an overgrown pasture that sloped down to a creek. He couldn't even see the creek for it was hidden by the trees and underbrush that grew thickly along its sandy banks. They had talked about horses when they first moved here, when the children were little, and they'd had a few chickens and, briefly, some goats to eat out the poison ivy and stinging nettles. The youngest child was in college now. Their only animals were a couple of dogs and some stray cats that nobody had the heart to take to the pound, and small pine trees were starting to spring up in the pasture.

Although they'd both grown up on working farms—or maybe it was more accurate to say that because they'd both grown up *working* on farms right here in Colleton County, North Carolina—they had no romantic illusions about getting back to the earth. Tobacco was already loosening its stranglehold on the area and even if it weren't, neither Sam nor Kate any desire to spend their lives in such hot, sweaty, dirty work. No, when they came back to the country, it was on *their* terms: with college degrees that allowed them to work in Raleigh yet still raise their children in a loving community of aunts and uncles and grandparents, on a ten-acre piece of land where there was space for the children to run and play freely, safely.

"What are you looking at?" he asked again, his chin brushed by the softness of her hair, hair that was gently going gray, like the first random flakes of
snow falling lightly on brown autumn leaves.

"Nothing," she said, leaning back against his chest in the circle of his arms.
"Not a thing." Yet she continued to gaze out the window, so he did, too.

And then, of course, he saw it. How odd that he'd never noticed before. By
some trick of architecture, this was the only window in the house that was
high enough to overlook the trees along the creek bottom to where the land
rose beyond. Near the top of the rise was a ruined chimney, two stories tall, a
visible reminder of the house that once stood there.

"Do you ever feel time fold back against itself?" she asked him. "Sometimes I stand here and I can almost see the house the way it used to look with
Tim and me racing down the hill with our fishing poles, heading for the creek
after a day in the fields. As if those two kids were the reality and I was a ghost
out of their future."

"The future doesn't have ghosts."

"Doesn't it? Remember when we were building this house? I stood right
here—it was the same day they put the roof trusses on—and you and the
children were outside picking up nails where the driveway was going to go. I
remember thinking to myself that I'd grow old in this house and I would stand
at this very window and watch a grown-up child come up from the creek. It
felt so real, I could almost see it. Last weekend, when Chris was out here—"
Her voice trembled and broke off.

He turned her in his arms then and looked down into her troubled face.
"Kate, the kids are back and forth all the time. Of course they're going to go
down to the creek. They spent half their lives splashing around down there.
There's nothing odd about seeing Chris through this window."

"No? Then why did I have the exact same feeling I had twenty years ago?
As if I ought to be able to look up and see the sky through the trusses."

"*Déjà vu* all over again?" he teased. Then, as he felt her shoulders tighten,
he added sympathetically, "You've been working too hard. And all this strain
with your mother. You were out there this afternoon, weren't you?"

She nodded. "It's not that though. She's adjusting to the place very nicely.
Likes the food, likes the staff, likes her room."

"What then?"

A small shrug of her shoulders. "The aide was changing the sheets when I
got there and Mama was up in her wheelchair. The aide said something about
her cold feet and Mama said that was one of the things she missed the most

after her husband died. Not having somebody there beside her that she could warm her cold feet on."

"And?" he asked in puzzlement.

Even though his family had known the Cole family when they were children, they were in different school districts and hadn't met till high school. Like the rest of the community, he'd heard of the tragedy though—how Mr. Cole had fallen asleep with a lighted cigarette after being up half the night with his wife when she miscarried their third child, how Kate and her older brother Tim blamed themselves because they might have noticed the fire in time to raise the alarm if they hadn't skipped their chores and gone fishing.

Not that Kate ever talked much about it or about their father either, for that matter. Even after they were married, it was years before she confided that her father had been drinking that day. In that time, in that churchly community, excessive drinking—drunkenness—had been a shameful secret that every affected family tried to keep hidden. She chattered freely of the poor but loving grandparents who took them in, the aunts and uncles who'd helped out. Only rarely did she speak of her father, and never about his death. When Tim reminisced about the water wheels Mr. Cole built for him on the creekbank or the times they went hunting together, Kate would somehow drift away to the kitchen to make coffee or fill a glass or check on the kids.

It was years before Sam actually noticed and when he did, he put it down to the pain and embarrassment she must have felt.

Mrs. Cole was a different matter. A sickly woman who shied from any sort of confrontation, she had bravely borne her widowhood, devoting herself to the welfare of her two children. Her two *fatherless* children. She had a way of reminding you of how she had sacrificed her health to make up to them for their loss. And hers, too, of course. A hot-tempered man, folks said, but a good man and a hard worker. Made the children work hard, too, they said. Hard work never hurt anybody and look how good those children turned out, both of them teachers, both of them upright pillars of the community.

"After all these years, don't you think it's sort of sweet that she still misses him?"

"Daddy's been dead almost thirty-five years," Kate said. "And she quit sleeping in his bed long before that."

That surprised him. "But I thought that was why she was in the hospital with a miscarriage."

"Even a poor marriage can still have sex," Kate said dryly as she turned back to the window.

But someone to warm her cold feet on? Kate wondered what Mama would say if suddenly reminded of the way she flinched whenever he grabbed her breast in front of them and pulled her up the rickety stairs to his bedroom and slammed the door, leaving Kate and Tim to pretend nothing unpleasant was happening up there? Not that she had really understood, but Tim was two years older and he certainly had. That must have been why he always tried to distract her during those bad times. Protecting her emotions. Unable to protect his own. She shuddered to think of the lasting damage to his emotional psyche if their father hadn't died when he did. So why should it bother her if Tim had managed to bury the pain and angry humiliation of their childhood, if Mama pretended her marriage had been as warm and loving as Sam and Kate's?

Most of the time, she didn't care, just let her mind go blank. But today, standing at this window, staring across to the ruined house of her childhood, Kate wondered if she were the only one who remembered how things really were....

They were tenant farmers. Sharecroppers. Un-landed gentry.

Maybe that was the acid that ate at him and corroded his soul. Moving from farm to farm every few years. Living in tiny little shacks or huge dilapidated houses like this one, with no indoor plumbing as though it were the 1870s, not the 1970s. Knowing that the labor of his body and that of his wife and children would never earn enough to buy back the land that his own father had gambled away in the forties. Or maybe it was just the alcohol. Rotgut whiskey or a case of Bud when he had a few dollars. Fermented tomato juice or aftershave lotion when he didn't.

Not that he was drunk all the time. That's what made it so horrible. The unpredictability of his rages. He could go months without a drop, months where, when the field work was done for the day, he'd help little Katie plant flower seeds or whittle slingshots, and yes, water wheels for Timmy. Then, for no reason they could ever fathom, he'd go roaring off to town and come home in a black drunken rage that could last for days. Near the end, those rages seemed to come more often, with more violence.

Like the day he'd carried Mama to the hospital because she was bleeding so badly. She and Timmy were scared and wanted to go with them, but he'd ordered them out to the field.

"And I'd better see every one of them tobacco plants suckered by the time I get back," he'd told them.

All morning, they'd toiled up and down the rows of sticky green plants, snapping off the suckers that tried to grow up where the money leaves met the plant's stem. At lunchtime, they stopped just long enough for sandwiches and glasses of cold milk before heading back into the broiling field with only their wide-brimmed straw hats for shade. Feet bare on the hot dirt, their bare arms and legs burned brown by the sun.

An hour later, Timmy had gone back to the house for a jug of water and that's where he was when their father came home and accused him of slacking off while his sister was out there working as she'd been told.

Katie heard his screams from the edge of the field, but experience had told her there was nothing she could do except blank her mind and keep on snapping the suckers.

When Timmy took his place beside her in the next row, his legs were red and raw. The welts from the belt marched up and down her brother's backside like rows of newly-seeded corn.

"Did Mama come home?" she whispered. Not that Mama had ever been able to step between Timmy and the belt.

Timmy shook his head and kept moving.

They finished the field a little before four. Timmy didn't want to go back to the house, but Katie was bolder. Their father almost never hit her. Just Timmy and Mama. "Besides, I'll bet he's passed out on the bed by now."

Something else that experience had taught her.

But Timmy couldn't be persuaded. Instead he fetched a hoe and headed for the vegetable garden. "He said for us to start chopping grass if we got through early."

She crept into the old wooden house quieter than the mice usually were. Silence was all around. At the foot of the staircase, she hesitated until she heard deep snores from above. Relief flowed down like healing waters on her sore heart then, and she tiptoed up the stairs, the stairs he'd knocked Mama down this morning though he said it was an accident when he saw all the blood.

His bedroom was at the top of the stairs and as her eyes got level with the landing, Katie could see him sprawled on his back, his head on the pillow, loud ragged snores issuing from his open mouth. She tiptoed closer. The sheet had come untucked and there was a cigarette-shaped scorch mark on the mattress ticking. At least this time, he'd put his cigarette in the ashtray on the night stand, she thought. It had burned right down to the filter, leaving an acrid smell in the room. There were more little scorch marks all around on the carpet where cigarettes had dropped from his fingers when he fell asleep. Last winter, he'd actually burned his chest and fingers when he passed out with a freshly lit one. Mama kept saying they'd all be burned in their beds one night.

She thought of Timmy's raw legs, of Mama's bloody dress and the way she'd held her swollen belly and moaned as she hobbled to the car.

Timmy's legs.

Mama's blood.

"It's okay," she told Timmy, whose eyes were almost as red as the welts on his legs. "He's drunk as a skunk and won't remember how much chopping needed doing today. Let's you and me go fishing, okay? Catch a few sun perch for supper."

She pulled a couple of cane poles from the shed and sidetracked Timmy when he headed for the compost pile with a small shovel to dig for worms. "Wait and dig 'em out of the creekbank," she said. "It'll be cooler there."

As they hurried along toward the path that led through the thick underbrush down to the creek, she paused and looked back.

A tendril of gray smoke leaked from the upstairs bedroom window.

Abruptly, like a startled doe who feels the hunter's eye upon her, she whirled around and searched with her own eyes the pasture that rose on the other side of the creek, an empty pasture where no house was yet built.

No one was there though. No one had watched her before and no one cried out in alarm now.

No one.

"So your mother sees her marriage through rose-colored glasses," said Sam. "After thirty-five years, let the old woman rewrite her past if she wants to. Haven't you ever wanted to?"

Kate stood so long without answering, that Sam tightened his arms around her. "Hey, it was just a rhetorical question. It's not as if you really have a choice."

No choice? When out there, across the creek, she could almost see the ten-year-old child she'd once been looking straight at her? If she leaned forward, rapped on the window, would the child turn? Run back to the house? Raise the alarm?

"No, of course not," she told Sam. "And even if I could rewrite the past, I wouldn't."

"C'mon, Katie!" Timmy called impatiently. "Whatcha looking at?"

"Nothing," Katie said. "Not a thing." And ran down through the underbrush to join her brother.

Malice Domestic 10, 2001

The Dog That Didn't Bark

This story actually began as I've written it when I decided to do another circuit of our evening walk and my husband said, "If you don't come back, I'll send the dogs." We do not currently own a dog (his choice) so it made me laugh and say, "I'm tempted to stay out and see just what kind of dogs you'd send." But as I walked away into the twilight, I thought, What if I didn't come back? What if I vanished? *This story almost plotted itself at that point.*

Feel like another round?" Donna asked as she and her husband neared the lane that wound through a stand of tall and bushy cedar trees and led to their back terrace.

Their lot here in central North Carolina was less than five acres, but she had mowed a long path though the property, a sort of lazy-eight shape that meandered though woods and field. It was more than wide enough for two people to walk side by side. Three times around was exactly one mile, and walking that mile with two-pound wrist and ankle weights was usually all that James felt like doing now that he was retired—especially in this muggy August weather to which his northern-bred body stubbornly refused to adapt.

"No, I think I'll go on in and make our drinks." Their regular evening walks were for physical health. Their regular evening cocktails maintained their mental health. "You go ahead, though, if you like."

"Maybe I'll just zip around one more time," said Donna, who had barely broken a sweat. There was a radiance about her lately, as if she'd discovered the fountain of youth since their move from northern Pennsylvania.

The setting sun cast long shadows around them.

"If you don't come back soon, I'll send the dogs."

She laughed. "I'm almost tempted to stay out till you do. Just to see what kind of dogs you'd send."

"What did she mean by that?" asked Major Dwight Bryant of the Colleton County Sheriff's Department.

"It was a joke," said Greggson. "You know—like, send the Marines? I don't care much for dogs and we've never had any, although she thinks we really ought to now that we're living in the country."

Country was a relative term, thought Dwight. The lots might be big out here, with tall leafy oaks and maples spreading deep shade around the houses and natural tangles of kudzu, honeysuckle, and cedars left along the road fronts to maintain the illusion, but they were still lots, not unbroken countryside.

"And you say that was about seven-thirty?"

It was now almost midnight, more than four hours since Donna Greggson disappeared. Normally they would have waited twenty-four hours before searching for an adult, but it was a slow evening and Dwight had been nearby when the call came in that a woman was missing—a beautiful woman somewhat younger than her husband, judging by the snapshots he'd seen. She had wide brown eyes, soft brown hair, and a teasing smile. At the moment, there were no smiles here in the Greggson living room, only anxious concern as her husband and their three nearest neighbors answered his questions.

Once, thought Dwight, he would have known all the faces living in this end of the county by sight if not by name. But there had been so much development over here in the last few years that the people in this room were total strangers to him.

He had learned that Mr. and Mrs. Zukowski were neighbors to the east and that Walter Malindorf's property touched both pieces at the rear. Like James Greggson, the other three looked to be in their mid to late fifties. Mrs. Zukowski—Marita—was tall and lean, with a strong-willed chin and the sturdy air of an outdoors person. Her husband Hank was lanky and thin-faced under a thick crop of rusty brown hair. He had the kind of boyish good looks that ages well. Time would be kinder to him than to his wife, thought Dwight.

Malindorf, on the other hand, reminded him of a bantam rooster, loud and puffed with the self-importance that came from owning the largest "farmette" in this upscale development. Texans had a phrase for people who bought a sliver of earth and acted as if they held title to a kingdom, thought Dwight: All hat, no cattle. In Walter Malindorf's case, it was all car, no crops. Shorter than the others by five or six inches and chubby where they were slim and fit, the man owned one of those outsized all-terrain SUV's. When Greggson called to ask if his wife was there, Malindorf had immediately come roaring through the wide mowed paths, shining his four headlights and side-mounted spotlight deep into the woods and across the open meadow, effectively destroying any physical traces that might have helped them determine what happened to the missing woman.

"Now you see here, Bryant," Malindorf blustered, his round face flushed with annoyance. "If she'd been lying out there hurt, you'd have been glad enough to have me find her pretty quick."

"But you didn't, did you?" said Hank Zukowski. "And now you've messed it up good for them."

Malindorf's red face turned even redder and he glared at his neighbor, rising on the balls of his feet to get closer to Zukowski's face. "Yeah, and if you'd kept your eyes open when you walked over, maybe you'd have seen who was sneaking around the place. *If* there was anybody to see."

"It's too early to say who should've done what," Dwight said, holding up a placating hand as he turned to Greggson. "Was there anything out of the ordinary about your routine today? Any visitors, unusual phone calls?"

"Nothing," James Greggson said firmly. "We worked on the yard this morning. It was getting so hard to mow under some of the trees that I cut a lot of lower limbs. Donna hates the sound of the chainsaw so she went inside for that. We drove over to the clubhouse for lunch, then trimmed up some bushes this afternoon. No phone calls that she mentioned. The cleaning woman came yesterday, so there was no one else here today unless you count the Mexican that comes in every week. He mowed the lawn, finished up the pruning, and hauled all the limbs down to the bonfire, but I don't think Donna said five words to him the whole time."

"Bonfire?"

"Yeah. We're planning a big Halloween party and we've been piling up all our burnable stuff on it for the last six months. Zukowski and Malindorf, too. It's going to be huge."

Dwight wondered if they planned to get a burn permit or if they knew how quickly bonfires could get out of hand with just the least little breeze? Well, one thing about these big lots, a fire truck could get here before a carelessly set fire burned more than three or four of their own acres.

"What's the worker's name?"

"Rosie's all I know. I always pay him cash, so I've never needed his last name."

"Rosario Fuentes," said Marita Zukowski helpfully. "He mucks out the stable for me. Lives in Cotton Grove."

Dwight made a note of the name. "Was he still here when you went for your evening walk?"

Greggson shook his head. "Left at five sharp. Said his kid was pitching in a

Little League game. I remember when my sons were in Little League," he added, his voice suddenly wistful. "I never missed a game. It's great the way people assimilate, isn't it? Man can hardly speak English and his son'll be American as apple pie."

He gave a rueful smile. "Or should I say American as tacos and enchiladas?"

From the woods out back came the sharp bark of a dog. Dwight stepped to the heavy French doors and opened them. Even at midnight, the air outside was still hot and muggy. No breath of wind stirred. He stepped out onto the broad, multilevel cedar deck and the others followed.

"They find her?" asked Malindorf, almost shoving Dwight aside.

Flashlights bobbled toward them through the trees and several officers walked into the light cast by lanterns on the deck railings.

"No luck, Major," one of them called. "The dog's just going around in circles. If she left the path, she wasn't walking. We stayed to the edge much as we could, but all them tire tracks—" There was the suggestion of a shrug in the officer's voice. "Maybe in the daylight we'll be able to see something."

"That's it?" asked Greggson.

Malindorf's face began to redden again. "You're quitting? Just like that?"

"If the dog couldn't find her, there's nothing more we can do out there tonight," said Dwight. "We'll be back by sunrise, though. I'll post an officer and I don't want anybody else crossing the area till we can take another look at it in the daylight."

Greggson turned to Hank Zukowski. "You *sure* you didn't see her, Hank? The way she was headed was over toward your side of the property."

"What's that supposed to mean?" Zukowski asked mildly, a frown wrinkling his youthful brow. "I've told you no a dozen times tonight."

Greggson gave an impatient flip of his hand and turned away but the taller Zukowski grabbed his shoulder.

"No! First Malindorf here and now you. If I'd seen Donna, don't you think I'd tell you?"

"Unless—?" said Malindorf, deliberately leaving the word to dangle accusingly.

"Unless what? Christ! You think I had anything to do with her disappearance? I was with James here. You said it yourself, James. I got here about five minutes after you left her and I haven't been out of your sight since then. When the hell did I have time to do whatever you're thinking?"

Dwight watched the distrait husband shake his head in weary frustration.

"Sorry, Hank. I don't know what I think. I just want her to come home."

Marita Zukowski glared at the other two men and put out a comforting hand to lead him back inside the house. Dwight followed.

"I'm sorry, Mr. Greggson, but I have to ask you. Is there any reason your wife would leave on her own? Any trouble here that maybe made her want to get away for a while?"

"Of course not!" Greggson's steel-gray hair had begun to thin across the top, but his voice was still as youthful and vigorous as his handsome face.

"Then why did you wait so long to start calling your neighbors?"

"I told you. I thought she was playing with me. About sending dogs. Hank and I were here talking about the book he brought back, not paying attention to the time. I just assumed she was over with Marita. That's why I walked home with Hank—so she wouldn't have to come back in the dark alone. Then Marita said she hadn't been there, and that's when I called Walter. They're the only people out here we know well enough for Donna to drop in on."

Dwight's people had already searched the house from attic to basement, paying special attention to the auxiliary freezer in the basement and to the trunks and boxes in the attic. James Greggson might indeed be a loving and worried husband, but every officer was experienced enough to know that when a spouse goes missing, the remaining spouse is often responsible. So they looked very carefully at every container and cubbyhole large enough to hold a small woman. They even unrolled the large tent and sleeping bags stored there from the years of wilderness camping with his sons and grandsons.

When they finished with the house, they had moved on to the "barn," a three-car garage with a guest loft above and storage spaces the size of horse stalls to the sides, all under a gambrel roof. Working barns in Colleton County tended to be sided in sheets of tin, but Dwight supposed the dark red paint looked more authentic to somebody from Pennsylvania.

"Her purse is still here," Marita Zukowski said now, pointing to a side table near the door.

The summer bag was a feminine froth of multicolored straw. A tangle of keys lay beside it.

They all watched as James Greggson opened it and pulled out a slim wallet. They saw cash in the bill compartment and credit cards neatly slotted.

"Anything missing?" asked Dwight.

"We only have four cards," he answered, fanning them in his hand. "ATM, telephone, Visa, American Express. They're all here. Her driver's license, and medical insurance, too."

"So she *didn't* leave under her own steam," Malindorf said. "I *knew* it! Just because this piddly-assed excuse for a sheriff's department's giving up doesn't mean we have to. Come on, guys, let's get our flashlights and go find her."

Dwight rose to his full six-foot-three, topping Walter Malindorf's take-charge pomposity by a good ten inches. "You go blundering out there again, Mr. Malindorf, and I'll arrest you for trespassing on a crime scene."

"Crime scene?" Hank Zukowski looked shocked.

"Until proven otherwise," Dwight said grimly.

"But she may be hurt," said Greggson. "Bleeding."

"The dog would have found her." He hated having to speak so bluntly, but they'd done enough damage between them and he wasn't going to allow more if he could help it. "We'll get an early start in the morning. Maybe something will give us a clue."

At that, the others rose, too.

Marita Zukowski gave Greggson a neighborly hug as she left. "Try to get some sleep, James. It won't help Donna if you worry yourself into a break-down."

Dwight heard Malindorf offer the Zukowskis a lift since they couldn't take the shortcut to their house, but would have to walk around by the road As the monstrous SUV roared away down the drive, he paused by a display of photographs atop a console table. Most were of children and young adults. "Your children?"

"Mine, yes," said Greggson. "This is a second marriage for both of us, but Donna never had children."

"Any of them in the area?"

Greggson shook his head. "No. All back in Pennsylvania. Carrie, my baby—" Here he touched the picture of a younger woman holding two little boys. "—her husband was almost transferred to the Research Triangle, but it fell through."

"I'm surprised you could leave them," said Dwight, thinking of his own son up in Virginia, a good four hours away.

"I didn't want to," he admitted. "Not really. But the winters there are hard and Donna's brother's here, so—oh, Lord! I forgot all about Phil. He's in Raleigh. I'd better call him."

When it was clear from the one-sided phone conversation that Greggson's brother-in-law hadn't heard from the missing woman, Dwight let himself out into the warm August night.

He spoke to the officer he'd left on watch, then got in his patrol car.

The mosquitoes were wicked tonight. Even though Marita Zukowski had slipped one of Hank's long-sleeved cotton shirts on over her bare arms, one buzzed around her face and another bit her bare ankle.

Everything that could be said between them had been said by the time they reached their own front door and Hank had gone on up to their bedroom. She told him she was going to walk their dog but that was only an excuse to hurry back down their long drive before that deputy could go away thinking what he must think.

Duncan was as sweet-tempered and patient as most golden retrievers, and he lay quietly at her feet as she waited. She slapped at the buzzing near her ear and wondered if mosquitos bothered him. In the middle of that thought, the patrol car finally pulled out of the Greggson drive down the road and she stepped from the shadow of the trees so that his headlights washed over her and her dog.

Dwight slowed to a stop and lowered his window. "You wanted to talk to me, Mrs. Zukowski?"

"Yes." Her voice was as tight as the skin stretched across the bones of her face.

He cut his lights, got out of the car, and leaned against it to listen to what this tall thin woman wanted to say here in the darkness, away from the others.

"James and Walter. They're making it sound as if Hank had something to do with Donna's disappearance."

"Were they?"

"Don't play games, Major. It may suit you to let Walter Malindorf think you're a country bumpkin, but I read that piece in the paper about you a couple of years ago. Ex-Army Intelligence? They don't take just anybody. You heard what James and Walter were saying, all right."

The moon had long since set, but there was enough starlight for him to see the urgency in her eyes. "So?"

"So, I just want you to know there's nothing to it," she said. "Hank and I had a light supper about six-thirty and he walked over to return a book about an hour later, just as he and James told you. Donna's a flirt and a tease and maybe Hank had his head turned for a minute or two when they first moved here, and maybe he did kiss her a little longer than he should have last New Year's, but you can't blame Hank for that. She's very pretty, you know. Doesn't look a day over forty though I know for a fact that she's fifty-one. Small and cuddly, too," she added bitterly.

Small and cuddly women made some men feel even taller and more manly, thought Dwight. Whereas a wife this tall, this angular—?

"There was absolutely nothing more to it than that," said Mrs. Zukowski, "but when you asked if there'd been any trouble and James said no, I couldn't contradict him right there, could I?"

"They were still fighting over a New Year's Eve kiss? Eight months later?"

"No, no!" she said impatiently. "They fought, but not about Hank. It was about staying here. You see, Donna wheedled James into moving to North Carolina even though he didn't want to leave Pennsylvania. He misses his old friends, his children, going camping with his grandchildren. I think he even misses the snow. The bargain was that he'd give it a try for two years and then they'd move back if he really hated it. She was so sure he'd love it as much as the rest of us do."

"Do you?" He was genuinely curious about the influx of new people, of why they came, and whether they found what they hoped for.

"Oh, yes! I've wanted a horse of my own ever since I was a little girl and now I finally have two. That was the big draw for this development. All the boundary lines are bridle paths held in common by the association. We can ride for miles out here. And Hank can golf three hundred days a year if he wants. I can't say I'm crazy about your summer humidity, but it doesn't bother me as much as it bothers James."

"Mr. Greggson doesn't ride or golf?"

"That's not the point," said Marita Zukowski. "Donna made a bargain she had no intention of keeping. It was just a way to get him down here near her precious brother and away from his children. The two years are up at the end of October, but last week, when he told her he wanted to put the house on the market next month, she just laughed at him. Said he hadn't tried to adjust and that North Carolina was their home from now on. James was furious. Ask Walter. He was there. We could see how angry James was, yet he just turned away and walked into the house and poured us all another round of drinks." She hesitated. "Something else, though."

"Yes?" asked Dwight.

"They've only been married a few years. The Pennsylvania house was his. This house is in both their names and North Carolina's a no-fault state, isn't it? If James left her, he'd have to split his assets and there goes a big chunk of his grandchildren's inheritance."

And what about Mrs. Zukowski? mused Dwight on the drive back to Dobbs. No-fault divorce cuts both ways. Would she have to give up those long-wished-for horses if her husband and her neighbor really were having an affair and it led to two divorces?

Daybreak came 'way too early next morning, but Dwight Bryant kept his word and was back at the Greggson home before the sun was fully up.

James Greggson met him in the driveway with his brother-in-law Phil Crusher, a compactly built man with the same wide brown eyes as his sister.

"Tell Bryant what you told me," Greggson said, when introductions were over.

"C'mon, James. It really doesn't mean what you're thinking," the younger man protested.

"Tell me what, Mr. Crusher?"

"It's just a coincidence," he answered reluctantly. "Last week, when Donna came into town for lunch, we got to talking about some movie she'd watched the night before. I forget the name of it. Something about a man who decided to disappear? How he put together some secret cash, got new identity papers and just walked away from his old life? She said that it might be fun to try it, except that if she did, the hardest thing would be never again seeing people you did love. Like me. But it was *nothing*, Major Bryant. She was just making conversation."

"You're sure?"

"I was till James here—" His voice wavered with uncertainty. "I thought we were too close for that."

"Then where's her passport?" James demanded.

"What?" said Dwight.

"When Phil told me what she said, I went upstairs and looked in the desk drawer where we keep our passports. Hers is gone. We keep some extra cash on hand, and that's gone, too."

"How much extra cash you talking?" asked Dwight.

"Fifteen hundred, two thousand. It varies. But she could easily have another twelve or fourteen thousand squirreled away. She isn't extravagant and I don't question what she spends as long as the accounts aren't overdrawn at the end of the month."

Must be nice, thought Dwight, who was paying his son's orthodontia bills in addition to child support and hadn't had an extra hundred since the divorce, much less an extra thousand.

"I hate to be so blunt here, Mr. Greggson, but was your wife maybe seeing somebody else?"

"No!" he said angrily.

"Yes," said his brother-in-law.

Dwight and Greggson both stared at him.

Phil Crusher was clearly embarrassed but determined. "I'm sorry, James, but I think she was."

"Who?" they asked.

"I don't know. She just laughed when I called her on it, but I've seen her like that before. Happy. Excited. Running on adrenaline. Just like the time she started with you."

"I didn't know she was still married then," James said stiffly. "She told me she and her first husband were legally separated."

The brother's assertion opened up other possibilities, but Dwight wasn't going to jump to conclusions. First things first.

Together, he and his team walked every inch of the wide paths, beginning at the huge brush pile in the middle, where the looping paths crossed. It was going to be another hot day. The green leaves on yesterday's freshly-cut tree limbs were already wilted and limp and the sun had begun to bake the open meadow where flowering weeds grew head high.

Above them, in the hard blue sky, a helicopter sent out from one of the Raleigh news channels made noisy sweeps back and forth over the whole area. The trees were too thick to see beneath, but if Donna Greggson's body were lying in the open, they saw no sign of it.

They fanned out across the property six to eight feet apart.

Not even a stray cigarette butt beneath the trees.

As a last resort, they dismantled the bonfire pile limb by limb, until it became clear that nothing was there except brush, scrap lumber, cardboard, and easily burned bits of household furnishings. Among the castoffs were a perfectly useable oak captain's chair with only one broken rung, a stuffed dog that didn't look as if a child had ever played with it, old magazines that should have been recycled, and some threadbare cotton bath mats.

By this time, pudgy little Walter Malindorf had driven over in his bright red SUV with Hank Zukowski. Both men seemed anxious to help in any way they could and offered to repile the brush. They acted grateful for the work and toiled away under the hot August sun until Malindorf's shirt was wet with sweat and even Zukowski was breathing hard. Dwight had seen this reaction before. It was the male equivalent of bringing casseroles to a house of bereavement.

Greggson came down for a few minutes, his handsome face haggard and drawn, and he watched Zukowski with suspicious, resentful eyes before abruptly turning away and stalking back to the house.

"What's bugging him?" asked Zukowski uneasily.

Malindorf picked up the stuffed dog, a golden retriever made of silky plush, pulled a handkerchief from the pocket of his chino shorts, and wiped sweat that trickled down his round cheeks. "Donna's missing," he said, his voice heavy with sarcasm. "Or didn't you notice?"

Zukowski stared at him, then shrugged and threw a final limb on the pile.

The pile was much taller than Malindorf, but with a sort of solemn dignity, he stood on tiptoe to set the little dog as high up as he could, as if to leave it standing guard.

When Dwight asked if his people could search their outbuildings, both men agreed. He really wanted to search the Zukowski home, but without a warrant, he doubted they'd allow it and not even his favorite judge would give him one without probable cause.

Since the Greggsons' path edged the communal bridle path between their property and Malindorf's, and since golf carts and occasional light trucks also used the bridle path as a short-cut to the development's golf course and club house, it was clear that Mrs. Greggson could easily have disappeared by that route, willingly or unwillingly.

"But you'd think the dog would have found her scent," argued one of the deputies.

"Not if she was in somebody's truck," said another

"Or on a horse," said a third.

As they broke for lunch, Deputy Mayleen Richards arrived with the first results of her electronic inquiries.

"No records of anything more serious than speeding tickets," she reported glumly. "All solid citizens with triple-A credit ratings—the men anyhow. Mrs. Zukowski and Mrs. Greggson haven't held paying jobs since they married."

In her voice was the disdain working women often have for women who don't have to.

"Any dirt from the cleaning woman?"

"Just the usual. If they fought, it wasn't in front of her."

"And Fuentes?" Dwight asked.

Her freckled face brightened. "I checked his alibi myself with my brother's son. Billy Jim's on the same team as the Fuentes boy, who's got a slider that falls off the edge of the earth according to Billy Jim. Their game started at six-thirty and the boy's daddy was there from the get-go."

If Greggson was correct about the time he last saw his wife, then he and Zukowski alibied each other. Except for their dogs, Malindorf and Marita Zukowski had been alone in their respective houses. Malindorf had no apparent motive though and if Marita Zukowski had gotten rid of the woman she feared as a rival, then she was a damned good actress with nerves of steel.

By mid-afternoon, there was nothing left for Dwight Bryant to do except face Donna Greggson's husband and brother and promise that they would continue to canvass the neighborhood and follow up any leads their APBs produced. If she had left of her own volition, then sooner or later, they'd probably hear from her.

He let them vent on him the frustration he himself was feeling and promised to keep in touch.

And that's where matters stood through the rest of a torrid August and an unusually hot September. On a drizzly and cooler day near the middle of October, Dwight Bryant got a phone call from James Greggson. Once more he had to tell the man that there was nothing new to report.

"Actually," said Greggson, "I called to tell you that I've sold the house. I'll be moving back to Pennsylvania next week. You have Phil's phone number and I'll send you my new one as soon as I know it."

Nothing in his tone accused the Colleton County Sheriff's Department of incompetence, but neither did it sound as if he ever expected Dwight to use the new number.

This was not his first unsolved missing person, thought Dwight, and it wouldn't be his last, but he kept feeling that somehow he'd messed up here, that there must have been one more thing that would have made all the difference if he'd only noticed in time.

The drizzle ended in the afternoon and cool westerly winds blew away all the gray clouds, giving a hint of the beautiful autumn weather to come. As Walter Malindorf stepped outside to give his three spaniels a run, the tubby little man smelled something odd. He followed his nose around the corner of his house and saw wisps of smoke lifting above the woods that separated his place from Greggson's. Curious, he opened the back of his SUV, let the dogs pile in, then drove through the woods, across the bridle trail, and onto the wide path Donna had kept mowed until she disappeared.

Tall weeds with small yellow aster-like flowers had grown up in the past two months. Soon, he thought sadly, there would be no sign that a path had ever been here, that a small brown-haired woman with laughing brown eyes had ever passed along it.

As the path curved to the crossing, he saw that a ring of tiny flames edged across the damp grass toward the brushpile in the middle. Greggson had set a backfire to keep the main fire in check when it kindled and was standing alertly with pitchfork and shovel to take care of any stray sparks.

Since Donna's disappearance, relations had been strained between the three neighbors. Malindorf knew that Greggson suspected Zukowski of sleeping with his wife. He also knew that Zukowski denied it. Having no desire to listen to either man's bitterness, Malindorf had avoided them both. He wouldn't even have known that Greggson had sold the place if Marita Zukowski hadn't mentioned it when he ran into her at the club a few days earlier.

He climbed down from the SUV, well aware that Greggson considered him a ridiculous figure for buying such a vehicle. It would never occur to Greggson that someone could so enjoy the companionship of dogs that he'd buy a van for their comfort rather than his own. Well, the man was leaving. Wouldn't hurt to maintain the facade a little longer.

"Help you with that?" he asked as the flames reached the bonfire and began to eat at the base.

"That's okay," said Greggson. "The rain this morning damped everything down and there's not enough wind to worry about. In fact, if you don't mind, I'd rather do this by myself."

To take away the suggestion of insult, he added, "Donna was looking forward to our Halloween party and burning this with the whole neighborhood around. This is sort of for her, you know?"

"Yeah, sure," said Malindorf. He started back to the SUV, then hesitated. "Where's the dog?"

"The what?"

"The stuffed dog. A toy golden retriever. I set it up there near the top the day after Donna went missing—when Zukowski and I restacked the pile. Remember?"

Greggson shrugged.

Heavy gray smoke began to billow up from the center as the fire encircled the base and climbed the sides, growing in intensity. The broken captain's chair now lay atop the bonfire, yet Malindorf distinctly remembered throwing it on before covering it with some heavy limbs. And that blue cardboard box was one of his own contributions. It had been stacked on the other side of the pile.

"You restacked the pile?" he asked curiously. "Why?"

The answer came to him immediately. "My God! She's in there, isn't she? You killed her and now you're burning her body!"

Greggson glared malevolently, then charged toward him with the pitch-fork. Malindorf dodged, barely escaping the icepick-sharp tines, and the momentum of Greggson's lunge carried him through the charred grass circle. He caught himself just short of the roaring blaze, but the points of the pitchfork pierced the blue box. He tried to jerk it free and a tangle of burning limbs tumbled toward him.

He abandoned the pitchfork and grabbed the shovel, but when he turned for Malindorf, he saw the little man scramble into his SUV and lock the doors. Howling with rage, Greggson swung the shovel at the windshield. The glass spider-webbed beneath the blow yet did not break. The dogs inside barked furiously and leaped from seat to seat. Greggson barely heard. Again he swung at the window on the driver's side.

Malindorf ducked automatically but when his head reappeared, he had a cell phone against his ear and Greggson saw his lips moving above the mouth-piece. At that, James Greggson slammed the window a final time, then dropped the shovel and ran unsteadily through the cedars toward his house.

The volunteer firemen got there first. By the time they quenched the fire, Dwight Bryant had arrived with several deputies. They entered the house cautiously, weapons drawn, and called out for Greggson to give himself up.

They were too late.

James Greggson had drawn his own weapon.

They found his body on the bed. There was no note.

"But where did he hide her all that time?" asked Malindorf. It was several hours later and they stood on the flagstone terrace of his house to gaze across at the glare of portable floodlights that still illuminated the bonfire site. The spaniels lay at his feet, alert to his every move. "We looked. I looked. Your people looked. You even had a tracking dog."

That had puzzled Dwight, too, until he saw the heavy green nylon bag and the ropes that the West Colleton Fire Department volunteers had pulled from the center of the bonfire. The contents sickened them. It had been a very hot two months. But the bag and the ropes made him remember the six-man tent in Greggson's storeroom and that in turn reminded him of his Army survival training.

"He sealed her body in a couple of large plastic bags, which hid her scent from the dog, then he put her in the tent bag and hoisted her up into one of those bushy cedar trees. That's what you do to keep bears from getting your food if you're camping in the wilderness. Hang it from a high limb. He must have hung her against the trunk so that our eyes would pass right over another limb shape. People don't look up much when they're searching. We found the tree, by the way. Just off the path where they grow so thick. We spotted a pulley screwed high up in the trunk."

One of the spaniels came and laid its large head against Malindorf's knee. Absently, he scratched the silky ear. "So he had it all planned and lied about the time he last saw her?"

Dwight nodded. "It's a good thing you noticed he'd restacked the pile."

"The stuffed dog was gone."

"Observant of you."

"Not especially." Malindorf looked at him sadly. "I gave it to her. The week before she died. A stand-in for the registered pup I was going to buy her for a divorce present."

"Divorce?" Dwight said. "She and Zukowski really were having an affair?"

"You, too?" Malindorf's voice was sardonic. "Good old Hank Zukowski. Tall, handsome, good physique—the automatic suspect when Greggson realized Donna was in love with someone else. He thought Zukowski gave her the dog. That's why he threw it on the burn pile. Never dawned on either of them that she might be tired of tall handsome men whose egos need massaging. That she might be ready for someone who could make her laugh, who could adore her."

"You?" asked Dwight.

Grief and wonder shone in Walter Malindorf's chubby face.

"Me," he said and began to cry.

Ellery Queen's Mystery Magazine, December 2002

Mystery Novels and Short Stories by Margaret Maron: A Checklist

BOOKS

One Coffee With. Raven House 1981. Reprinted by Bantam 1988 and Mysterious Press 1995.
  Sigrid Harald novel.
Death of a Butterfly. Doubleday 1984. Reprinted by Bantam 1991.
  Sigrid Harald novel.
Death in Blue Folders. Doubleday 1985. Reprinted by Bantam 1992.
  Sigrid Harald novel.
Bloody Kin. Doubleday 1985. Reprinted by Bantam 1992 and Mysterious Press 1995.
  Deborah Knott prequel novel.
The Right Jack. Bantam 1987. Reprinted by Mysterious Press 1995.
  Sigrid Harald novel.
Baby Doll Games. Bantam 1988. Reprinted by Mysterious Press 1995.
  Sigrid Harald novel.
Corpus Christmas. Doubleday 1989. Reprinted by Bantam 1991.
  Sigrid Harald novel.
Past Imperfect. Doubleday 1991. Reprinted by Bantam 1992.
  Sigrid Harald novel.
Bootlegger's Daughter. Mysterious Press 1992. Reprinted as a Mysterious Press paperback 1993.
  Deborah Knott novel.
Southern Discomfort. Mysterious Press 1993. Reprinted as a Mysterious Press paperback 1994.
  Deborah Knott novel.
Shooting at Loons. Mysterious Press 1994. Reprinted as a Mysterious Press paperback 1995.
  Deborah Knott novel.

Fugitive Colors. Mysterious Press 1995. Reprinted as a Mysterious Press paperback 1996.
Sigrid Harald novel.

Up Jumps the Devil. Mysterious Press 1996. Reprinted as a Mysterious Press paperback 1997.
Deborah Knott novel.

Killer Market. Mysterious Press 1997. Reprinted as a Mysterious Press paperback 1998.
Deborah Knott novel.

Shoveling Smoke, Selected Mystery Stories. Crippen & Landru, Publishers 1997.
Short story collection, including cases solved by Sigrid Harald and Deborah Knott.

Home Fires. Mysterious Press 1998. Reprinted as a Warner Books paperback 2000.
Deborah Knott novel.

Storm Track. Mysterious Press 2000. Reprinted as a Warner Books paperback 2001
Deborah Knott novel.

Uncommon Clay. Mysterious Press 2001. Reprinted as a Warner Books paperback 2002.
Deborah Knott novel.

Slow Dollar. Mysterious Press 2002. Reprinted as a Warner Books paperback 2003.
Deborah Knott novel.

Last Lessons of Summer. Mysterious Press 2003.
Non-series novel.

Suitable for Hanging: Selected Stories. Crippen & Landru Publishers, 2004.
Short story collection, including cases solved by Deborah Knott.

High Country Fall. Due from Mysterious Press 2004.
Deborah Knott novel.

Mystery and Crime Short Stories

"The Death of Me," *Alfred Hitchcock's Mystery Magazine*, January 1968.
Collected in *Shoveling Smoke*, 1997.

"The Compromised Confessional," *Alfred Hitchcock's Mystery Magazine*, January 1969.

"The Roots of Death," *Alfred Hitchcock's Mystery Magazine*, August 1969.

"A Very Special Talent," *Alfred Hitchcock's Mystery Magazine*, June 1970. Collected in *Shoveling Smoke*, 1997.

"The Early Retirement of Mario Colletti," *Mike Shayne Mystery Magazine*, December 1970. Collected in *Suitable for Hanging*, 2004.

"The Beast Within," *Alfred Hitchcock's Mystery Magazine*, July 1972. Collected in *Shoveling Smoke*, 1997.

"Side Trip to King's Post," *Alfred Hitchcock's Mystery Magazine*, October 1972.

"To Hide a Tree," *Alfred Hitchcock's Mystery Magazine*, May 1973. Collected in *Suitable for Hanging*, 2004.

"Bang! You're Dead!" *Alfred Hitchcock's Mystery Magazine*, February 1974.

"When Daddy's Gone," *The Executioner Mystery Magazine*, August 1975. Collected in *Shoveling Smoke*, 1997.

"Lady of Honor," *Alfred Hitchcock's Mystery Magazine*, November 1975.

"Deadhead Coming Down," *Mike Shayne Mystery Magazine*, April 1978. Collected in *Shoveling Smoke*, 1997.

"Guy and Dolls," *Alfred Hitchcock's Mystery Magazine*, June 1979. Collected in *Shoveling Smoke*, 1997.

"Let No Man Put Asunder," *Mike Shayne Mystery Magazine*, May 1980. Collected in *Shoveling Smoke*, 1997.

"A City Full of Thieves," *Skullduggery*, June 1980. Collected in *Shoveling Smoke*, 1997.

"Mrs. Howell and Criminal Justice 2.1," *Alfred Hitchcock's Mystery Magazine*, May 1984. Collected in *Shoveling Smoke*, 1997.

"On Windy Ridge," *Alfred Hitchcock's Mystery Magazine*, Mid-December 1984. Collected in *Shoveling Smoke*, 1997.

"Lost and Found," *Woman's World*, February 16, 1988. Collected in *Suitable for Hanging*, 2004.

"Out of Whole Cloth," *Sisters in Crime 2*, ed. Marilyn Wallace, 1989. Collected in *Shoveling Smoke*, 1997.

"Lieutenant Harald and the *Treasure Island* Treasure," *Alfred Hitchcock's Mystery Magazine*, September 1989. Collected in *Shoveling Smoke*, 1997.

"My Mother, My Daughter, Me," *Alfred Hitchcock's Mystery Magazine*, March 1990. Collected in *Shoveling Smoke*, 1997.

"Small Club Lead, Dummy Plays Low," *New Crimes II*, ed Maxim Jakubowski, 1990. Collected in *Shoveling Smoke*, 1997.

"Deborah's Judgment," *A Woman's Eye*, ed. Sara Paretsky, 1991. Collected in *Shoveling Smoke*, 1997.

"Fruitcake, Mercy, and Black-Eyed Peas," *Christmas Stalkings*, ed. Charlotte MacLeod, 1991. Collected in *Shoveling Smoke*, 1997.

"Lieutenant Harald and the Impossible Gun," *Sisters in Crime 4*, ed. Marilyn Wallace, 1991. Collected in *Shoveling Smoke*, 1997.

"Hangnail," *Deadly Allies*, ed. Marilyn Wallace and Robert Randisi, 1992. Collected in *Shoveling Smoke*, 1997.

". . . That Married Dear Old Dad," *Malice Domestic II*, ed. Martin Harry Greenberg, 1993. Collected in *Suitable for Hanging*, 2004.

"That Bells May Ring and Whistles Safely Blow," *Santa Clues*, ed. Ed Gorman and Martin Harry Greenberg, 1993. Collected in *Shoveling Smoke*, 1997.

"What's a Friend For?" with Susan Dunlap, *Partners in Crime*, ed. Elaine Raco Chase, 1994. Collected in *Shoveling Smoke*, 1997.

"With This Ring," *Crimes of the Heart*, ed. Carolyn G. Hart and Martin Harry Greenberg, 1995. Collected in *Shoveling Smoke*, 1997.

"No, I'm not Jane Marple, But . . . ," *Vengeance Is Hers*, ed. Mickey Spillane and Max Allan Collins, 1997. Collected in *Suitable for Hanging*, 2004.

"Shaggy Dog," *Funny Bones*, ed. Joan Hess and Martin Harry Greenberg, 1997. Collected in *Suitable for Hanging*, 2004.

"Craquelure," *The Store of Joys*, ed. Huston Paschal, 1997. Collected in *Suitable for Hanging*, 2004.

"The Stupid Pet Trick," *Murder She Wrote 2*, ed. Elizabeth Foxwell and Martin Harry Greenberg, 1997. Collected in *Suitable for Hanging*, 2004.

"Prayer for Judgment," *Shoveling Smoke: Selected Mystery Stories*, 1997.

"Half of Something," *Irreconcilable Differences*, ed. Lia Matera and Martin Harry Greenberg, 1999. Collected in *Suitable for Hanging*, 2004.

"Growth Marks," *Mom, Apple Pie, and Murder*, ed. Nancy Pickard, 1999. Collected in *Suitable for Hanging*, 2004.

"Roman's Holiday, *Mary Higgins Clark Mystery Magazine*, Summer 1999. Collected in *Suitable for Hanging*, 2004.

"Virgo in Sapphires," *Eiskalte Jungfrauen*, ed. Thea Dorn, 2000 (First US publication: *Ellery Queen Mystery Magazine*, December 2001.) Collected in *Suitable for Hanging*, 2004. Edgar, Anthony, Agatha Nominee.

"The Third Element," *A Confederacy of Crime*, ed. Sarah Shankman, 2000. Collected in *Suitable for Hanging*, 2004.

"What's in a Name?" *The Mysterious Press Anniversary Anthology*, 2001. Collected in *Suitable for Hanging*, 2004.

"Mixed Blessings," *Women Before the Bench*, ed. Carolyn Wheat, 2001. Collected in *Suitable for Hanging*, 2004.

"Till 3:45," *Love and Death*, ed. Carolyn Hart, 2001. Collected in *Suitable for Hanging*, 2004.

"The Choice," *Malice Domestic 10,* presented by Nevada Barr, 2001. Collected in *Suitable for Hanging,* 2004.

"The Dog that Didn't Bark," *Ellery Queen's Mystery Magazine,* December 2002. Collected in *Suitable for Hanging,* 2004.

"Devil's Island." *Suitable for Hanging,* 2004.

"Croquet Summer." *Suitable for Hanging,* 2004.